By Mike Blakely
from Tom Doherty Associates

SPANISH BLOOD

Mike Blakely

FORGE®

A TOM DOHERTY ASSOCIATES BOOK
NEW YORK

SPANISH BLOOD

Cover art by Jeffery Terreson

A Forge Book
Published by Tom Doherty Associates, Inc.
175 Fifth Avenue
New York, NY 10010

Forge® is a registered trademark of Tom Doherty Associates, Inc.

ISBN: 0-812-54831-0

First edition: September 1996

Printed in the United States of America

0 9 8 7 6 5 4 3 2 1

This book is dedicated to Kim Golden Blakely:
my sister-in-law, my original fan,
and my tireless supporter.

Thanks to Layne Preslar, of the Bug Scuffle Ranch, Cloudcroft, New Mexico, for showing me around the Sacramento Mountains from Wild Boy Springs to Burnt House Canyon.

For their hospitality and love of their land, I thank the people of the great state of New Mexico.

Special thanks to the Mescalero Apache people.

This work of fiction is inspired by, but in no way intended to represent, the exploits of James Addison Reavis, the "Baron of Arizona."

Part I

One

❧

RATTLESNAKE EGGS
Territory of New Mexico

The label on the package was stamped in ink, as if with an often-used woodcut daubed on a blotter. The postmark came from Santa Fe. The address, hand printed, was to Bartholomew Cedric Young, Tulane University, New Orleans, Louisiana.

Bart slid the small package across the saloon table to his friend, and glanced out through the beveled glass at a passerby on Bourbon Street.

"Rattlesnake eggs?" Randy Hendricks said. "What in the world?"

"I ordered them from a Santa Fe trading company. Those are registered diamondback eggs. Take a look."

Randy regarded the postmark, the address, the authentic ink stamp. It was just like Bart Young to raise venomous reptiles from eggs. "What are you gonna do with rattlesnakes?"

"Pull their fangs out, and you can have all kinds

of fun with 'em. You know, leave 'em in peoples'
beds and things like that. Mailboxes—whatever.
Go on, take a look. Bet you've never seen rattlesnake eggs before."

Randy picked up the box and judged its weight.
He donned a skeptical smirk, and opened the card-
board lid.

Even before his eyes could find the source, the
noise burst from the package—a loud, aggressive
rattling. Randy's knees banged against the bottom
of the table, his warm beer sloshing from the mug.
He felt his heart throb in his ears, and looked wild-
eyed into the open box as he scrambled in his seat.

Where he expected to find a coiled snake, he
saw instead a dismantled alarm clock with thin
pieces of wood tied to where the alarm bells would
ordinarily go, the tiny hammer still winding down,
tapping against the wood with diamondback
rapidity.

Across the table, Bart Young was almost choking
on his own laughter, his head rolling all around on
his shoulders, his eyes moist with gladness, his
mouth wide and bellowing.

"Damn you, Bart!"

The prankster took an ink-stained woodcut from
his pocket and tossed it on the table in front of
Randy. "You can get 'em down at the jetty. The old
man there will carve anything you want on 'em.
As for the postmark—well, I just mailed the box to
the Santa Fe postmaster, and asked him to send it
back to me."

"I don't care how you did it." Randy shoved the
box back at his grinning friend.

"Notice how I attached the alarm trigger to the
lid of the box?"

"Ingenious," Randy said, his sarcasm thickening. "I've been wondering who made off with my alarm clock."

"You can have it back now. I won't need it where I'm going. The roosters wake you up there."

"Where?"

Bart tapped the box labeled RATTLESNAKE EGGS. "New Mexico."

"New Mexico!" Randy Hendricks rubbed the knee he had banged on the bottom of the table. "When?"

Bart shoved two train tickets across the table. "I leave for Dodge City tomorrow afternoon. From Dodge I take the stagecoach to Santa Fe."

"What'll your old man say?"

Bart shrugged. "He's in Houston. He won't know a thing about it until I'm long gone."

Randy fell back in his chair to study Bart's face. It looked sincere this time, but with Bart Young, you could never be certain. "Who's the other ticket for?"

"You."

Randy scoffed, rolling his eyes. "Now I know you're insane. You'd better cash in those tickets and start paying attention to your studies if you ever want to pass the bar."

Bart's grin flashed quickly across his face. He had perfect teeth and flaunted them often. He used the grin to draw attention away from his forehead, which worried him a great deal. He was only twenty, but his hairline was already receding. He planned to grow a beard to make up for the loss, just as soon as he was safely beyond the reach of his father in New Mexico. "That's just it," he said, "I've already passed the bar."

"You couldn't pass the bar examination given free run of the library."

Bart shoved his beer mug aside, opened a manila envelope on the table, and pulled some documents out. "Take a look at these."

Randy's brow wrinkled above his green eyes, and he scratched his curly red hair like a dog with fleas. It was an annoying habit with him. Suddenly, though, his fingernails stopped working his scalp and he sat perfectly still, staring at the papers in his hands. "Where did you get this diploma?" He shuffled the documents. "And this is a certificate from the Texas bar! How did you get these?"

"I found some old diplomas nobody ever claimed in the files of the bursar's office when I worked there last year. I just bleached the old names off and ..."

"Never mind. I don't want to know." Randy shoved the papers back at Bart as if they were burning his hands.

"As for the bar certificate, my father won't miss it for another—"

"I said, I *don't want to know!* Someday one of these little tricks of yours is going to get you into trouble."

As the redhead put his mug to his lips and tilted it, Bart reached across the table and lifted the bottom of the glass, causing beer to cascade down Randy's chin.

"Dang it, Bart! You're going to chip a tooth doing that!"

Bart slapped the table and laughed. "But seriously, don't you think it would be funny to pull one over on the whole university *and* the bar association?"

Randy glowered as he dried his chin. "When you talked me into leaving the milk cow on the second floor of the library—now, that was funny. Loosening the hubs on Professor Stangle's buggy was funny. But this . . ." He paused to look over his shoulder. "This is *forgery*," he said in a whisper.

"That's not what you called it when I faked your father's handwriting."

Randy squirmed a little in his chair. Once, when he had spent his quarterly allotment on a Bourbon Street harlot, Bart had helped him out by forging his father's signature on a check.

"That was different," Randy said. "That was between me and my old man. But this . . ." He gestured fearfully toward the manila envelope.

"They won't know the difference, or care, out in New Mexico. It's wide open out there."

Randy frowned and shook his head. "Why New Mexico, of all the godforsaken places?"

"Because a good lawyer can make a fortune out there with those old Spanish land grants."

"The only problem is you're not a good lawyer. You're not a lawyer at all. Do you know the first thing about acquiring a Spanish land grant?"

"We'll figure it out. We'll have more money and land than you ever dreamed of."

"So, it's the land thing again. Bart, you wouldn't know what to do with my granddaddy's forty-acre farm. What makes you think you could manage a New Mexico land grant?"

"There's nothing to it. We get some old Spanish grant, make a few improvements, sell it off at a huge profit, then buy a bigger place. You can handle all the legal stuff, and I'll take care of the land."

Randy started to argue but knew it was useless.

Bart Young would persist. With exams coming up, he didn't have the time to waste in debate. He simply sighed and looked away.

"My old man fought there during the war, you know. He told me about the mountains. Most beautiful place in the world, he said. It's got to have something if even my old man can rave about it."

Randy looked at Bart straight-faced and threw his arms into the air. "All right." He picked up one of the railroad tickets and rose from the table.

"You mean it?"

"If we're leaving tomorrow. I'd better go pack. And you'd better get to work on my diploma."

Bart's face made a rare reflection of surprise. He had doubted he would succeed in uprooting Randy from his studies even if he talked all night, which he had been prepared to do. But now it appeared the redhead was finally loosening up and deciding to live. "Well, I'll be damned! My good influence is rubbing off on you." He got up to follow his friend out of the saloon.

They squinted against the afternoon sun as they stepped out onto Bourbon Street.

"You won't regret it," Bart said. "This is the best decision you'll ever make." He burst into a sudden and joyful fit of laughter. "Rattlesnake eggs!"

Bartholomew Cedric Young was a flatlander, born and raised in Houston, Texas. He had never even seen a hill that amounted to anything and had begged his father to send him to study law in some mountain state. He went instead to New Orleans.

There had never been any question that Bart

would become a lawyer. His father was a lawyer, and Bart was to join the family firm once he passed the Texas bar. He didn't like his father very much. The only fond memories he had of George Young revolved around Sibley's Civil War campaign in New Mexico.

Bart's father had ridden with General Sibley out west to El Paso and engaged Union troops all the way up the Rio Grande, helping to capture the city of Santa Fe. He had been badly wounded at the battle of Glorieta Pass, where the Yankee forces destroyed the Texans' supply lines and ran them all the way back to El Paso. He had spent weeks recuperating at the rancho of a rich native New Mexican near Santa Fe. When he finally recovered, he was granted amnesty by the Yankees and allowed to return to Houston.

When Bart occasionally got his father to talk about New Mexico, the descriptions of the mountains, the high plains, and the deserts engrossed him. His father never spoke of the battles, but Bart wasn't interested in that, anyway. He wanted to see the ground rising five thousand feet above him. He wanted to taste snow. He wanted to find out for himself if adobe walls really made the houses feel that cool, even under the blistering summer sun.

Most of all, he wanted to escape the suffocating Gulf Coast air. Even though he had never lived anywhere else, he knew there was better wind to fill his nostrils with. He smelled it on the winter northers that blew down all too infrequently from the northwest.

Bart didn't have much use for law school. New Orleans was much like Houston, except bigger. He had convinced himself that he should have been the son of a High Plains rancher. He should have inherited a spread instead of a law firm.

After his first year of law school, Bart discovered something about his father that truly angered him. George Young had once owned a league and a labor of land south of Austin. He had never seen it, but he had held the deed on it. The place had been settled by George's grandfather, who had come to Texas when it was still part of Mexico. The claim was part of an old Spanish land grant, and George was the only heir. He had sold it to finance his education.

When Bart found out his father had traded more than four thousand acres for a lousy law school sheepskin, he started planning his escape from New Orleans. He felt his destiny had been denied him by a mere generation. That old Spanish land should have been his.

Then he read an article in a legal magazine about land-grant speculation in New Mexico. He decided he would go to Santa Fe and acquire some huge old Spanish grant for pennies an acre. But instead of parceling it up and selling it off at high profits as most speculators did, he would keep it. He would become a cattle king or a land baron or a mountain lord.

It was a very vague image, however, and that's why he decided to rope his friend, Randy Hendricks, into the plan. Randy was good at fleshing out details. He actually enjoyed wading through statutes and manipulating technicalities. No one had forced *him* into law school.

In fact, Bart was rather surprised that Randy had so readily agreed to quit law school for New Mex-

ico. He assumed the talk of acquiring land grants
had done it. If Randy loved thinking law in school,
he would doubly enjoy putting his skills to practice in the real arena of a New Mexico land office
or courtroom.

When he put the ink on Randy's fake credentials
that night, he felt as if he were charting the course
for his own glorious future, signing the deed to his
own Spanish land grant.

Bart found Randy at the depot the next day, sitting on a bench, scratching his scalp, two suitcases
at his feet.

"Where have you been all day?" Bart asked.

"Classes."

"You attended classes *today*? We're heading
west, boy. What were you thinking?"

"My father doesn't live in Houston. If I had
missed a lecture, some professor might have sent a
message across town to the old man, inquiring as
to my whereabouts. He's got them all looking after
me like watchdogs."

Bart sniffed at his friend's paranoia, but resisted
taunting him. "I guess you have a point."

They boarded the train and took their seats.
When the locomotive jerked the couplings together, Randy nudged his companion. "Let me see
my papers," he said.

Bart grinned with pride as he produced the
forgeries from his portmanteau. "I've prepared
everything you'll need. Diploma, transcripts, cer-
tificates . . . I even wrote you a letter of recommendation from Professor Stangle."

The train was inching out of the station.

Randy thumbed through his false credentials.

"Stop looking over my shoulder!" He took a gold piece from his vest pocket and handed it to Bart. "Go back to the smoker and order us a couple of drinks while I check these documents. I'll be along in a minute or two."

"Now you're talking sense." Bart rose, turning the coin between his fingers, and strode down the aisle.

He bought two whiskeys in the smoker and took a seat by the window where he could watch the scenery pass. The train was slowly increasing in speed, and his excitement seemed to build with the pace. He was free of the wretched university. Soon he would smell the high, dry air of the West. Someday he would peer down from a mountaintop he called his own to survey his personal kingdom. His goal was a league and a labor—the inheritance his father had traded away. He didn't even know how much land that was, really, but he envisioned it rolling away under him from one horizon to the next.

As he smelled the whiskey and took his first sip, Bart heard a knuckle rap on the window at his elbow. He turned and found Randy Hendricks's fake law school diploma plastered to the glass. The forged document pulled away from his eyes, and he saw a grinning Randy taking long strides to pace the train, waving the forgeries in his hands.

"Hey!" Bart shouted, oblivious to the other men in the smoker. "What in the hell are you doing out there?"

Randy yelled something that the steam whistle obliterated, and tore his fake diploma in half. He threw his head back and laughed, wild-eyed. He ripped another forgery in two, and let the pieces flutter into the air. He was trotting now to keep up with the train.

"You son of a bitch!" Bart yelled. "I worked all night on that!"

"Hey, boy," the bartender warned. "Mind your language in this car."

Bart ignored the bartender and ran to the door at the end of the car. Bursting out onto the platform, he leaned over the rail and found Randy loping along beside him, still laughing, shredding papers, and throwing them into a cloud of locomotive smoke. "Randy, get your ass back on the train!"

Randy broke into a dead run and pulled his train ticket from his pocket. "Who do I look like? Sancho Panza?" He tore the ticket in two and let the pieces flutter to the ground behind him. "You don't need me to tilt at your New Mexico windmills!"

"Have you lost your mind, boy? Give me your hand! Jump aboard!"

Randy slowed and let the gap widen between himself and Bart. "I got you, Bart! I got you good! Beat you at your own game!" His laughter died as the train rushed away from him.

The reality hit Bart like a wave of steaming New Orleans air. He almost got mad, until he saw the beauty of it. "You son of a bitch!" he yelled, shaking his fist at the shrinking figure trotting beside the cars. "Damned if you didn't!" A smile pulled across his face, and he laughed to the rumble of the steel wheels. Randy had learned something from him after all. His fist opened, and he waved.

Two

✤

"Do you mind?" Lieutenant Delton Semple said, elbowing his fellow passenger in the ribs.

"Huh?" Bart grunted, waking with a start.

"Wake up. You're falling all over me!"

The stagecoach was hot and uncomfortable. The trip from Dodge City had been a long one, and the snotty little lieutenant had made it more miserable than necessary for everyone—complaining constantly, bossing the other passengers, exaggerating his military authority.

"Sorry, Lieutenant," Bart said. "It's just that I've made this trip so many times, the scenery lulls me to sleep." It was, of course, Bart's first day in New Mexico Territory, as it was the lieutenant's, but Semple had been asking for it, and Bart was going to pull one over on him.

"You didn't tell me you were familiar with the territory. What do you do here?"

"Land grant speculator. I've lived here for years."

"Then you know about the Indian problems."

"Know about them? The Red Devils?" A lurch pitched him against the coach door, and he used the sudden commotion to cover a wink he sent to the passengers sitting across from him. "They're worst around . . . Where did you say you were going to be stationed?"

"Fort Union."

"Oh." Bart made his face go pale and looked out under the rolled canvas at the dry New Mexico plains. "Well, think positively, Lieutenant. You can make rank quicker at the more dangerous posts." He smiled sympathetically, then turned back to the scenery.

The other passengers, two hard-bitten miners and a scar-faced gambler, caught on and started telling stories of Indian butchery. Bart grinned out of the far side of his mouth as he listened to the men branch out.

So far, he hadn't been very impressed with New Mexico. The only timber he had seen grew in the form of scrubby piñon and juniper trees. He had left New Orleans during the greenest time of year, and the lack of vegetation here awed him. But there were mountains on the horizon to the west, and Bart suspected there was much more to see.

"Just wait till we get to Maxwell's Ranch tonight at Cimarron," one of the miners said to the lieutenant. "You'll see your first Indians there, sure."

"Maybe we'll see some action, too, it they're on the warpath," the gambler added.

Semple tugged at the almost invisible wisps of his yellow mustache, lifted his campaign hat, and smoothed back his slick blond hair with an immaculate hand. "If you gentlemen are trying to scare me, you'll have to do better than that." His face was smooth and fair, except for the red patches high on his cheeks.

Bart laughed as if he were on Semple's side. "You can't hoodwink this one, boys. He's too smart for you. We could use more like him out here in the territory."

The lieutenant beamed with victory and gazed through the window, until a bump in the road pitched him almost across the coach. "How much longer to Maxwell's Ranch?" he asked Bart.

"We should make it about nightfall." Bart knew only because he had asked the driver at the last stop.

"I understand Mr. Maxwell exerts quite a lot of influence over the Indians," Semple said.

"You'll want him on your side if you're going to be stationed at Fort Union," the gambler said. "He's the only thing standing between the Indians and war right now. The Utes, the Jicarillas, even the Comanches respect him."

"A *civilian*?" the lieutenant said. "Is he the Indian agent there?"

"Not officially, though the agency is located at his ranch on the Cimarron. No, it's mainly the fact that he's not afraid to fight them on the one hand, and he respects them a great deal on the other hand. He lets them live and hunt on his grant. He owns well over a million acres, you know."

Bart had to restrain himself to keep his eyes from bugging out. A million acres! He had no idea.

"So I've heard," the officer said. "It's criminal that one man should be allowed to take up so much land."

One of the miners laughed. "I'd keep those opinions to myself, if I was you, Lieutenant. Maxwell has some of the best grazing lands, timber, and working gold mines in the territory, and as far as he's concerned he's earned them. He'll treat you with the finest hospitality if you stay on his good side, but don't cross him."

"Maxwell's a fine gentleman," the gambler added.

"But damn near deaf as a post," Bart suddenly said, flashing his eyes at the other civilians. "Make sure you speak up loudly when you talk to him. He gets terribly upset if he can't understand you. Don't be offended when he shouts back at you, either. That's the only way he can hear himself speak."

He turned back to the window and looked across the dusty plains. He saw a small herd of antelope grazing in the distance. Beyond them, the Sangre de Cristo Mountains rose on the western horizon. They were too far to pass judgment on, but Bart sensed their beauty. Those were the mountains that had moved even his stolid father.

With a resonant thump, an arrow shaft suddenly appeared near the shoulder of the scar-faced gambler sitting across from Bart. The gambler looked at it as he would a pesky fly, snapped the shaft off and quickly studied the markings.

"Comanches," he said, looking at the other passengers.

A blast from the shotgun rider's double-barrel spurred the men to action. Bart clawed at the

latches of his portmanteau. As he searched for the
Remington revolver he had bought in Dodge City,
Lieutenant Semple stepped over him, crawled out
through the coach window and climbed onto the
roof. Bart could see the canvas-covered boards
above him bending with the officer's weight.

"Git up there with him, young fella'," a miner
said to Bart, waving the barrel of his single-shot
pistol out the window. "You've got a six-shooter.
Don't let the son of a bitch show you up!"

Bart stood in the rocking coach and shoved his
pistol under his belt. He could hear the war yells
of Indians as he swung out through the coach window and searched for handholds that would get
him to the top. When an arrow ripped through the
canvas top beside him, he all but flew to the roof,
uncertain how he had gotten there.

There were two seats facing each other on the
roof—one looking forward, one back—where passengers rode on the more crowded runs. Semple
was on his knees on the rear seat, holding his Colt
revolver with two hands, squeezing off shots. Bart
pulled his Remington from his belt as he took in
the situation.

About a dozen Indians were chasing the coach,
but keeping a safe distance. They were short,
paunchy men, much to Bart's surprise, but their
horsemanship surpassed everything he had heard
about them. They were fanning out far to the right
of the coach, slowly gaining on it. It looked as
though some of them intended to get in front of
the mule team.

Looking past the driver and the shotgun rider,
Bart saw that the road ran between the head of a
prairie arroyo on the left and the base of a bluff on

the right. It seemed the Indians intended to get in front of the stage and meet it at that bottleneck. He saw timber in the arroyo and knew it would serve well as cover.

Semple was firing methodically at the Indians.

"Save your rounds!" the shotgun rider yelled.

"*You* fired!" Semple replied. "Why shouldn't I?"

"I've already reloaded, and you'd better do the same by the time we pass between that arroyo and that bluff. That's where they'll try and turn us!"

Semple looked ahead, speed plastering the front brim of his campaign hat against its crown. "We're not going under that bluff! We're going to run for that timber down there in the gully. We'll make a stand there!"

"Like hell!" the driver yelled, shifting the quid of tobacco in his cheek, and streaming its juices into the wind. He shook the reins and cussed the mules. "That's where they want us to go!"

"I order you to steer for that timber in the gully!" Semple shouted.

"Go to hell!" the shotgun rider replied.

Bart tapped the officer on the shoulder. "We call it an arroyo out here, Lieutenant, not a gully." He had Semple primed for ridicule—assuming the two of them lived beyond the encroaching attack.

The Comanches fired a few long shots as they rode to get in front of the coach. Bart watched the arrows they lobbed, amazed that the Indians could come so near hitting their target while galloping full-out at such a distance. He put his knees on the seat behind the shotgun rider and got ready to meet the attackers at the bottleneck in the road. Semple came up beside him, obviously flustered at his lack of control over the battle.

"Don't you boys shoot till we git right on 'em," the driver said. "Wait'll Bob shoots his scatter gun; then make every shot tell."

Semple didn't wait for the shotgun. Fifty yards from the waiting Indians, he stood up on the coach seat and fired—a round that completely missed the attackers. The driver swerved his mules, shifting the coach out from under the lieutenant's feet, almost slinging him off the top.

"Damn you, boy! I said wait!" the driver yelled.

By the time Semple crawled back onto the seat, the men in the coach below had already opened fire on the Indians closing in from the right. The shotgun spoke, crippling a warrior's horse. Bart saw the nostrils of the Indian ponies flaring, streaks of war paint almost near enough to touch. He fired but realized he wasn't aiming. He had never shot a handgun before, anyway. He saw muzzle blasts and blurs of arrow shafts, one passing between his shoulder and Semple's.

The shotgun took one Indian. Semple's revolver hit two others. Bart tried to find a target to aim at, but they were now going past him too fast. Then he saw the sinewy arm of a mounted brave reach for the mule harness. The shotgun rider was reloading. Semple was firing behind. Bart aimed for the brave and jerked the trigger. His shot hit the Indian pony in the spine, just in front of the rump. The collapsing horse pitched the unlucky rider under the stagecoach wheels.

"That's smart shootin'!" the shotgun rider yelled, looking over his shoulder for more targets.

Bart was still feeling the unpleasant bump of the coach wheels over the screaming brave as he floundered to the backseat with Semple and emptied his revolver. It was more lucky shooting than smart. He had aimed for the brave's head. He couldn't say he had killed the warrior. Not directly, anyway.

As the coach left the crippled war party behind at the bottleneck, the passengers heard another war whoop, double that of the original. Looking east, they saw scores of braves pouring out of the timbered arroyo Semple had ordered the driver to steer into. The stagecoach men said nothing, but Bart couldn't let it alone.

"See there, Lieutenant," he said. "If we'd have driven in there like you said, we'd all be hairless about now."

The larger war party only feigned giving chase. The driver let the mules slow down a little, then looked over his shoulder, grinning with relief.

Bart nudged the unhappy lieutenant good-naturedly. "Let's go see how the boys down below fared."

As the driver had predicted, the coach neared Maxwell's Ranch just before sundown. Bart was leaning out the window, squinting against the dust and holding his hat to his head, when he caught sight of the ranch headquarters. New Mexico suddenly looked better.

The coach passed a few poor Mexican's coming in from their irrigated fields on the Cimarron, then rumbled by a small collection of tepees near a cottonwood grove. The mules slowed to a trot at a huge stone mill. Across an open plaza, Maxwell's whitewashed adobe mansion rambled among shade trees, surrounded by a low rock wall.

When the coach stopped in the plaza, Bart

wasted no time getting out. Smoke rose from several chimneys, and the whole compound smelled like food. He suddenly realized that he had a real Spanish land grant under his shoes. The vague vision of empire became a little clearer. Maybe he would never have a million acres, but someday he would build a mansion like Maxwell's on his own mountainside.

The other passengers tested their legs behind Bart. The two miners got their luggage out of the boot on the back of the coach. They were quitting the stage line at Maxwell's Ranch, and heading west to Elizabethtown—"E Town" as it was called. They were going there to work in Maxwell's Aztec Mine.

The coachmen encountered some difficulty in getting the harnesses off of the mules, so naturally Lieutenant Semple found it necessary to advise them on the problem. The rest of the passengers strolled toward the mansion, where a hot meal waited. Maxwell's Ranch was the finest stage stop on the line.

Just as they came through the gate, Lucien Bonaparte Maxwell appeared on the front gallery of his mansion. He looked about fifty years old—and prosperous. "Welcome, gentlemen," he said, raising his hand. He wore a suit of fine black cloth, well-filled with muscle. He removed his hat, revealing a bald pate that made Bart immediately sympathetic toward him, and strode down a flagstone walk to greet his guests.

The gentlemen exchanged introductions and were telling Maxwell about their scrape with Indians—until they heard the stagecoach driver shout. The driver had been cussing his mules all day, but not with the rancor he was voicing now.

"Goddamn your hide, Lieutenant!" he yelled. "Go to hell and let us handle our own mules!"

"Who's that?" Maxwell asked.

"A new kid for Fort Union," the gambler explained. "His name's Delton Semple."

"He has aggravated the business out of us ever since Dodge City," Bart added.

"How do you mean?" Maxwell asked.

Bart glanced at the coach to see Semple stalking toward him. "Said he had an accident on parade recently. Got too close to the cannon when it went off. Temporary deafness. He can't hear a thing unless you shout at him, and he can't even hear himself unless he yells his lungs out. Most aggravating thing I've ever put up with."

Maxwell turned a skeptical eye toward the fair lieutenant as he came through the gate.

"Lieutenant Semple!" Bart shouted. "Allow me to introduce Lucien B. Maxwell, our host!"

"How do you do, Mr. Maxwell!" Semple shouted back, leaning toward the land baron as he spoke.

"Pleased to meet you, Lieutenant!" Maxwell answered, speaking loudly. "I understand you're to be stationed at Fort Union!"

The coach passengers backed off a few steps from the two yelling men, working hard to stifle their smiles.

"Yes, sir!" Semple said, leaning toward Maxwell again, shouting ever louder. "That is correct!"

Bart turned giddy over the way his prank had played out. He was holding his breath to keep from busting out in laughter. Even the stagecoach employees had turned to see what all the yelling was about.

"We're always in need of good young officers!" Maxwell shouted. "The Indians are a constant menace!"

"So I've seen!" Semple hollered, leaning ever closer to Maxwell.

"Have you any experience with Indians?" the rancher asked loudly.

"Only that skirmish today!" the lieutenant replied. He was about to fall over on his host, yelling almost in Maxwell's ear. "But I graduated near the top of my class at West Point, and—"

Maxwell, wincing at the volume of the officer's voice, put his hand on the uniformed shoulder and pushed Semple away.

"Lieutenant!" he yelled. "Why the devil are you shouting in my ear. *I'm* not deaf! *You* are!"

Semple's astonished face turned pink as his four fellow passengers exploded in laughter. "But . . . Young told me . . ."

Maxwell's eyes darted among the laughing men, then glared at Bart. Slowly, a sly grin curled his lips. "If you're going to play the trickster in this territory, Mr. Young, you'd better be able to take a joke as well as you played that one."

"I'll consider that fair warning," Bart said, bowing slightly.

"As well you should." He allowed himself to chuckle. "Now, come on in, gentlemen, and let's have supper!"

Five men went laughing toward the mansion, but Semple stood in his tracks, his confusion turning to rage as he realized how gullible he had been. He might have stayed there until the stage left for Fort Union, but he heard the coachmen laughing at him from the plaza, and decided he would just as soon face the men in the house as the two stage line employees.

Three

❧

After supper, Lieutenant Semple asked where his quarters might be located, then excused himself. The other men repaired to Maxwell's study for brandy and conversation. It was a warm adobe room, with tile floors, a large fireplace, hand-hewn furniture, and a chandelier made of deer antlers. The evening became considerably more enjoyable with the absence of the brash young officer. Bart was even moved to offer a toast to Semple's speedy delivery southward.

"I'll drink to that!" Maxwell said, raising his glass. "I thought that was a rather rank trick you pulled when you all arrived—telling him I was deaf. But I see now how he must have deserved it."

"Rank?" Bart said defensively. He had considered it rather ingenious.

"Well, it was a little amateurish, you must admit," Maxwell said.

"Amateurish?" Bart said.

"I thought it was hilarious," the gambler said. "Bart was so convincing that I almost believed you were deaf myself, and I've known you for years."

Maxwell chuckled. "Well, it was amusing. But who will remember it ten years from now? You've got to think bigger than that, Bart. Not just in pulling pranks, but in everything you do. That's my philosophy. Take Kit Carson, for example. Now, Kit was one to play jokes now and then, but he did them in a big way."

"You knew Kit Carson?" Bart asked.

"Knew him? We were the best of friends for twenty-five years. He pulled jokes on people that will go down in history. In Santa Fe they're still talking about the time he had fake menus printed and switched them with the real ones at the Rico Café: rat-tail soup, roast mule, coyote cutlets . . . He pulled some beauties. Even got me with them sometimes. But not even Kit could beat the joke Daniel Boone played on me back in 'forty-two."

Bart looked quizzically at the rancher. "Daniel Boone wasn't even alive in 'forty-two."

"That was the beauty of the joke," Maxwell said, tapping his temple with his finger. "It was still tricking people twenty-two years after old Daniel died."

"What kind of joke was it?" Bart asked, pulling himself to the edge of his cowhide chair.

"The biggest. The best I've ever seen. Don't know that it will ever be beat."

The scar-faced gambler was interested now.

"Well, are you going to tell us about it or not, Lucien?" he asked.

Maxwell sat back in his chair and stared at the ceiling timbers for a moment while he stroked his chin. "Me and Kit were scouting for Colonel Fremont that summer on his first expedition. Kit wasn't there the day we found the stone. He was leading another party off somewhere else. I was with Fremont on the South Platte when we found it."

"Found what?" Bart asked.

"The Daniel Boone stone."

"What's that?"

"Well, sit back, boy. I'm trying to tell you." He chuckled, and reached back through the decades again. "I was riding ahead on the south bank of the South Platte—somewhere between Plum Creek and where Julesburg is now—looking for a good campground, when I came across a big slab of rock. I glanced at it, and you'll never guess what I saw on the top face of it."

"What?" Bart demanded.

"Writing! Chiseled letters on the flat side of that boulder. Well, I got off my horse, brushed the dirt away and had a look-see. I'll never forget what it said as long as I live. In four lines—big letters that took up most of the smooth face—it said, 'Here passed Daniel Boone in the year of 1816 en route to the Rocky Mountains,' Then, at the bottom, it said, 'Read more information on the other face.'

"Well, I see what the joke was already," Bart said. "Daniel Boone lived in Kentucky. What would he be doing way out on the South Platte."

"That's what I thought," Maxwell said, pointing his cigar at his guest. "I figured it for a hoax. But it was still a sight, I tell you. A chiseled stone out there in the wilderness! I rode back to tell Fremont, and then I learned a thing or two about Daniel Boone.

"Like you said, everybody knows Boone lived in Kentucky. But in his old age, he moved to Missouri, and when he was eighty-some-odd years old, he made a trip to the Rockies. And that was in 1816. Colonel Fremont knew all this some way or another. That man knew just about everything—and thought he knew what he didn't. Still does, I guess.

"Anyway, Fremont got all interested in reading the bottom face of the stone. I guess I was, too. The year of 1816 was two years before I was born, so the thing was an antique to me. I was pretty excited to think I was exploring the same ground Daniel Boone had, and was reading something he had chiseled, so when Fremont told me to chop a pole to prize that slab up, I went to it like a contest.

"Well, one pole wouldn't prize a rock that big. Hell, four poles wouldn't. We had to hitch a horse. But even a horse and seven men couldn't turn that stone! It was getting on to dark, and we were hungry and hadn't even made camp yet, but Colonel Fremont was determined to read that bottom side. He figured old Daniel had left us some secret map to a mountain pass or some such thing.

"We must have hitched every horse and every strap of leather and every rope we had in the whole party to that damned stone, and finally started it turning over after dark. I was driving a horse when it started to move. It angled up a little, and I turned to whip that horse on and get the boulder turned over so Fremont would let us rest. Then it came over quicker than anybody could have guessed, and I fell down right where it was going to land. And that's the reason I will never know what the Daniel Boone stone said on the other side. . . ." Maxwell hung his head, sighed, and closed his eyes.

Bart was hanging on the very edge of his cowhide chair, about to fall into the fireplace with anticipation. "What do you mean? Why don't you know what it said?"

Maxwell raised tearful eyes to his young guest. "Because," he said, "The damned thing rolled over on me and squashed me dead right there!"

The gambler and the two miners joined Maxwell in a mighty salvo of laughter aimed at Bart Young. They doubled over in their chairs, sloshed their brandy, stomped the tiles, and sent echoes down the labyrinth corridors of Maxwell's mansion.

Bart reeled back at first, but it only took him a moment to realize how badly he had been taken in. He ground his teeth and pursed his lips. "Damn," he said.

But Bart knew how good it felt to execute a clean one, and Maxwell had pulled this one off flawlessly. He would not deny the land baron his fun. He covered his face as if in embarrassment and joined the laughter.

"Bart," Maxwell said, wiping the tears away from his eyes, "you went along so well, I just couldn't resist it. But, now, let me tell you what really happened with Fremont on the South Platte." He stood by the fire with his brandy and turned back to his guests. The memories flooded back again: the Daniel Boone stone, Fremont's first expedition, the days of his youth—a landless, care-less vagabond adventurer, friend to the greatest frontiersmen who ever lived.

"Oh, no, you don't," Bart said. "I won't fall for another one."

"Just sit still and listen. I'll explain everything. The stone didn't really kill me, of course, but everything else I told you was true. And, actually, the thing came near crushing my leg when it flipped over. It was dark. I slipped. The boulder came down like a tall timber and landed on my boot heel. We had to unlace my boot to get me loose and dig under it to get it out.

"Anyway, Colonel Fremont jumped up on the stone then, and cleared off all the dirt while I made him a torch to read with. Those of us who knew our letters—and for me, that was just barely—well, we gathered around to have a look-see with Fremont."

Maxwell looked at his young guest, calling the image to mind, and smiled. "It was the damnedest thing, Bart. In four lines—big letters that took up most of the smooth face—it said, 'Here passed Daniel Boone in the year of 1816 en route to the Rocky Mountains.' Then, at the bottom, it said, 'Read more information on the other face.' Right about then I felt like you did a minute ago. I had been roped, tied, blindfolded, and branded gullible by the best joke ever. Old Daniel Boone got me, twenty-two years in the grave."

Bart did not laugh, but he smiled and felt a heartthrob of something—maybe admiration or envy or awe. He sat back and visualized the chis-eled boulder. Maxwell was right. It was pure ge-nius. The greatest prank ever. It possessed the lasting quality of stone. Once sprung on one victim, it lay ready for the next. It was large and simple and permanent.

Bart knew then that he would have to start thinking bigger. If he came to New Mexico for a league and a labor, he would probably get no more than he sought. If he satisfied himself with rank tricks, he would enjoy only the laughter of an amateur.

Lucien B. Maxwell had taken nearly two million acres. Daniel Boone had chiseled the world's best prank in stone. How was Bartholomew Cedric Young going to top that?

Four

∽∾∽

W hat was his name again?" Antonio Montoya asked the youth at his gate.

"Young. George Young. He was a captain in Sibley's Brigade."

Don Antonio stroked his black mustache that was turning gray where it met his sideburns. "I am sorry, my friend. There were so many wounded men here. Some from Texas, others from Colorado. Both armies. I cannot remember their names."

Bart stepped deeper into the shadow of the grapevine arbor. "He was wounded bad in the stomach. Said he was one of the last to leave because he took so long to heal."

The old don's eyes widened and met Bart's. "*Un momento*. There was one who stayed here a long time. Yes, I think I remember. He said he lived near the ocean. He told me about the waves, and the green grass everywhere. Houston!"

"Yes!" Bart said. "That was my father. I'm Bartholomew Young!"

"*Por Dios!*" Antonio said, holding his arms wide. "And now you have come to tell me how my old friend is doing!"

Bart returned the unexpected embrace when it came, slapping the dignified old man heartily on the back.

"You will stay here with us," Antonio said, "until you are completely recovered from your long trip. Tell me, how is your father doing?"

"All right," Bart said, removing the loop handles of his portmanteau from the saddle horn. "His gut still bothers him some, but he's still practicing law and making good money." He obeyed Don Antonio's gesture, urging him to the house. A boy led his horse away.

The invitation to stay came as a welcome relief. It had been a hard trip from Maxwell's Ranch for a young man unaccustomed to the saddle. He had planned to ride the stage all the way to Santa Fe, until Lucien Maxwell invited him to ride over the mountains.

"I have to go to E Town and check on the mines," Maxwell had said. "I'll loan you a horse, and you can ride with me. From there you can ride down to Taos and into Santa Fe. That beats the hell out of taking the stage through Fort Union. If you pass through there, Lieutenant Semple's liable to have some corporal shoot you as a comanchero."

So he had ridden with Maxwell up the Cimarron, into the mountains, among the tall pines and the running streams. This was the New Mexico he had envisioned. He held his horse back on occasion to take in a choice view. He loved to see roll after roll of timber falling away to the valleys.

In E Town, he had asked if Maxwell knew Antonio Montoya.

"Everybody in the territory knows Antonio," Maxwell had answered. "Those land-grant speculators you're going to join have been trying to buy his grant for years, but he won't sell."

After E Town, Bart had gone on alone, with more than a borrowed horse to show for his acquaintance with Maxwell. He also carried a general letter of introduction from Maxwell, and a personal letter to Don Antonio.

He had found Antonio's hacienda looming on the hillside east of Santa Fe, like some medieval castle overlooking the fields of its peasants. It had been built in the old colonial style, with a high adobe wall surrounding it for protection against Indians.

Now he was inside the high wall, strolling with Don Antonio toward the hacienda, looking forward to the cool relief of the adobe walls. A few boys were tending a small herd of sheep in one corner of the compound. A fruit orchard shadowed another. Elsewhere, cottonwoods lent greenery and shade.

Like the wall that surrounded it, the hacienda could be made nearly impregnable. It had only two entrances—the main one facing west, and the other around back on the east. The huge wooden gates stood open, and Bart could see all the way through the shady courtyard to the corrals. But with the two entrances closed, he knew the mansion would stand as solid as a fort. Not one window opened to the outside.

As he entered the mansion, he was telling Antonio what his father had been up to since the Confederate invasion. George Young wasn't Bart's favorite subject, but his father was his only link to Antonio Montoya, and he intended to exploit it. He did not know a soul in Santa Fe. An acquaintance with Don Antonio might prove beneficial.

There was something else, too. Lucien Maxwell had taken him by the sleeve at E Town, and, looking over both shoulders to make sure nobody would hear, had said, "Antonio has two daughters of marriageable age, Bart. It wouldn't hurt to ask him if you could marry one. That would put you in line to inherit some of that community grant he's been buying up over the years. I think it covers fifty thousand acres or so."

Bart had narrowed his eyes suspiciously. "You think I'd marry a girl just to get my hands on her daddy's land?"

"How else are you going to get ahold of land out here? You'll be competing against every speculator in the territory, and you don't know a one of their tricks. Besides, Antonio's daughters are renowned for their looks." Maxwell had then launched an explanation of the old Spanish courtship customs, so Bart would know how to go about getting a Montoya bride.

Now he was searching Antonio's courtyard for a glimpse of the renowned beauties. The courtyard in itself was a thing to behold. It covered almost as much space as a town square. Every room in the hacienda opened out to it, the upper rooms by means of balconies. Tree branches and grape vines shaded the gardens and stone walkways below. A well stood near one corner.

"I am happy to hear that your father is doing well," Antonio said, leading his guest into the courtyard. "And what about your lovely mother?"

"Oh, she died," Bart said. "Yellow fever, the year after my father came back from the war."

"I am very sorry," the don said, removing his sombrero.

Bart saw a young Spanish woman breeze under an archway across the courtyard. Maxwell, it seemed, had been right. She wasn't hard to look at. She was dressed fetchingly but tastefully in a close-fitting white blouse and a long red skirt, a lace rebozo wrapping her shoulders.

"Sebastiana!" Antonio said. "Come here and meet our guest. Bring the gourd with you so that he may have a drink of water."

The young beauty obeyed, dipping the gourd in the well bucket and sweeping across the courtyard toward the *rico* and his guest. She was definitely of marriageable age, Bart thought. Certainly desirable enough. Her eyes searched him without a hint of timidity, and a faint smile made him stand a little taller and strike a more gallant pose.

"Cool your throat, amigo," Don Antonio said as Sebastiana handed the gourd dipper to Bart. "It has been a long, hot journey for you."

Bart ogled the woman between his hat brim and the gourd as he drank. He had expected a teenager. This woman was mature—his own age, if not a year or two older. How long was Antonio going to hold on to her?

"Sebastiana, *querida*," Antonio continued, "this is Bartolome Young, from Texas."

Bart liked the sound of his name in Spanish. He

embraced the senorita's hand with a warm grip, not too firm.

"Bartolome . . ." the *rico* said, "my wife, Sebastiana."

Bart's hand went cold as a dead fish. This was the old man's wife! And she wouldn't turn loose of his hand! She wet her lips and raised one eyebrow at him.

"M-m-m-my pleasure," he stammered. Her fingers caressed his palm with something more than the customary welcome. The handshake lingered until Bart was sure the hacendado would grow suspicious. Still, Sebastiana refused to release his hand.

To his relief, a racket that sounded remarkably like a fight between two rabid cats echoed sharply through the courtyard, causing Sebastiana to lose her grip. She rolled her eyes at the shrill voices and turned away with indifference, glancing back at Bart only once before she disappeared in the cool shadows of the adobe walls.

Two awkward girls marched into the courtyard, each one trying to stand in the way of the other. They snapped at each other like hens, rattling off Spanish with such momentum that Don Antonio could not quiet them from where he stood. The hacendado marched toward them, but just before he reached them, one grabbed the other's hair, and a battle of fingernails and shin kicks began, the likes of which Bart had never seen.

"Tomasa! Gregoria!" Antonio shouted, pulling them apart.

Bart beheld them with awe: two clumsy girls of tangled tresses, large flaring nostrils, snarling lips, clenching fists, and cheeks billowing with the angry breaths they heaved.

"Can you not see that we have a guest here in our courtyard?" Antonio shouted.

The girls glanced around until their wild eyes found Bart. They started pulling hair back from their homely faces and straightening their disheveled clothing. When they smiled, he saw they had crooked teeth.

"Now, that is better," Antonio said. "Bartolome, these are my two beautiful daughters, Tomasa and Gregoria."

Beautiful daughters? Where? These poor things were as fat and ugly as bloodhound pups. Still, Bart had to smile back. Maxwell had pulled a good one on him. Renowned for their looks? Yes, they probably were! He held back a guffaw and smiled at the two Montoya girls until he saw Sebastiana leering at him from the shadows of an archway, where only he could see her. The hacendada allowed her eyes to rake him from the heels of his boots to the crown of his hat and back again. He looked away from her before Antonio could catch him blushing.

And he was going to stay in this hacienda where all the women looked at him as though they had never seen a man before? This was going to be dangerous. Maybe even amusing.

Five

❧

Don Antonio Geronimo Montoya de Cordoba y Chaves de Oca was one of the last of the old *ricos*, and one of the few who had learned to profit from the Yanqui invasion. But he had always understood capitalism, even before the Americans came. He had started building his fortune with a string of ox carts that he kept busy on the old road to Chihuahua. Later, he realized even larger profits on the Santa Fe Trail to Missouri. He had established a trading house in Santa Fe, still operated by his two sons, one of whom also served in the territorial legislature.

Years before the Yanquis took over New Mexico, Antonio had organized a group of settlers to petition the Mexican government for a grant of land. In due time, the governor had approved the grant and placed Montoya's people in possession of eleven square leagues, about forty-eight thousand acres, situated on the mountain slopes east of Santa Fe. To earn title, the settlers had to grow crops, become virtually self-sufficient, and weather the occasional assault by Utes or Jicarilla Apaches.

The land did not belong to Antonio Montoya himself. It was a community grant, intended to populate the Northern Frontier with Mexican citizens. Like the other settlers, Antonio claimed only a small piece of land for his hacienda and a small field irrigated by a mountain stream. The vast remainder of the grant belonged to all of the settlers in common. There they grazed their herds of cattle and flocks of sheep, they cut timber, and they hunted.

As trade increased on the Santa Fe Trail, many settlers decided to sell their rights to the grant and move into Santa Fe to work. They found a willing buyer in Antonio Montoya. He paid fair prices for the small houses and fields, and with each he acquired another share in the common lands. It was his aim to someday gain exclusive ownership to all eleven square leagues.

After the United States won New Mexico, the Anglo land speculators came and began trying to buy shares in what had become known as the "Montoya grant." Antonio advised his people against dealing with the Anglos.

"If you want to sell your titles to the grant," he told them at a meeting one night in his hacienda, "sell to me. I will pay more, and I will let you stay in your houses and plow your fields as long as you live. The Anglos will make you leave if you sell to them. They do not care about you. All they want is the land."

Now only a handful of old settlers continued to

hold on to their grant rights. Antonio knew that as they grew older or died off, he could buy the rights from them or their heirs and ultimately gain exclusive right and title to the entire Montoya grant—its irrigated fields, pastures, and timber.

But it would have to happen quickly. The Anglo lawyers were getting trickier. They had figured out ways to force Mexican landowners to sell their grants—ways to trick them out of their land— ways even Don Antonio could not prevent. The Anglo legal system differed so markedly from the old Spanish and Mexican courts that Antonio couldn't grasp its complexities.

That was why this Bartolome Young seemed like such a godsend. The son of a lawyer. New to the territory. Befriended already by the likes of Lucien Maxwell, whose horse he had ridden in on. Just the sort of man he could use on his side.

So Antonio showed the visitor to one of his finest guest rooms, on the second floor with a balcony overlooking the east side of the courtyard. Bart found no bedstead in the room. The New Mexicans slept on thick mattresses of wool, which during the day were rolled and placed against a wall. Along with the mattress, Bart found a candle, a washstand, and a small fireplace.

"My sons will arrive soon from Santa Fe," the hacendado said. "Then we will eat. You have time to refresh yourself and relax before they get here."

"*Gracias, Señor,*" Bart said. He dropped his portmanteau on the floor as the *rico* left him. He took off his shirt to get closer to the coolness of the adobe walls. After washing his face and hands, he unrolled the mattress and stretched out on it to take a short siesta. He dozed off staring at the peeled timbers above him. He felt strangely at home with the architecture of New Mexico.

He hadn't been asleep very long when he heard his door latch click. His eyes opened and saw a person moving toward him. Pulling himself up on his elbows, he found Sebastiana descending on him. The young hacendada put her hand on his bare chest and pushed him back down onto his mattress. She let her eyes pass over him as if feasting on his flesh.

Bart smiled nervously.

"You are a very light sleeper," she said.

He could think of no reply.

"Antonio is a very sound sleeper."

"You mean your husband?"

"He never wakes up. I will prove it to you tonight."

"That's not necessary. I believe you."

"After he goes to sleep, I will come to you here."

His eyes shifted. "I think that might be asking too much of Antonio's hospitality."

"You will see. After he goes to sleep, he never wakes up. He is an old man." She searched him with her eyes again. "You are young. Tonight."

Sebastiana parted her lips and leaned over Bart's face. Her hair fell from her shoulders and tickled his neck. He held his breath and shrank as deeply as he could into the mattress as she put her lips very near his. But she didn't kiss him. She smiled wickedly and left the room like a breeze.

He lay there, contemplating Sebastiana, until he heard the hoofbeats. Stepping out on to the balcony as he buttoned his shirt, he saw two paunchy, well-dressed young men alighting from a carriage.

Antonio's sons, he presumed. In minutes, Antonio was at his door, inviting him to supper.

The dining hall was filled with rustic New Mexico furnishings, accented with a few Spanish-colonial pieces. Planks comprising the table top had been hand-hewn and smoothed. The chairs around it were small, square specimens. As Bart had learned at Maxwell's Ranch, the men would dine in this room alone, while Antonio's wife and daughters, and the other women in the hacienda, would eat in a dining room of their own.

Bart met the hacendado's sons, Francisco and Vicente. They extended little of the hospitality Antonio had shown. Both around thirty years of age, they behaved with a great deal of arrogance. Vicente was the legislator, but Francisco seemed more apt to lead.

"Bartolome's father was one of the wounded Texans here during the war," Antonio explained.

"Where is the food?" Francisco replied.

"Yes, I am starving," Vicente added.

They seated themselves at the table as two señoritas began bringing in the food. When the brothers started speaking to Antonio in Spanish, Bart let his attention wander to the girls who were serving the meal. They were dressed in neat peasant skirts and blouses. The Montoya men did not so much as glance at them. They were rather plain looking, their eyes lacking energy. They served the men by routine.

Then the third girl came in, carrying goblets and a bottle of wine. Bart knew instantly that she was different. She wore the same peasant dress, but her beauty was striking, though she was only fifteen or sixteen by his estimation. Her bright eyes darted among the men. When they met his, they cut quickly away, but she smiled slightly as she went about her duties. Bart could hardly keep his eyes off of her.

"What?" Antonio said, in a suddenly louder voice, in response to something one of his sons had said. He looked at Bart. "Bartolome, when you stayed with Maxwell, did he tell you he had sold his grant?" The pretty servant girl was at his shoulder, pouring the wine.

"Yes," Bart said. "That reminds me"—he reached into the pocket of his jacket—"Maxwell asked me to carry this letter to you."

When he handed the letter to Don Antonio, Bart caught the servant girl's eyes and held her stare long enough to make her spill the wine on the hacendado. Antonio leaped back from the table and let fly a string of what Bart took for Spanish cuss words. But when he turned his angry eyes on the girl, he became suddenly silent.

"Bitora!" he said, after taking a moment to compose himself. "What are you doing in here?"

"I wanted to meet the guest," she said, glancing at Bart. "Tomasa and Gregoria got to meet him, and I did not."

"How dare you dress like that! And you should be eating with your sisters and your mother."

"That witch is not my mother," Bitora said.

Antonio raised his hand. "Watch your tongue! I will slap you for such talk!"

Bart could tell by the way Bitora smirked that she had never been slapped in her life.

"I want to be introduced to our guest, like everyone else," she demanded.

"Yes, but you are *not* like everyone else!"

Antonio roared. "You do not know your place!" He grabbed his youngest daughter by the arm and led her to the door. Her bright eyes settled on Bart for a moment before the door shut her out.

"My apologies, Bartolome," the old man said, his eyes flashing as if he had really enjoyed the confrontation. "That one has always been trouble."

"The prettiest ones always are," he replied.

The hacendado returned to his chair and opened the letter from Lucien Maxwell. "I hope you will not consider me ill mannered if I read this letter in your presence, Bartolome, but I haven't heard from Señor Maxwell in a long time."

"Not at all," Bart said.

Antonio scanned the letter for a few seconds, then raised his eyes to his sons. "It is true," he said. "He has sold his grant to some Englishmen. Ha! He is suggesting that I do the same thing. He says he will find the buyers if I wish."

"Are you trying to sell, too?" Bart asked.

"Never. No price is high enough. I will be buried here."

Instantly, Bart's admiration for the hacendado doubled. He had finally found someone who knew what land was worth. A man could become a part of his land, like a tree taking root.

"Maxwell has bought Fort Sumner from the army," Antonio said, astonished, "and he is going there to live! *Incredible!* Why would he want to live so far from the mountains? It will kill him!"

The *rico* shook his head as he turned to the second leaf of the letter. Then his worried eyes brightened. "This part is about you, Bartolome. Maxwell says you have come to New Mexico to get some land and become a rancher."

Bart nodded. "As soon as I figure out how the speculators do it," he said. "I want a piece like yours—reaching into the mountains, with timber, pasture lands, and running water."

As Don Antonio came to the bottom of the page, his face went blank. He stared long enough to let Bart know he was reading the last paragraph over and over. Finally he folded the pages, slipped them back into the envelope, and turned his chair to face Bart. "Now I understand why you have come to see me," he said.

"Sir?" Bart said.

"Señor Maxwell has made your proposal for you, as you wished, and he speaks very well of you. You will receive my fairest consideration."

"Thank you," Bart said, wondering what Maxwell had written about him.

"Now, tell me. Which of my daughters do you wish to marry? Or does it matter to you?"

The jaws of the Montoya brothers locked as they turned their dark eyes on Bart for the first time since they had met him. They had no desire to share the family fortune with a new son-in-law.

Bart almost choked on a large bite he had just taken. He remembered Maxwell explaining the Spanish courtship customs. It was common for a friend to recommend a prospective groom in a letter, and it seemed Maxwell had done so. Bart didn't even have to know the customs to realize how deeply he would offend Antonio now by telling him he didn't want to marry any of his daughters.

Thankfully, he had the mouthful of food to chew, which gave him some precious time to think of a way out of this. He couldn't imagine himself standing at the altar with either of the snarling butterballs he had seen scrapping in the courtyard earlier. And Bitora was a mere child.

Even in his panic, he had to admire Maxwell. The land baron had given him fair warning, and Bart still hadn't seen it coming.

He reached for his wine glass, not yet knowing what he would say. But then it came time to speak, and the inspiration seemed to come to him out of pure ether.

"It matters a great deal to me which of your daughters I would marry," he began. "I'll name her if you'll let me explain my circumstances."

Antonio nodded.

"I'm new to the territory. I have no money or land. I don't even have a job yet. Despite what Maxwell says, I am certainly not much of a prospect for your daughters at this time." He found the brothers nodding in agreement with him, and Antonio listening with curiosity.

"However," the Anglo continued, "I intend to have all those situations remedied in four or five years. By that time I should think that I would be a highly favorable prospect."

"Perhaps," Antonio said. "But which daughter will wait that long for you? Tomasa and Gregoria have each received several proposals. I intend to see them married within the year."

"Yes, but my interest is in Bitora."

The old don bristled. "Bitora!"

"She's only a girl now," Bart said, "but in four or five years, she will be of marriageable age."

"You wish to marry my little Bitora?"

"Only if she is in agreement. I insist she be given her choice."

Francisco's eyes sparked, and he nudged Vicente, thinking the guest wouldn't notice. Both brothers realized how easy it would be to turn Bitora against this Anglo over the course of four or five years.

The stern look on Don Antonio's face lost some of its edge as he saw the many ways around the proposal. Bartolome might not get rich enough in five years to warrant serious consideration. He might not even last a year in the territory. On the other hand, if he proved ambitious enough to become wealthy and landed in five years, he might prove to be a valuable son-in-law.

Still, he did not reply. It was better to let the young man sweat. He turned his attention back to his food, and the men ate the remainder of their meal without conversation. When Antonio finally looked up from his plate, it was as if there had never been any talk of marriage.

"Let us retire to the courtyard," the hacendado said, rising. "Sebastiana is going to play the guitar for us. Wait until you hear her sing, Bartolome." He grinned boyishly. "I would kill for that woman."

As they left the dining hall, Bart asked Antonio to wait a moment before proceeding to the courtyard. "I don't mean to sound ungrateful," he began, "but it's about my room."

"What is wrong with your room?"

"Absolutely nothing. It's the finest room I've ever seen, but . . ."

"Please, what is it?" Antonio said.

"Well, I was wondering if I might have a room on the west side of the courtyard. I want to look across it and see the sun rise over your mountains in the morning."

Antonio smiled. "Of course, amigo. I should have thought of it myself." He put his hand on Bart's shoulder and started him walking toward the courtyard.

"But please don't mention to your wife about my changing rooms," Bart added. "I would die of embarrassment if she thought I was in any way ungrateful."

"Of course not," the *rico* said. "I will keep it just between you and me."

Six

❦

"I am not going to marry you," Bitora said.

She had come up behind Bart so silently in the courtyard that her voice startled him, making him slosh coffee from his cup. He rose from his bench, slinging the scalding liquid from his hand. Again he was struck by her youthful beauty.

The rising sun was on her face, lending a fiery light to her eyes, bathing her warm complexion in golden hues. She had lost her peasant skirt and blouse, and now wore a blue organdy dress with ruffles and a matching rebozo. Silver pins held her hair up, and high-heeled leather shoes had replaced her sandals, as if she had risen in wealth and standing overnight.

He smiled. "Can't say that I blame you."

"My father cannot make me marry you. The old customs are ridiculous."

"I agree. Don't worry, Miss Montoya, I didn't come here to marry you or anybody else."

She appeared suddenly insulted, and glanced up and down at him as if she couldn't believe his nerve. "What do you mean? My brothers told me you brought a letter of proposal with you."

Bart chuckled. "A friend of mine tried to trick me into marrying one of your sisters. I didn't like the idea of that, so I used you as an excuse to get out of it. I said it was *you* I wanted to marry, when you got old enough, figuring that would give the whole thing four or five years to simmer down."

She stepped back and glowered at him indignantly. "So, I am just your *excuse*? You should know that there are many handsome young men around here who would like to marry me."

"I'm sure there are, but I'm not one of them."

She put her hands on her hips. "And so now I am not good enough for you? It is because I was dressed like a peasant girl last night, isn't it?"

"What are you getting so riled about? You said you didn't want to marry me, anyway. I had to use you as an excuse to keep from insulting your father. I surely wasn't about to marry one of your sisters."

Her hard stare finally relented, but she held her defiant pose. "And so, you did not come here to marry me?"

"No offense, Miss Montoya, but no. I didn't even know you existed until I saw you last night."

Suddenly Bitora laughed and looked away.

"Now, what's so funny?"

"Francisco and Vicente told some terrible lies about you."

"I don't doubt it. What did they say?"

"That you were addicted to opium, that you cheat at cards, and that your parents never married."

He turned red and trembled, embarrassed and incensed to hear an innocent repeating such lies about him.

Bitora regretted telling him. "I didn't believe them," she said quickly. She was trying to think of a new topic of conversation when she heard Sebastiana's taunting laughter across the courtyard. Her stepmother passed briefly under a shadowy archway, another figure following close behind, reaching for her.

Bart couldn't tell if it was Vicente or Francisco pursuing Sebastiana, but right now one was no different from the other to him. He took a step toward the archway, bent on teaching whichever brother it was what he thought about liars, but Bitora grabbed him by the arm.

"Don't make trouble," she said. "If my father finds out about them, something terrible will happen."

"If he finds out about who?"

"That witch and my brothers."

He looked down at her hand, still clenched tightly around his elbow. "You mean, your brothers . . ."

"That is why they leave their wives in Santa Fe when they come here. But they are so stupid, they don't even know about each other. She is making a fool of every man in this house, and I am the only one who can see it. She will probably try to make a fool of you, too."

"She already has," Bart admitted, "but I threw her off my trail last night."

"How did she do it?" Bitora asked, her eyes flashing.

"She came to my room yesterday afternoon." He was suddenly a bit stunned to think of himself telling such things to a sixteen-year-old girl, but he found her easy to talk to. "Dang near pounced on me right there on the floor."

"She will not stop there. Vicente resisted her for a while, but she finally got him, too. Francisco did not resist at all. Now she sneaks into their rooms in the middle of the night. Or she leaves messages in their beds, telling them to meet her someplace. I know all about it. There is something wrong with her. She is a crazy witch."

"Maybe you should tell your father."

She shook her head and stepped back in dread. "No! I am afraid he might kill them. And her, too. You don't know my father. He believes in the old customs. He would kill you, too, if he caught you with Sebastiana. I am warning you. He doesn't care what the Yanquis would do to him. He would murder someone if he found out."

"There you are!" a voice suddenly called.

Bart flinched, and turned to see Antonio, smiling and approaching him across the courtyard.

"Are you ready to take our ride?" the old don said.

"Yes, sir," Bart replied, composing himself.

"Bitora, what are you doing here?"

"I want to go, too," she said.

"You are not going. Leave us. Go do something else."

"There is nothing else to do. I'm bored!"

"Go away, child. You cannot ride with men."

Bitora glanced at Bart, then stomped away, holding her ruffles above her ankles.

Antonio chuckled. "To tell the truth, Bartolome, she can ride better than either you or I. She hates the sidesaddle I bought for her. She would rather straddle her horse like a boy. She has always been the one to cause trouble!"

Bart spent the rest of the morning touring the Montoya grant with Antonio. Four servants came along to care for the horses, and to serve the food and wine. They ate on a mountain ridge, under tall pines. From their vantage they could see the plaza of Santa Fe, miles distant.

The day was one to fix the vision of empire in Bart's head. There was no other place like this in the world. He was glad he had dropped out of law school and come to New Mexico while there was still a chance of acquiring an old Spanish land grant.

"When I die, this is where I want to be buried," Antonio said to his guest. "This is the highest point on my grant. Here I am close to heaven, and my journey will not be so long."

Seven

❧

Vernon Regis sat hunched over a copy of the old papers for the Lopez grant, trying to figure out a way to trick the Lopezes out of it. The Spanish government had made the grant to two Lopez brothers in 1767. Their heirs still lived on the land, grazed it, farmed it. None of them would answer his inquiries, nor come to Santa Fe to talk about selling.

The only piece of land Regis wanted more than the Lopez place was the Montoya grant east of town. He just wanted the Lopez grant to parcel up and sell at a profit. The Montoya grant was different. He would divide most of it, but he wanted to keep the Montoya hacienda as his own weekend retreat. Old Antonio had the finest mansion in the county.

On this day, however, he couldn't figure out a way to get his hands on either grant, and it was frustrating the devil out of him. To make things worse, he had heartburn again. Damn Mexican food tore his stomach up something terrible. He stood and unbuttoned his vest to give his gut some room. He was a large man, poorly built. He had narrow shoulders and hips, a large head, a bulging stomach, and tremendous feet. His hands were soft, pale, and thin-skinned, with fingers like pitchfork tines.

He paced, then stood at the window to look out at the plaza. The view depressed him. Cottonwoods cast shadows on the dusty streets. Rambling adobes surrounded the square like so many dirt dobber nests. To the left was the Palace of the Governors; it held the archives where he had schooled himself in the particulars of Spanish and Mexican land grants.

A black sombrero passed in front of his window, and Regis turned back to his desk, determined to study the Lopez grant until the answer came to him. He heard the brass bell ring on the door of his outer office. Whoever it was, his office manager would take care of it.

Just as he was delving back into the grant papers, a knock came at his door, and his office manager stuck his head in.

"There's a fella here who says he wants to talk to you about a land grant."

Regis frowned. "Send him in. Do me good to cuss somebody out today." He slipped the Lopez grant papers under some others on his desk and stood ready to greet the visitor. A young Anglo holding a big black sombrero entered, and Regis wondered what self-respecting American would wear such a hat.

"Bart Young," the visitor said, "lately of Texas."

"What can I do for you?"

"I hear you speculate in land grants."

"I'm a lawyer," Regis replied.

"I'd like to work for you."

Regis invited the visitor to sit in the chair facing his desk. "I don't need any help right now."

Bart handed Regis a few leaves of paper. "Here are my credendials."

Unwillingly, the speculator sat down behind his desk and began perusing the documents. The first appeared to be a letter of recommendation from none other than Lucien B. Maxwell. The next was a Tulane University diploma, then came a certificate from the Texas bar. This wasn't the first time some snot nose had skulked in here to horn in on Vernon Regis's empire.

"Very impressive, Mr. Young, but I really don't have any use for some greenhorn Texas ..." He was about to hurl a few unabridged profanities when he shuffled to the last document in the stack: a letter of introduction from Antonio Montoya. In midsentence, he smiled and looked up at the fledgling lawyer: "... some greenhorn Texas legal genius come here to put me out of business. Tulane's a very good school. Where are you staying?"

"At the hacienda of Don Antonio Montoya. I have a letter from him there."

Regis smirked and tossed the credentials back to Bart's side of the desk. "I know of Montoya. Good fellow. But, like I said, I really have no need for a clerk or what-have-you."

"I'll work strictly on commission," Bart said. "I just want to learn the ropes."

Regis opened a hardwood cigar case and urged

his guest to take one. "I don't have time to be anybody's mentor, son, but maybe we can find something appropriate for you in town. What exactly is
your relationship with Señor Montoya?"

"He and my father were best friends."

Regis covered a giddy streak he felt coming on.
"And what is your interest in Spanish land?"

"I want to own a chunk of it."

"For what purpose?"

"To live on. Start a ranch."

"I see," Regis said. He stroked his chin, leaned
back in his chair, and propped his huge feet on his
desk. "When do you expect to acquire this cattle
empire of yours?"

"I figure it would take a number of years to
learn the business of acquiring the land grants—
and to find the right piece of property."

Regis's big head nodded on his skinny neck for
several long seconds. "I admire your ambition,
young man. I think I know just the place for you."

"You do?" Bart said, pulling himself forward in
his chair.

"Now, keep this to yourself, because the information is confidential. I happen to know that a position will soon be vacant in the archives division
of the territorial government. That's the best place
in the territory to study land grants. Do you read
Spanish?"

"Not much," Bart admitted.

"Doesn't matter. You'll learn. When can you
start?"

"As soon as I can get a room in town."

"Good. I'll arrange the position for you. Come
see me after you get yourself situated. The job
should open up within the week."

Bart shook the speculator's hand, then strode triumphantly from the office. He couldn't wait to get ahold of pen and ink so he could write Randy back in New Orleans.

After his visitor left, Regis crossed the corner of the plaza to the Palace of the Governors. Passing beneath the flimsy porch roof the Americans had tacked on to the venerable adobe, he marched to the office of Alfred Nichols, secretary of the territorial government's records division.

"Morning, Al," he said, entering the small, windowless room.

"Vernon." The bureaucrat slid a file drawer shut. "What brings you over?"

"I have a favor to ask. I want you to fire that Mexican who handles the Spanish archives for you."

"Gonzales?"

"Whatever his name is."

"But, he knows the archives better than anybody. He was here when Kearny took the territory from Old Mexico."

"He's also so damned old that he can barely open the files. He's got a pension coming doesn't he?"

"Yes, a small one."

"Then get rid of him."

"What do you care who handles the archives?"

Regis sank into a chair and crossed his legs, swinging one foot like a sledge hammer. "I know somebody who will be perfect for the job."

"Does he know Spanish?"

"He said 'adios' when he left my office."

"What makes him perfect for the job?"

Regis paused and raised one of his skeletal fingers as his dry lips formed a smile. "He's a friend of Antonio Montoya."

Nichols wrung his hands together nervously as his eyes shifted around his tiny office. "You're going to recruit him?"

"Hell, no. Then he'll want a share of the grant, like you and everybody else. I intend to use him without him even knowing it."

"How?"

"That's my worry. All you have to do is get rid of Gonzales and hire this new kid. Bart Young is his name."

"And?" Nichols said.

"I made you a deal years ago, and it still stands. You help me acquire the Montoya grant, I'll see that you get a one-eighth share in the land. All you have to do is hire Young."

Eight

∾⧫∾

How are your Spanish lessons coming?" Antonio asked.

"*Bastante bien*," Bart answered.

They sat alone in the dining hall, sipping their after-dinner drinks: a brandy for Bart, and a rich port for Antonio.

"Are you able to read the documents in the archives?"

"Not as well as I'd like," Bart admitted. "Those old Spanish pen scrolls take some getting used to. But from what I can translate, they tell some great tales. There are stories of Spanish noblemen, bands of peasants—exploring new places, fighting Indians, settling the land grants."

"So you like working there?"

Bart grinned, his eyes sparkling. "I've got documents in there over a hundred years old. Some of them have sailed back and forth across the ocean, and have signatures of dead Spanish kings on them."

Antonio dismissed the servant girls and poked at the fire for a while. It was November, and the flames went well with the port to pierce the cold creeping down from the mountains. "Have you discovered the name of Nepomeceno Montoya on any of the old papers?"

Bart scratched at the beard he had been cultivating in preparation for the winter. "No, but I can look if you want me to. Ancestor of yours?"

The *rico* pulled a chair up to the hearth and asked Bart to join him. "He was my great-grandfather. The first in my family to come to New Spain. It was 1769 when he arrived on the frontier as a captain of dragoons. One hundred and one years ago, Bartolome. I don't know much about him except for the campaign against the Indians in 1775."

"I've seen references to that campaign in the archives."

"It was maybe the biggest war ever fought between the Spanish Army and the Indians. It made my great-grandfather a famous hero."

"How did it happen?" Bart asked, sliding to the edge of his chair like a boy.

"A man named Hugo O'Conor was the Comandante Inspector then. That was the highest ranking military post on the frontier."

"O'Conor?" Bart snorted. "What kind of name is that for a Spanish officer?"

"I think he was born Irish. Anyway, in 1775 he ordered two thousand men in presidios all across the Northern Frontier to march into the Apache country to punish the Indians for raiding. Nepomeceno Montoya, my great-grandfather, was garrison captain at San Elisario, down the river from where El Paso is now. He was ordered to march north with about a hundred men into the Sacramento Mountains.

"I remember my father and my grandfather telling me about it. They said it was August, and very hot on the desert. But when Nepomeceno got high into the Sacramento Mountains, he found it very cool, with plenty of water running from the mountains in streams. And there were tall trees there, and plenty of rain.

"Nepomeceno found the Mescaleros, but he did not do very much fighting with them at first. He had orders to meet Hugo O'Conor on the Rio Grande, so he had to take his men west. Then he led O'Conor back to the Sacramentos—and that was when the real fighting began.

"The Mescaleros were great warriors. They still live in those mountains, and they are not finished fighting yet. But O'Conor had the best soldiers on the Northern Frontier with him, and they had some bloody battles.

"One morning, when Nepomeceno was leading O'Conor to one of the Indian villages he had discovered, the Mescaleros surprised them and got between O'Conor and my great-grandfather. It was on a steep mountain trail through tall trees, and the soldiers were marching in single file. The Indians attacked the middle of the file to divide the command, and surrounded O'Conor and a few of his men.

"The soldiers scattered all over the place, but Nepomeceno pulled them together and broke through the circle of Mescaleros who had surrounded O'Conor. He led the attack himself, and was shot twice with arrows, but not badly wounded. He fought with his saber and—so the story goes in my family—took the head off a warrior who was trying to kill O'Conor with a knife."

"No wonder he became a hero," Bart said.

"O'Conor recommended Nepomeceno for the Order of Carlos the Third—a very great honor in Spain."

"He should have gotten a land grant in the Sacramentos where he saved O'Conor's life. I've read in the archives where war heros sometimes got big Spanish grants."

"That would have been a fine place for a grant."

Bart poured the last of his brandy down his throat. "You've been there?"

"Once. A long time ago. I had been taking my ox carts to Chihuahua for a few years, and the road along the Rio Grande goes not too far from the Sacramentos, so I decided to take some of my men on horses and see where my great-grandfather saved the life of the Comandante Inspector. We took plenty of powder and bullets, because the Mescaleros were very powerful then."

Antonio smiled, and the firelight flared in his eyes. "We went above the piñons and came to the big timber, and the trees were the tallest I have ever seen. That night we camped and it was very cool, though it was the middle of summer.

"We explored the mountains for seven days. There was water and grass, and deer and elk to hunt. And I heard wolves and lions in the night. We climbed very high, and I think we could see California from up there. I got the idea that I could build a great ranch there, in the Sacramento Mountains. It was so cool that I didn't want to come down."

"So why did you?" Bart asked, rolling a log on the andirons.

"The Mescaleros," Antonio whispered, widening his eyes. "On the seventh day, we were riding on a trail when I saw an Indian brave watching me from the forest. He was so close, a whip could have cut him. I pulled the reins back, and stopped in the trail. One of my men followed my eyes to see what I was looking at. Before I could stop him, he pulled an old horse pistol out of a saddle holster and shot at the Indian."

"Killed him?" Bart asked.

Antonio chuckled. "No, he blasted some bark away from a big tree, and the wood chips got in the Indian's eyes, and made him scream and fall back on the ground. Then the forest came alive with those Apaches. They seemed to spring down from the trees and up from the ground like magic. There were only six of us in my party, and there seemed to be a hundred warriors with bows and arrows that would shoot ten times as fast as our old muskets."

"What did you do?"

"I knew that if we fired, we would be slaughtered, so I told my men to draw their weapons, cock them, aim them, but not to shoot unless the Indians shot their arrows first. They were afraid of our guns. When we aimed at them, they jumped behind trees to hide.

"The Indian who had the wood chips in his eyes finally stopped screaming and sat up on the ground, rubbing his eyes. I told my men to keep their guns pointed at the Indians. I put my rifle in the saddle scabbard and, taking my canteen, got down from my horse."

"Canteen? What were you going to do? Drown them?"

"No, *idiota*, I helped that Indian wash his eyes clear of the tree bark, and then I drank with him from the same canteen, like brothers."

"And they let you go?"

"A chief named Ojo Blanco came down from the forest. He spoke very good Spanish. He was a young man—maybe not a head chief, but just a leader of that band or something. He told us that if we would give them our weapons, they would let us go."

"Did you?"

"What would you have done, Bartolome?"

Bart paused to pick his teeth with a wood splinter. "I don't believe I'd ever give up my guns to Indians."

"But Ojo Blanco said he would kill us if we didn't give up our guns."

'Well, I hope you told him there would be a lot of widows and orphans back at his camp before he got your guns away from you."

The *rico* smiled and smoothed his mustache into his sideburns. "I didn't say it that way, but Ojo Blanco understood me. We argued for a while and threatened to kill each other a dozen times, until finally the chief told me I could take my men out of the mountains if I promised never to come back. If I did return, he said, he would kill me for certain."

"Did you ever go back?" Bart asked.

"Never. But the memory of that place is always with me. I wish I could go back there." He sighed and shook his head as if to clear the thoughts from his mind. "I will probably never see it again. It is a wild place and I am an old man."

"You mean it's an old place, and you're a wild man," Bart suggested. "If you want to go there again, why don't we just get up an expedition?"

Antonio chuckled. "I have other pleasures to divert me here. I could not stand to spend that much time away from Sebastiana. Not even one night, amigo." His eyes twinkled.

"Afraid you might miss something?"

"I know I would."

"Every night?" Bart asked.

"Each and every night." The hacendado grinned and raised his eyebrows.

Bart shook his head in disbelief. "You amaze me," he said. But he was thinking of the way Bitora so often spoke of her stepmother: That woman was not natural.

Nine

~∞~

Vernon Regis sucked the match flame into his cigar as he leaned across R. T. Fincher's desk. "It sounds simple, but it took me a long time to think of it," his thin lips said around the stogie. He was bragging to the surveyor general about his recent acquisition of the Lopez grant.

"How did you do it?" Fincher asked, blowing smoke rings over his leaded-glass lamp.

"I just had some associates send letters to various members of the Lopez family until I had half of them convinced that the other half was going to sue for sole possession of the land. After I got them feuding amongst themselves, they couldn't wait to sell their shares, just to keep their own uncles and cousins from taking them."

Fincher chuckled and puffed smoke at the ceiling. "Now, don't gloat, Vernon. It's no great feat

to take land from people as ignorant as these
Mexicans."

Regis's big head bobbed. "You're right, as
usual," he said.

Hobnobbing with the surveyor general was a
crucial part of his job. One of Fincher's duties was
to recommend approval or denial of Spanish land
grants to Congress. He knew more Greek than
Spanish and understood little of land grant history,
but Congress almost always followed his recommendations. Without congressional approval, the
Lopez grant would become public domain, and
Regis's title to it would be worthless.

Regis was hoping to get Fincher to invest in the
grant. The surveyor general speculated openly in
Spanish land and saw no conflict of interest there,
though he virtually had the power to confirm or
deny the grants he invested in with his congressional recommendations.

"Did you look over the papers?" the speculator
asked.

Fincher smirked. "It all looks like gibberish to
me. I sent them to one of my title experts." He
glanced at the grandfather clock standing against
the adobe wall. "He should be here any minute to
report to me on it. You might as well stay and hear
what he has to say."

"Don't mind if I do," Regis said. "But I know the
title is firm. I wouldn't be asking you in on the
deal if there was any question about it."

"I trust you," the surveyor general said. "But I
have all the grants checked by experts so I'll know
what to write in my reports to Congress. Now, we
might as well sip some whiskey until the grant papers get here."

"Anything but tequila," Regis said.

They had poured the liquor and drank their first toasts when they heard a knock at the door. Regis burst out laughing when Bart Young came in carrying a box of papers. "This is your so-called expert? He hasn't even been in the territory a year!"

Bart put the box down and brushed the snow-flakes from his coat. "I didn't know you would be here, Vernon." He snapped his fingers. "I've got a new riddle for you."

"Bart's partial to riddles," the speculator said.

"So am I," Fincher replied. "Let's hear it."

Bart pulled up a chair. "Let's say you have five eggs in a bowl. How can you divide the five eggs among five men, yet leave one in the bowl?"

Regis scratched his head with a cadaverous finger as if actually contemplating the puzzle. He hated riddles. They were a ridiculous waste of time. But it was important to string the archivist along if he was going to own Montoya's hacienda someday.

R. T. Fincher broke the silence with his voice in a state of near hysteria. "I know! Scramble them! Leave one in the bowl, scramble the other four, and let the five men divide the scrambled eggs!"

"Good try," Bart said, "but that would only be dividing four eggs. How about you, Vernon? Care to try?"

"No, you've stumped me again, Bart. What's the answer?"

"You simply give the fifth man the egg *and* the bowl!"

Regis spread his arms to the ceiling, like a vulture taking sun on his wings. "Now, let's see if you're as clever with land titles as you are with riddles. What did you find out about the Lopez grant?"

Bart put on his professional demeanor and removed the first sheet of parchment from the box. "The earliest document pertaining to the grant is this petition from two Lopez brothers, Juan and Filipe, dated 1765." He put the petition aside and reached for the next document in his box. "Now, here is the governor's report on the petition, dated several months later—you know how slow things move in government."

"Mr. Young," Fincher suddenly said, "I assume all these details are in your report?"

"Of course."

"Then get to the point. Is the title to the Lopez grant valid, or not?"

Bart almost withered. He had rehearsed this presentation document by document. "There's no doubt in my mind that it's a good grant, and Vernon has acquired full possession of it."

"That's all I wanted to know," the surveyor general said.

"However . . ." Bart added. The speculator and the bureaucrat looked at him with wrinkles of concern on their brows, and he felt himself in control again.

"Well?" Regis said.

Bart made furious excavations into the box of old papers. "It doesn't affect the validity of the grant, but I thought you would want to know."

"Know what?" Regis said.

"Here it is." He extracted a wrinkled page. "You paid some Lopez heirs up in Taos for their share in the grant, right?"

"Three sisters and a brother. What of it? I paid Lopezes all over the territory to get that grant."

"Yes, but these particular Lopezes had no real claim to the grant."

"They had the last will and testament of their great-grandfather," Regis argued.

"You mean this?" He handed the will to Regis. "It's a forgery."

The speculator studied the leaf of parchment. "How do you know?"

"It's written with a steel pen."

"So what?"

"It's dated 1769, and the steel-point pen wasn't even invented until the 1790s. I'm afraid they took you, Vernon."

Fincher broke into a laugh. "Hoodwinked by ignorant Mexicans!"

Regis held his composure, but the forgery burned his fingers like hot coals. He could not tolerate being made a fool of.

"It's an excellent forgery, except for the steel pen they used," Bart said. "After I noticed it, I did some checking, and it seems this great-grandfather who supposedly wrote this will never even existed."

An ugly, rambling grin stretched across Regis's face. "Good work, Bart." He looked at Fincher, who was still chuckling. "Oh, shut up, R. T."

Regis offered to help Bart carry the documents back to the archives. Leaving the surveyor general's office, they turned toward the plaza, bowing their heads to the snow whipping down the street on a north wind.

"You're getting awful proficient at this archive business," the speculator said. "Not even I caught

that forgery, and I've seen dozens of them. I'll remember that thing about the steel pen."

Bart stiffened with pride. "Antonio got me to
thinking about that. He remembers using quill
pens when he was a boy."

Regis sensed the opening he had been awaiting
for months. "Speaking of Don Antonio . . ." he began. His unwieldy shoes left long streaks in the
snow as he shuffled out on to the Plaza. "I probably shouldn't be telling you this. . . ."

"What?" Bart asked.

"Some of my colleagues would consider it trea-
sonous, letting you in on their plans, but, dammit,
they've gone too far this time. They're going to
give us all a bad name if somebody doesn't do
something about it."

"What are you talking about?"

"I heard a rumor. Some lawyers are going to
challenge Antonio's claim to his grant."

Bart laughed. "The Montoya grant is the most
well-documented grant in the archives. Who
would be fool enough to challenge it?"

"The challenge is just a trick to get Antonio into
court," Regis said. "He'll need a lawyer. So, some
lawyer who is in on the scheme will come out to
his hacienda and offer to fight the challenge for
him. But only if Antonio pays in land. They'll
probably demand a third of his grant. That's the
going rate. The same scam has been played on
other grants in the territory."

Bart stomped the snow from his boots under the
shed porch of the Palace of the Governors. "He
won't fall for that. He'll just hire his own lawyer."

"That's the problem," Regis said. "Any lawyer

who represents Antonio will incur the disfavor of the Santa Fe ring."

"I thought that whole business about the Santa Fe ring was a myth," the archivist said, leading Regis into the building.

"It's nothing organized, but it works. It's hard to explain. The more connections you have, and the more favors you can call in, the deeper you are in the ring. If somebody went against the ring on the Montoya grant, he would find legal roadblocks everywhere he went for months, maybe years. It would take somebody of high caliber to pull it off."

Bart stopped at the door to his office and struggled to get a hand on the knob. "Somebody like you?"

Regis put on his best look of surprise. "Don't drag me into it. I'm only telling you this because I think it's criminal what some of these speculators are getting away with these days."

"That's why you're just the man to fight it," Bart replied, finally putting his burden down on his desk. "You have the influence to survive the Santa Fe ring."

Regis appeared nervous as he put his load next to Bart's. "Now, don't jump the gun. If they really challenge Antonio's claim, tell me; then we'll decide what to do about it. Hell, it's probably just a wild rumor, anyway. I wouldn't worry about it. I thought you might want to warn Antonio, though. Just don't tell anybody you heard it from me."

"I won't," Bart promised.

"Now I have to get back to the office and deal with these Lopezes in Taos who defrauded me with that forgery you discovered."

"All right," Bart said. "Thanks for the help with these documents. Say, before you go, I've got one more for you."

"One more what?"

"How many eggs could the giant, Goliath, eat on an empty stomach?"

Regis sighed and feigned his look of concentration. These riddles were beginning to irk him, and he was still boiling mad over those Taos Lopezes. He couldn't wait to get back to his office where he could kick something.

Ten

The fire in the back room of the Paisano Club roared up the chimney, and Domingo Archiveque sat with his feet propped on the hearth. A hole in his boot had let in the slush from the Santa Fe streets, and the heat pricked his toes as they thawed.

He was alone, his back to the darkened room. Only the firelight moved in his emotionless eyes. It flickered across his spotty beard and the ugly knife scar that started at the nostril and ended at the earlobe. He wore his grease-stained sheepskin coat draped over his shoulders like a cape, and under it he had his hand on his pistol grip.

There was nothing fancy about the old Colt—it had seen decades of service in many hands. But none was as ready to use it as Domingo's.

When he heard the door latch move, he turned sideways in his chair, making certain the Colt would slip from the holster if he needed it. The door opened, and Vernon Regis stood silhouetted by the light in the saloon, waiting for his eyes to adjust to the darkness.

"Is that you?" he said.

Domingo grunted.

Regis grabbed a coal-oil lamp off the wall of the saloon and filled the back room with its light. He put a bottle of tequila on the table as he sat. Domingo moved like a cat to the bottle and poured a glass.

"How did things go down at Torreon?"

"There are still three who will not sell their farms," Domingo said.

"Did you threaten them like I told you?"

He nodded.

"You'll have to go back and get rough, then."

Domingo said nothing, but his lips formed a smile as he touched them with his tequila glass.

"I have another job for you to take care of, first, though." The speculator removed a piece of paper and several gold coins from his pocket. "These are the names of four Lopezes who live up in Taos. Three sisters and a brother. They cheated me out of some money. Make them sorry for it."

Archiveque held the paper between his fingers for a moment, then threw it in the fire.

"Don't kill them," Regis said. "They only took me for fifty dollars a head. I don't suppose that's worth their lives. But make sure they know I sent you."

Archiveque nodded as he picked up the gold coins.

The speculator rose from the table. "Want me to leave the lamp?" he asked.

The Mexican shook his head.

"No, I don't suppose you were ever afraid of the dark, were you?"

"Once, I was," Domingo said. "I was afraid the old man I lived with would start beating me if I went to sleep. But then I killed him."

Regis was never sure whether or not to believe Archiveque's many boasts of murder. "How old are you, Domingo?"

"Almost twenty."

Regis laughed as he grabbed the lamp. "You must have killed a man a month from the stories you tell." He stopped at the door and turned back to the gunman. "One of those Lopez sisters in Taos is damned good to look at," he said. "You'll know the one I mean when you see her. Give her one of those so she'll remember what she did to me." He traced his long gaunt finger from nostril to earlobe.

Archiveque nodded and smiled again as he was left in darkness.

Eleven

❧

One?" Bitora said, wrinkling her nose under the flat brim of her riding hat. "Goliath was a giant."

"But he could only eat one egg on an empty stomach," Bart explained, "because after that his stomach wouldn't be empty any more."

"How was I supposed to guess that?"

"I guessed it the first time I heard it."

"You are lying!"

They argued as they wound down the trail, returning from their Saturday ride in the mountains. When they came within earshot of the hacienda, an angry shout interrupted them.

"That's my father's voice," Bitora said, spurring her mount to a gallop.

Bart's horse kicked rocks from the rough trail as he pursued her. He caught her just before they entered the corrals at the rear of the hacienda, but

Bitora pressed her horse right into the courtyard,
ducking under the archway. Bart came to her side
again as they heard the old *rico* shout over the rattle of hooves on the stone walkways.

"He's out front," Bart said. "Wonder what he's
so mad about?"

They raced their horses through the front archway and found Antonio shouting at a Santa Fe
lawyer named Lefty Harless who was scrambling
into a buggy. Tomasa and Gregoria stood agog,
watching. Francisco and Vicente looked on with
satisfaction as their father berated the Anglo in
Spanish. Sebastiana was there, too, standing apart
from the others.

It had been weeks since Vernon Regis's warning
about the challenge to the Montoya grant. Bart had
almost dismissed it as rumor. But now Lefty
Harless, one of the least ethical land speculators in
the territory, had set foot on the Montoya grant.
Bart could tell by Don Antonio's threats what had
brought Harless out: Somebody had challenged the
authenticity of the Montoya grant in district court,
and Harless had offered to defend the case if
Antonio would pay with a third of the grant.

After the lawyer's buggy bounced away toward
Santa Fe, Antonio turned to Bart. "It is just as your
friend warned, Bartolome. We must go to Santa Fe
immediately and find out what we can do."

Vicente and Francisco glared at Bart with
jealousy for knowing more than they about the
problem.

They saddled four fresh horses and galloped
into the territorial capital, passing Lefty Harless on
the outskirts of town. Bart led the Montoyas to
Vernon Regis's rambling adobe house on the Santa

Fe River and asked the scar-faced guard at the gate to take a message to the speculator. They let the spring sunshine take the chill of the brisk ride from their faces as they waited.

In a few minutes Regis appeared at the front gate to ask what was wrong. When Bart told him, he frowned and nodded. "So, the rumor was true. I was afraid it might be."

"What do you recommend that I do?" Antonio asked.

"Get a lawyer, of course," Regis replied.

"Will you take the case, Vernon?" Bart asked.

Regis chuckled. "You don't want me, Bart. I've got too many irons in the fire. But I'll refer you to some decent attorneys who might help."

Bart and the Montoya men spent the rest of the day tracking down the lawyers Regis had recommended. None of them had the time to fight the challenge.

"Why won't they help me, Bartolome? I have the money to pay them."

"The Santa Fe ring is behind it. They're all afraid of being blacklisted."

"I will have to get a lawyer from the States," the *rico* suggested.

"He wouldn't know anything about Spanish land grants. Let's go see Regis again. This time we won't take no for an answer."

Regis flatly refused at first, but Bart argued until it was pitch black, and Regis finally gave in.

"Oh, all right, Bart," he said. "It'll be the end of my career in Santa Fe, but I'll do it. I guess you're right. The ring has gone too far this time, and if I don't fight it, I might as well be part of it. It will take time, though, and I don't work cheap."

"I can pay your fee," Antonio assured him.

"It might go higher than you ever dreamed, Antonio. The plaintiffs will drag this thing out as long as they can, and they'll have the judges on their side. They'll get postponements and cause delays for months in order to wear us out. They'll want to make an example of you for having the audacity to fight the ring."

"And I will make an example of them!" Antonio said with fire in his voice. "There is not a Mexicano in Santa Fe who will not spit at that little coward who came to my hacienda today! His servants will leave him! The cafés will not feed him! Not even the whores will take his money!"

Regis chuckled to think of Lefty Harless being turned away from his favorite whorehouse. "That's the spirit, Antonio. That's the only way to deal with these greedy bastards. Hit them where it hurts."

As Regis had warned, the proceedings dragged on for months. Bart testified several times, explaining to the court in great detail the validity of the Montoya grant, using the old papers from the archive to bolster his position and pointing out that Congress had confirmed the grant several years before.

As the trial dragged on through the summer, public sentiment began to favor Antonio Montoya. The newspapers mocked the tactics of the land-grabbing plaintiffs. Vernon Regis grew into something of a crusader.

Through it all, Bart was more excited than concerned by the trial. He felt as if he were bringing about changes of great importance in the

territory, in addition to protecting the Montoya
grant, which he had begun to think might someday be his if he were to actually marry Bitora. He
wrote letters about the trial to Randy Hendricks,
who had passed the bar and was now working on
the staff of a Louisiana congressman in Washington, D.C. He even wrote to his father in Houston,
for the first time since coming to New Mexico. He
thought the old man would be impressed with his
involvement in legal matters. George Young, however, failed to write back.

Only one thing truly concerned Bart about the
entire affair. Regis had started spending weekends
at the Montoya hacienda to report to Don Antonio
on the case and discuss strategy. Bitora noticed before he did that Sebastiana had cast her spurious
eyes on the speculator. Bitora said her stepmother
was sneaking out of her room at night to spend
time with her father's lawyer.

Bart was stunned. He had never thought of
Regis as a lady's man. "Are you sure?" he asked
Bitora that night in the courtyard as Sebastiana
played the guitar and sang. "He's not all that
handsome."

"He's ugly," she answered. "Look at how big his
head is on his neck. He has hands like a skeleton.
But that doesn't matter to her. She would go to bed
with a leper."

The case dragged on until leaves began to fall
from the cottonwoods on the Plaza. When the
plaintiffs had exhausted every attempt to prolong
the proceedings, Regis finally succeeded in getting
the suit against Antonio dismissed. He and
Antonio walked arm-in-arm from the courtroom as

citizens slapped their backs and hailed them as great reformers.

They settled accounts that weekend at the hacienda. The first hard freeze had come down from the mountains, and the house servants had stoked a crackling fire in Antonio's office. The lawyer, the hacendado, the two brothers, and Bart cradled brandy snifters in their palms around Antonio's huge hand-carved desk.

Antonio paid the victorious lawyer in cash, and his sons frowned when they saw how high Regis's fees had mounted. But Bart and Antonio smiled with gratitude. The grant was safe, more secure than ever. They cared little for the money. The title to the land was solid.

Regis, on the other hand, seemed rather solemn. He stacked the money several ways as the men conversed, but seemed reluctant to put his earnings in his pockets.

Finally he sighed and said, "Antonio, I have a proposition for you. One that I think will benefit us all. If you accept, I can leave this money right here on your desk."

The Montoya brothers raised their eyebrows and turned their ears.

"But you have earned every penny," Antonio said.

"Yes, I know, but coming out here so often over the past several months has given me an idea."

Antonio was intrigued. "What is your proposition?"

"Let's say I take this much of my legal fees," he said, setting aside a stack of cash on the desk, "and buy your livestock—cattle, sheep, and goats. Not the horses, because I know you're partial to them.

Then I take the remainder of my fees and lease your grazing lands for a year. That way you get to keep all this money, and I get a herd of livestock."

"But, my friend, what do you want with all those animals? You are no ranchero."

"No, I'm not," Regis agreed. "But for years I have wished I had ready access to livestock when I needed it. I buy and sell a lot of land, and some buyers want livestock included when they buy a spread. Why, just a couple of months ago, I had a deal fall through on a large tract of land across the mountains because I couldn't find a herd for sale to throw in as part of the deal. Now, if I had my own herd, right here on your place, and could lease your lands to graze them on, I would never have to worry about finding livestock when I needed it."

"But you have ranchland all over the territory," Bart said. "Why not stock one of your own places with a herd?" He felt suddenly as if Regis were trying to horn in on his domain.

"Then I'd just have to hire cowboys and goat herders to look after them. Too damn much trouble. I might as well go into the ranching business if I did that. Antonio, on the other hand, already has vaqueros and herders right here. They would go on tending the animals as if he still owned them."

Vicente nodded and looked at the two stacks of money on the desk. "It is a good idea."

"A very good idea," Francisco agreed.

"Yes, but there is one problem," Antonio said. "Not all of the animals belong to me. And, more importantly, not all of the land belongs to me. You forget, Vernon, that this is still a community grant.

The common lands belong not to me, but equally to everyone who owns a share in the grant. They, as well as I, would have to agree to lease the land to you."

Regis's head nodded for several seconds as if his skinny neck were too weak to stop it. "That complicates things a little. But if you speak to all the shareholders, and convince them to sell their animals and lease the common lands, we could try it for one year to see how it works out. Then we could renew every year as long as things remain profitable for all of us."

"Think of it, Papa," Vicente urged. "For once, we would know exactly how much the land and herds would bring us for the year."

"Yes, regardless of the weather or the markets," Francisco said.

Antonio sloshed his brandy in his snifter for a moment, then admired its color against the fire.

"I'll tell you what," the speculator said. "I'll leave that money right there on your desk until tomorrow. That will give you an opportunity to talk to the other shareholders and try to convince them to lease to me."

Bart found it difficult to keep his mouth shut, but it was really none of his business. The Montoya grant was not his, and wouldn't be unless he married Bitora.

Vicente and Francisco, on the other hand, belabored their father with their advice. They cared nothing for cattle and sheep. Their interest was in the trading business in Santa Fe—and the fortune in the family vault. They saw it growing annually with predictable lease revenues.

That afternoon, Antonio went down to the fields

to talk to the farmers. All agreed to lease. Vernon Regis had saved the Montoya grant, hadn't he? So why not lease it to him?

Antonio came to Bart almost apologetically that evening. He could tell his young friend had reservations about the proposed transaction. "It is only for a year, Bartolome," he said. "We will see how it works out."

Regis promised he would draw up the appropriate papers and bring them for signing at the fiesta in two weeks.

That night as Bart lay awake, he saw Sebastiana's lantern light through his keyhole. She passed his door, and he heard her enter Regis's room down the hall. First Sebastiana, then the Montoya herds. What would Vernon want next?

Twelve

❧

Bitora dusted her face with a powder made of ground deer antlers before she came down to the courtyard. The fiesta had already begun, but its revelers made a collective pause when she appeared. Even Bart scarcely recognized her in the flowing silk gown and lace rebozo, her hair and face done up as he had never seen.

Some of Regis's lease money had been applied to the fiesta, making it the biggest one on the Montoya grant in years. Antonio had chosen a husband for Gregoria, and they were to be married before Christmas. It was a marriage Bart approved of, though he had no say in it, of course. The groom was a successful restaurateur in Santa Fe—not the sort Antonio would deed land to. Now if only he could get Tomasa married off to some merchant or other city dweller, then marry Bitora himself ... But he was thinking too far ahead again.

"She looks beautiful tonight, doesn't she, Bartolome?" Antonio said, retrieving Bart from his fantasies of the future.

"Yes, sir. She sure does."

"Where is Vernon?"

"I don't know."

"Will you find him, *por favor*, and tell him we are ready to sign the lease papers in my office?"

"Sure," Bart said. He worked his way around the courtyard, looking for the speculator. He passed a group of young men, including Gregoria's fiancé. Across the courtyard, at that moment, Gregoria and Tomasa were engaged in a squabble and the fiancé's friends were ribbing him terribly about having to put up with such behavior once he made Gregoria his wife.

When he came near Bitora, Bart detoured to speak to her. "You look lovely tonight."

"Tonight?" she said, looking at him scornfully.

"Well, I mean always, but especially tonight."

Bitora was fuming about something, but she thanked Bart anyway. Her anger did not make her any less attractive. It was energy, and that was what he liked about her.

"Have you seen Vernon?" he asked.

"Yes," she said. "He is over there in the shadows with that *puta*."

Bart followed her eyes and saw Sebastiana standing too close to Regis behind one of the archways. "This is getting out of hand. I'll have to talk with him."

Bart pulled Regis away from Sebastiana and led him down a lantern-lit adobe corridor to Antonio's office. "Don Antonio's wife is a beauty, isn't she?" he said as they walked.

Regis grunted, shrugging his narrow shoulders.

Bart stopped in the corridor and held the speculator back by the elbow before they reached the office. "He'd kill any man he caught fooling around with her."

Regis stared straight-faced at him. Though the lawyer did not say a word, Bart got an idea—for the first time—of how well he could lie.

"I suppose he might," Regis finally said. "These old *ricos* live by a different code. I thought you said we were going to sign the lease. What are we waiting for?"

"Nothing," Bart replied. He smiled and proceeded down the hallway with the land speculator, confident that he had made his point.

When they entered the office, Bart found Antonio putting his signature at the bottom of the lease contract. Eight farmers were lined up at the desk, ready to put their marks under his.

"Bartolome," the hacendado said, "you will sign with me as a witness when these men make their X. If that is agreeable with Vernon."

"Oh, sure," the speculator said, folding up like a collapsing trestle as he sat in a cowhide chair. "This is all just formality, anyway."

Bart witnessed the marks of the illiterate farmers, then handed the pen to Regis, who put his signature in the appropriate spaces.

"Now, let's get back to that fiesta," Regis said, folding his copies into his coat pocket. He shook hands with Antonio and each of the farmers, then led the way back to the courtyard, his huge feet slapping against the tiles.

Bart stayed behind as Antonio prepared to lock

the contract away in the iron safe. "I suppose you found the terms satisfactory," he said.

Antonio shrugged. "I did not read it all, but discussed it with Vernon earlier today."

Bart felt a tinge of panic. "Antonio, you're not supposed to sign something you haven't even read."

The *rico* chuckled. "Relax, amigo. What is wrong with you tonight? Vernon saved this grant, did he not? He has proven that we can trust him."

"I want to read that contract," he insisted. "You go on back to your guests if you want, but I'd like to find out exactly what I just witnessed."

Don Antonio scoffed, but handed the contract to Bart. "All right, Bartolome. But, you are forgetting that he was the one who told you to warn me in the first place about the challenge."

Bart sat down by the fire as Antonio left. To his relief, he found the contract exactly as Regis had represented it. One year. Grazing rights only. Hunting and timber rights reserved for shareholders of the grant. Antonio Montoya had control of stocking rates and all other matters concerning livestock.

He put the document on Antonio's desk and stared into the fire. He felt at home here. He was getting territorial, and the place did not even belong to him yet. He propped his feet on Don Antonio's ornate desk. Forty-eight thousand acres. Bitora by his side day and night. Mountains and adobes. He could see his future taking shape. He loved New Mexico. She had no banks or railroads, but her civilization was ancient and deeply rooted. He loved her native tongue. He was speaking it well now. He found he could readily say things in

Spanish that would have sounded ridiculously sappy in English.

He was where he belonged. It would all be his someday. He had been lucky. Randy Hendricks had made a mistake staying in law school, then going to Washington. He was missing everything.

Suddenly he flinched as if snake bit, and jumped up from his chair. Bitora was waiting to dance with him in the courtyard.

Thirteen

❦

But, honey, I'm on my knees," Bart said.

Bitora tore her hand from his grasp. "Not good enough," she answered. "You must propose the way my father did to my mother. I will have it no other way."

"But it's not the same with us," he said, dusting his knees of gravel as he got up.

"That is the only way I will marry you."

He sighed and rolled his eyes to the high walls of the courtyard. "It's ridiculous. I'm inside the hacienda right now."

"My father let you in. I want you to come back on Wednesday when he is not expecting you and the gates are bolted. My father proposed to my mother on a Wednesday night."

She had remained adamant for weeks, since the night he first bent his knee and asked for her hand.

She was nineteen now, beautiful beyond comparison and the object of every bachelor's desire for miles around. Even so, Bart knew he had no competition to fear. She wanted him. Antonio approved. He was going to marry her and gain control of the Montoya grant, its lands and hacienda. Everything would have been fine if not for this ridiculous insistence of Bitora's that she relive her late mother's romance.

"Why should I have to scale two walls and climb up to your room in the dead of night, when your father will let me in here any day of the week?"

"I insist," she said, stalking away. She glanced back once, a seductive glint in her eyes that suggested he might earn a reward for fulfilling her wishes.

For a moment, Bart wondered if Antonio's visit to Bitora's mother, many years ago, had included more than a proposal.

Antonio had found his bride in Chihuahua. Her father, a wealthy ranchero, had refused to let her marry a poor freighter. Antonio would not be turned away, however. He had invaded the ranchero's hacienda, snuck into his daughter's room, and proposed marriage. They eloped a few nights later.

Now Bitora demanded the same romantic exploits of Bart. They wouldn't have to elope, of course, but she wanted him to prove he loved her as much as her father had loved her mother. There was more to it than mere formality. There was some real risk involved. Bart had lately gotten on the wrong side of Antonio with a harmless practical joke.

The hacendado had invited him to hunt deer in

the mountains, taking a whole party of guides and servants. Carlos, a young cook whom Antonio had recently hired, conspired with Bart to pull one over on the old *rico*. They caught one of Vernon Regis's Merino rams, sheared it, rolled it in dirt to approximate the color of a deer, sawed its horns off short, and tied antlers to the stubs with wet rawhide. They staked the doomed sheep in a clearing and led Antonio there the next day. The hacendado made a perfect kill from two hundred yards. Arriving at the trophy, Bart and Carlos broke into fits of laughter, but Antonio was unamused.

There had been a time when his eyes would no more have mistaken a sheep for a deer than a house cat for a grizzly bear. The prank had made him feel old, and he had hardly said a civil word to Bart since, though he continued to receive him at the hacienda.

Bart didn't care to deepen the hole he had dug for himself on the hunt by getting caught sneaking over the hacienda walls to propose to Bitora. He would have to be careful. It wasn't Antonio's vigilance that concerned him, for he knew how much of a sound sleeper the old *rico* was. It was Sebastiana that had him worried. He might well bump into her tip-toeing around the hacienda at night. If she caught him, Lord knows what she would demand to keep the secret from Antonio.

But Bitora was adamant. He was going to have to scale the walls in the middle of the night like a thief.

When Wednesday night came, Bart found himself approaching the Montoya hacienda at midnight. He wore the most outlandishly dashing cowboy gear he could find in Santa Fe. He only wanted to do this once. He was sure his horse was making enough noise to wake the whole village of farmers below the hacienda, but no one challenged his right to pass. When he got to the outer wall, he found Carlos had failed him. The gates were locked.

There was nothing to do but climb over. He rode his horse up next to the wall, making the animal stand as close as possible. Gingerly, he raised himself up in the saddle until he was standing precariously on the highest ridge of the cantle. Just as he got one elbow on the top of the wall, the horse shifted its weight from one hip to the other. The smooth soles of Bart's boots slipped on the slick saddle leather. He kicked; the horse flinched. Rocks jabbed him and tore at his skin as his mount jumped out from under him, but he held on. Grunting, he managed to pull himself to the top.

He sat in the moonlight awhile, panting, checking his skinned palms. Descending would probably prove no more amusing.

He walked the wall like an acrobat, arms outstretched, until he came to a tree branch that reached over the rock barrier. Its girth did not satisfy him, but it had green leaves, so at least it wasn't rotten. This was ridiculous, he thought, as he grabbed hold of the limb. Fun, though. It was like pulling off a daring jest on somebody. And that look Bitora had given him kept playing before his eyes in the moonlight. What reward awaited him in her room?

The cracking of green wood brought him back to his senses. He swung apelike, hand over hand, as fast as he could, but before he reached the thicker base of the limb, it gave way. Luckily, the limb did not break completely away, but held by a splinter, slamming him against the tree trunk as it swung downward.

He nursed his scratches as he watched for movement from the hacienda. When he was sure he had woken no one, he got up, found his hat, and limped to the large gate at the front of the hacienda. This, too, he found bolted, and he cursed Carlos under his breath for not keeping his promise. He ran as quietly as he could to the back of the hacienda, climbed over the stable fences, and checked the rear gate—also secured.

But Bart had planned for the worse. Under the straw in one of the stalls he found the crude ladder he had built for emergency use. He leaned it against the adobe wall of the house and began climbing. He had made it barely tall enough. From the top rung he still had to scramble to get on the roof. The rest would be easy, he told himself as he lay on his back, catching his breath. Maybe Bitora was right to demand this. He would certainly remember it. It would make a good story someday. He opened the collar of his riding jacket and let the starry New Mexico night cool the sweat around his neck.

In the corner of the courtyard opposite the well, an old grapevine clung to a trellis mounted to the adobe wall. Bart had tested it a few days before. It would hold his weight. After creeping across the flat roof, he sat on the edge of the high courtyard wall and lowered himself on the vine. It was thick as his arms and firmly placed after decades of cultivation.

Halfway down, however, he felt the trellis coming loose from the adobes. Desperately, he reached for the younger, thinner vine. It held, but slipped through his soft archivist's hands, burning them. He stripped leaves faster than a herd of goats. The fall through the grapevine must have sounded like a bull in a rose hedge fence, and he was amazed that the entire hacienda hadn't been awakened. It was going to hurt to hold Bitora with those chafed palms.

He had to watch out for Sebastiana now, especially as he passed the wing that led to the servants quarters. Carlos said she had been taking turns with the housemen, threatening to blackmail any who refused her. Bart saw no sign of her, though, and tip-toed to the well, which stood under Bitora's corner of the courtyard.

The most logical route would have been up the stairs and in through Bitora's bedroom door. But she had ruled that out. He must climb the balcony as her father had done to win her mother, a generation ago.

With his sore hands and his battered shins, he crawled onto the little shingled roof that covered the well. Locking his boot heels over the peak of the roof, he stood precariously upright and looked with dread toward Bitora's balcony. He would have to leap to reach it. It looked much farther away in the dark than it had last weekend in the daylight. It was his final test.

He drew several deep breaths, searching for courage in the night air. Finally he gathered himself in a crouch and vaulted. His hands barely caught the bottom rail of the balcony. After kicking at thin air for a minute, he managed to pull himself up, pausing triumphantly to look down on the courtyard.

He caught his breath, then tested Bitora's balcony door, finding it unlocked. She had kept her word better than Carlos. She had even oiled the hinges as she promised. He whispered her name in the darkness of her room. He could hear her breathing deeply. He couldn't believe she had fallen asleep. He would have thought she'd be too excited. He had never visited her room before. The layout was a mystery to him, but he spied the bright value of linen in the dark, and eased toward her bed on the floor.

He knelt beside her and put his hand on her soft face. Her warmth at once soothed his injuries. He felt her stir, then heard her speak.

"Bartolome?" she said.

"Expecting somebody else?"

"You came."

"Of course. Now, for heaven's sake, will you finally agree to marry me?"

"Yes," she whispered, slipping her arm around his neck. "I was going to marry you even if you did not come."

"What?" he said, pulling back from her bed.

She held on to him. "But, because you have proven yourself, now you will have your reward."

Bart weakened as she pulled him onto her mattress. He had judged well that look she had given him in the courtyard. There was more to this test than a proposal. He could read her thoughts like poetry.

Then, like a sudden avalanche, the world seemed to cave in. Bart gasped with such a start that he almost sucked Bitora's upper lip from her face. He rolled off of her as light flooded the room, and he saw Antonio, wearing night clothes and a visage of murder, carrying a lamp and a sawed-off shotgun.

"Bartolome! You?"

"It's not what you think!" Bart said, scrambling to his feet. "Bitora, tell him!"

The hacendado shot a fierce glance at his daughter. She only screamed and pulled the covers over her head.

Antonio cocked both hammers of the double-barrel. "And to you I gave my trust," he growled. "Now you will pay for this insult."

"I can explain!" Bart said. "Bitora, tell him how it is!" He saw her peeking out from under her blanket.

"Enough!" the father cried. He backed Bart into a corner and put the twin muzzles against his chest. "Do you have any idea how I am going to make you pay for this invasion?"

"But . . . but . . ."

"I am going to make you . . ."—Antonio paused and grinned victoriously—"marry my daughter."

Bart gulped, then squinted. He couldn't quite gather what had happened. He heard Antonio laughing and saw the shotgun lowered from his chest. He heard Bitora shrieking and saw her throw back her blankets. She was lying fully dressed in bed. Gradually, the realization sank in, and he slapped his tender palm against his forehead in relief and embarrassment.

People began to flood into the room. Sebastiana was among the first. She did not laugh, but she glared at Bart with a look of contempt and satisfaction. The house servants came in after her. Many of them had suffered Bart's minor pranks over the past three years, and now they had their collective revenge.

"You, too, Carlos?" Bart asked as the cook entered.

"Who do you think bolted the gates?" Antonio said, "and sawed halfway through the limb of that tree, and loosened the trellis?"

Bart shook his head and gritted his teeth in a forced grin. "I could have broken my neck!"

Antonio put his arm around Bart's shoulder. "Perhaps you will think of that the next time you bind the antlers of a deer to the head of a ram!"

Howls of laughter rang in Bitora's room as she came to Bart's side to soothe his bruised pride. He had scaled the walls. Now he had his reward. He would marry Bitora. He let his own laughter join that of his tricksters.

Fourteen

∽⟨⟩∾

To satisfy Antonio's traditional streak, Bart had to accomplish the formalities of betrothal. First he wrote a letter of proposal, describing his genealogy and his personal financial circumstances. This letter he sent to Antonio, who answered it fifteen days later, approving the proposal.

Bart then wrote to his father in Houston, whom he had not heard from in over three years. He also wrote to Randy Hendricks in Washington, D.C., who had been appointed third assistant to the under secretary of Interior. George Young made no reply to his son's wedding announcement, but Randy Hendricks sent his kindest regards and best wishes.

The wedding was scheduled for the spring, soon after Bitora turned twenty. Following the honeymoon, Bart would resign his position at the Territorial Archives, move to the hacienda, and take over the operations of the Montoya grant's eleven square leagues.

In the meantime, the official betrothal ceremony, the *prendario*, would come in conjunction with the hacienda's annual fall fiesta. Since Vernon Regis had purchased the Montoya herds and begun leasing the grazing lands, the fiestas had grown yearly in size and revelry. The speculator seemed to enjoy them more than anyone, and even invested some of his own money in food and drink for the festivities.

To Bart's relief, Regis had ceased his frequent visits to the hacienda that had been common during the court case against the Montoya grant. It seemed the subtle warning Bart had given him in the corridor the night of the first lease signing had taken its desired effect. Even when he came to *fiestas*, Regis kept his distance from Sebastiana. Bart remained quite friendly with the speculator.

Bitora's *prendario* took place before the fiesta celebration could begin. First, she made her appearance before Bart, dressed stunningly in her finest gown. The onlookers gasped at her grace and beauty as she performed the traditional curtsy for her intended. Tomasa and Gregoria, both married to Santa Fe men now, appeared rather jealous of their younger sister's beauty, and the brothers, Francisco and Vicente, seethed throughout the entire *prendario*. Bart was the first Anglo to marry into the Montoya family, and they considered it a scandal.

As required by custom, Bart presented Bitora with her *donas*—her wedding dress, plus all the rebozos, silks, and linens he could afford. His offering was so meager that Francisco hissed audibly.

Then Antonio presented Bart with Bitora's dowry—two of his finest saddle horses, a stallion and a mare. With them, the couple would begin their own fine line of mounts.

After many toasts and much wine, Antonio gestured toward the musicians. But before Bart and Bitora could dance, he ushered them down an empty corridor and into his office, commanding them to sit before his desk.

"Perhaps you are thinking that I have been less than generous with the dowry, Bartolome."

"To the contrary. The horses are more than I expected. The main thing is that I'll have Bitora as my wife." He actually meant it. The land and livestock, the hacienda, the horses—all paled in comparison to the prospect of having Bitora by his side forever.

"Ahh!" Antonio said, swatting at Bart as if he were a fly. "You young people do not understand the importance of an advantageous marriage. I like you, Bartolome, but if I thought for one second that you would fail to provide for my daughter, I would never allow you to marry her."

"But I have no money," Bart said. "You could have married her off to a lot of *ricos*."

"Of money I have enough to last myself and my children a lifetime. I give you my blessing for a better reason, Bartolome. You have something this family needs dearly."

"What's that?" Bart asked. "A sense of humor?"

"No, *idiota!*" The old man chuckled. "Bitora and I have enough of that to make up for the others. But what you have, Bartolome, is a love for the land. I have watched your eyes when we ride together. I have seen you pull weeds and treat wounded trees and plunge your face into our springs. Tomasa and Gregoria married men of the city. Francisco and Vicente think only of money and business. But you, Bartolome. You are my hope that the Montoya grant will remain indivisible for generations to come."

Bart looked at Bitora. She shrugged. Neither knew exactly what Antonio was getting at.

"I would not say it in front of my other children, for they would ruin this evening for us all, but Bitora's dowry includes more than just a couple of horses, amigo. I have rewritten my will. The older children will divide equally among them all the money I leave, the buildings in Santa Fe, the trading houses, and the freight lines. Bitora will receive the land and the hacienda. And you, as her husband, will become master of it."

Bart felt a surge of glory, followed by panic. Forty-eight thousand acres! How would he manage it all? Then Bitora took his hand, calming him. And he realized that Don Antonio would be there to help him for years yet. The old man enjoyed vigorous health.

"I have already discussed it with Vernon," Antonio continued. "The latest lease you helped me to witness this afternoon is valid only until you and Bitora are married in the spring. At that time, I will purchase the livestock back from him, and you will have your work cut out for you."

The panic welled up in Bart again. "The lease! Did you read it this year? I didn't think about it!"

Antonio laughed. "Relax, amigo. You are taking your new responsibility too seriously. I glanced at the lease. It looked like the same one I signed last year, and the year before. Nothing is going to happen to your new rancho, Bartolome. You have the land you came to New Mexico for. You have my blessing to marry my daughter, and you have your life before you. What more could you ask?"

Bart smiled and sighed. "I won't let you down."

"Of course not, my friend. Now, let us go back to the fiesta, before Bitora's brothers and sisters guess that we are conspiring against them." He shook Bart's hand, kissed his daughter, and led them back to the party.

When Bart Young stepped out into the courtyard—*his* courtyard—the music and dancing almost dizzied him. He filled his lungs with cool October air as he put his arm around Bitora's waist. He found his eyes sweeping the courtyard, searching.

He located Tomasa, Gregoria, Vicente, Francisco, and all their spouses. Still, his eyes searched. He did not quite know why. He found Sebastiana, whispering in the ear of the guitar player. His eyes pulled away from her, too.

There was Carlos, the cook, carving the beef, a smile on his face. And Hilario, the agreeable young man who had recently taken the job as Don Antonio's valet and coachman.

Still, there was someone missing. Bart continued to search the crowd. Suddenly he realized that his ears were straining to separate from the music and conversation the voice of the land speculator, Vernon Regis. He didn't really know why, but he wanted to see the lawyer. His eyes probed every shadow and alcove. It was useless. Regis was nowhere to be found.

Fifteen

〰️

Bart had only been asleep a couple of hours when the shouts woke him. Someone was calling Antonio's name loudly from the courtyard. He rubbed his eyes, got out of bed, and squinted against the morning glare as he opened the balcony doors.

Below, he saw Vernon Regis and four armed men wearing badges. "A little early, isn't it?" he grumbled.

Regis shot a glance up at the balcony. "Where's Antonio?"

"Asleep. The fiesta went dang near till dawn. Where were you last night? We missed you."

"Just wake the old man up."

"Can't it wait?"

"Wake him up!"

"Something wrong?"

"Dammit, Young, I said wake the old man up and get him out here. Now!"

He woke Antonio, and they wondered together what had the speculator so riled. They went to the courtyard and found a crowd of groggy farmers and servants gathering. Regis was waiting with two U.S. marshals, and two deputy sheriffs.

"Amigo," Antonio said, "what brings you here so early?

"You knew our agreement. You're to be out of here today, so you'd better get started packing your things."

Antonio stared in confusion. "What is this?"

The speculator snapped his finger at one of the marshals, who stepped forward and put a court order in Antonio's hand. Bart looked over the hacendado's shoulder as they read it. It required the Montoya family to be out of the hacienda by midnight.

"This is madness!" Antonio cried. "Who orders me from my own home?"

"You mean *my* home," Regis replied.

"Vernon, what is this all about?" Bart demanded.

"You know what it's about, Young. You witnessed the contract yourself. I bought the Montoya grant last night."

A flood of worry came down on the hacendados. They suddenly saw beyond the court challenge of two years before, Regis's false friendship, the mutually beneficial lease agreement. They had been drawn stupidly into a snare that was now tightening around their necks.

Suddenly, Francisco was charging from the crowd, and Bart thought the younger Montoya would attack Regis. But, instead, he turned on his own father.

"You stupid old fool!" he shouted. "You have given away our land for nothing!"

"Shut up," Bart said, shoving Francisco in the chest. "As I recall, it was you who advised your father to lease to this son of a bitch in the first place."

"You brought this Anglo lawyer here yourself!" Francisco shouted. "You are with him in this!"

Bart felt so instantly insulted that he belted Francisco in the eye. The two of them traded punches and pulled at each other's jackets until Antonio came between them.

"Stop it!" he cried.

Regis was chuckling.

Bart saw a swift movement from the crowd, and knew it was Bitora, rushing forward to scratch the eyes out of the man who had taken her land. But before she could reach Regis, one of the deputies caught her around the waist and lifted her from the ground.

Bart sprang again, this time on the deputy who had grabbed Bitora. The three other lawmen wrestled Bart to the ground, one of them drawing a revolver and putting it against his head.

"Easy, son," said one of the marshals, a big blond-haired man. He looked up at Antonio. "Regis has a court order, Señor Montoya. We've got no choice but to escort you out of here. There's no use in fighting it this way."

The speculator's chuckle became an outright laugh.

"Bartolome!" Antonio said. "Stop kicking and get up from the ground! You, too, Bitora! Behave yourself! Hilario, saddle the horses! We are going to Santa Fe. Vicente, you will see the governor. Francisco, you will speak to the judge who gave this order. Bartolome and I will find a lawyer to fight this foolishness in court."

Regis's guffaws echoed throughout the courtyard. "You should have thought of that before you signed the contract and took my money. Now, get out. Everybody!" He lunged at the confused farmers, making hideous faces at them, laughing.

Antonio gave the orders in Spanish, and the crowd began to disperse. Bart moved with the Montoya men toward the stables, taking Bitora by the arm as he passed her. They had just reached the edge of the courtyard, when the astonished gasps of the farmers' wives turned their heads.

Sebastiana was embracing Vernon Regis right in the middle of the courtyard. The grotesque head bent on its toothpick neck over her comely face. Bart reached for Antonio's vest, not knowing whether the hacendado would try to murder them now, or wait until later. He felt the old man trembling, and turned to see his face contorted with ire. Antonio pointed a gnarled finger at the obscene couple in his courtyard, but could not conjure words. He turned into the stables, his eyes blazing with more hatred than Bart had ever seen any man display.

Every avenue they tested closed before them. Regis's case was sound. He claimed he had purchased the Montoya grant from Antonio fairly. Antonio's signature, after all, was on the paper that listed, explicitly, the terms of the sale.

Antonio argued that it had been drawn up to

resemble the lease agreement with the same number of pages and paragraphs, signatures in the same places, and that he had been duped into believing it was the same lease agreement he had signed twice before.

To win their home back, however, the Montoyas would have to prove Regis guilty of conspiracy, and not a lawyer in town would face him in court.

The *rico* came to Bart's boardinghouse room after dark with his mattress rolled under his arm. "May I stay with you?" he said.

"Of course," Bart replied, opening the door wide. "But, I thought—"

"Francisco turned me away. Vicente's wife would not let him take me in, either. Tomasa agreed to let Bitora stay at her house, but she was too angry at me. Gregoria said that I have lost the home of her childhood, and I deserve no other. I was too ashamed to go to a hotel. Everyone in Santa Fe knows what a fool I am."

Bart pulled his old friend into his room. "Did you have any supper?"

"I have no appetite." He spread his mattress on the floor. "I am going to sleep. That will give me some peace until I wake."

Bart sat on his own bed as Antonio lay down. The old man's eyes stayed closed for a long time, and Bart thought he was asleep. He dimmed the lantern and thought about turning in himself.

"Do you still want to marry my daughter?" the small voice said from the floor.

Bart stared for a long moment. "Don't insult me, Antonio. It was you who taught me the value of an advantageous marriage. I would marry Bitora if you were dirt poor. There are some advantages you don't measure in square leagues or silver."

The eyes did not open, but the face on the floor smiled.

Bart wrote a letter to Randy Hendricks, asking for assistance and counsel. He even wrote to his father in Houston. Perhaps George Young would come to his aid in this time of need. The reply from Houston arrived first. George Young had died weeks ago. He had told no one where his son could be found. Not until the letter from Santa Fe had arrived could Bart be notified.

Bart had once envisioned coaxing his father to Santa Fe—maybe even tricking him there. When the old lawyer saw how well his son had done, he would forgive Bart for not finishing law school to join the family firm. But now that dream had flown like dust.

The letter from Randy Hendricks proved almost as bad. Yes, he would like to help an old friend, but as counsel for Department of the Interior, he was advising the General Land Office not to get involved in any investigation. That would not be politically expedient at this time. It was a matter for the Justice Department. Let the courts handle it. He was sure Bart would understand.

But Bart did not understand. He knew all about Randy's ambition, but a friend was a friend. He wondered what men learned in that last year of law school that made them abandon their loyalties and ethics.

He kept assuring Antonio that they would find a way to fight back, but his hopes were dwindling.

With the first snowfall to blanket Santa Fe, Bart

found himself brooding in his office in the archives. A box arrived from the surveyor general's office. R. T. Fincher needed a routine title search accomplished before he could approve the sale of a tract of public domain to a speculator. Bart dove into the case, almost relieved to have some task to take his mind off Vernon Regis.

But the speculator's name was the first thing that leaped out at him from the land office documents. The second thing was the location: the Sacramento Mountains.

Regis was moving his operations into fresh country. He was buying canyons where he would establish cattle ranches, mountain slopes that he would strip of timber, gullies where traces of gold and silver had been discovered. It was almost as if the speculator had chosen the site to further humiliate Antonio. Hadn't Nepomeceno Montoya, Antonio's great-grandfather, won honors as a Spanish officer in the Sacramentos? Antonio had claims there that went back three generations. The idea of Vernon Regis moving in almost made Bart's stomach turn.

He virtually ransacked his own archives, searching desperately for the document that would deny Regis a claim in the Sacramentos. A lost grant. A forgotten pueblo or rancho. A title that preceded any Regis could ever buy.

There was nothing. The place was a virtual wilderness, never before settled by men who used plat maps. He would have done anything to find a paper claim to the mountains where Nepomeceno had saved the life of Comandante Hugo O'Conor. He would have coughed one up if he were able. He would have sweated one in blood. He would have forged one, were he so desperate.

Bart left his office in the middle of the afternoon. He could hardly think straight. He saw himself as an old man, trudging back and forth between the archives and the boardinghouse, day after day, never claiming his mountain domain.

The Montoya grant had been his overnight.

He wanted to see Antonio's face. He needed to talk to the old man. What could be done now? How would they right the wrong Regis had dealt them? When would the meek inherit the earth?

As he opened the door to his room, he found Antonio sitting on his bed with a revolver in his hand. He stared, shocked. "What are you doing with that gun?"

"Do not try to stop me."

"Stop you from what?"

Antonio pointed the muzzle to a newspaper on the bed beside him. "Did you see?" He picked the paper up and shook it at Bart, almost weeping as he spoke. "They have sold my grant! They call it the Regis grant now, and they have sold it!"

"Who's sold it?"

"Vernon Regis, R. T. Fincher, Lefty Harless, Alfred Nichols . . . They were all in it together, Bartolome. They have sold it all except for the hacienda, and that still belongs to Vernon Regis. He is going to *live* there."

Bart took a step forward. "Give me that Colt, Antonio."

"Go back to your archives. I have work to do with this pistol. I am going to kill Regis first. Then, if I get away, I am going to my old hacienda to kill that whore who called herself my wife."

"Then what?" Bart said. "You'll rot in jail if they don't hang you."

Antonio shook his head. "It is the only way, amigo. Now, leave me!"

"It's not the only way, it's just the stupid way. I just had a thought over at the archives. It seemed a little loco at first, but now I can see it working. We haven't been thinking big enough, Antonio. We've only been thinking of getting even with Regis. We should have been planning all along to go him one better."

"What are you talking about?" Antonio demanded.

Bart sat on the bed and put his arm around the old man's shoulders. "How would you like to play a little trick on Vernon Regis?" he said. "No, not a little trick. A big one. Maybe the biggest ever."

"What do you mean? How big?"

Bart grinned. "Let's say"—he looked blankly at the ceiling—"a million acres worth."

Part II

Sixteen

❧

The crate weighed a good twenty-five pounds, but Bart carried it almost without effort. The warm breath of spring was whispering across the Santa Fe plaza, the cottonwoods sprouting tender leaves. A butterfly perched on one of them, sunning its wings. Bart felt a hundred fluttering in his stomach.

Ulysses S. Grant was out of the White House, Rutherford B. Hayes was in, and with him had come a new contingent of political appointees all the way down to the Office of the Surveyor General of New Mexico.

R. T. Fincher had gone back East with his spoils, and one Rudolph Raspberry had taken his place. Raspberry knew perhaps six words of Spanish. His background in land title litigation did not exist. Of surveying he knew zero. A compass to Raspberry was something to draw circles with. Yet, he possessed unimpeachable integrity. Charges of corruption in the surveyor general's office had reached Washington. Raspberry was the only honest man available to clean the place up.

Today was Raspberry's first full day in office, and Bart had made one of the first appointments to meet with him. It was the perfect opportunity to launch his little prank on Vernon Regis. When he entered the office, he found Raspberry familiarizing himself with his new surroundings.

"Hello, Bart," said Raspberry's secretary, George Baird. Baird had served under Fincher and was helping his new boss get settled in.

Bart nodded and dropped his crate on Raspberry's desk. "Howdy, George. And you must be Rudolph Raspberry," he added, extending his hand. "Bart Young."

"Bart administers the Territorial Archives over at the Palace of the Governors," George explained. "He's one of our foremost experts on Spanish land grants."

"Pleased to meet you, Mr. Young," Raspberry said. "What brings you here today?"

Without waiting for an invitation, Bart sat down, crossing his legs casually in the uncomfortable chair. "I've a little story to tell you."

"You'll excuse me, then," George said. "I've heard enough of Bart's stories."

"No," Bart insisted. "Stay. This tale will fascinate you."

Raspberry shrugged and motioned for George to take a seat.

The archivist put his palms together in front of his lips, and stared at the ceiling. "Where shall I begin?" He paused for a long moment, building suspense.

"Fifteen years ago, my father came to New Mexico as a volunteer in General Sibley's brigade during the Civil War. He was badly wounded in the fighting at Glorieta Pass, and spent months convalescing at the rancho of Don Antonio Montoya, in the hacienda east of town that now belongs to Vernon Regis.

"During his recovery, my father became very friendly with Don Antonio. Because my father was a lawyer, Antonio shared a family secret with him. It seems that for generations, there had been a legend in the Montoya family about a lost Spanish land grant—one that would entitle the Montoyas to great expanses of valuable property. Antonio was unfamiliar with United States courts, and he wanted my father to find out what it would take to prove the existence of such a grant."

"Wait a minute," George said. "Antonio already had eleven square leagues at that time."

"I'm not talking about the Montoya grant here in Santa Fe County," Bart said, "lately referred to as the Regis grant. I'm talking about an entirely different grant—one that was rumored to have been granted to one of Antonio's ancestors by the king of Spain, a hundred years ago."

The new surveyor general was in a stupor, watching the conversation bounce between his secretary and the archivist.

"Anyway," Bart continued, "when my father returned to Texas after the war, his health never permitted him to pursue Antonio's request for help. But he confided in me, and I found the story so intriguing that I came to New Mexico myself to help

Antonio. I managed to get the job in the archives, and there I searched for years, until finally, with Antonio's help, I began to piece together the fascinating tale of the lost Montoya grant."

Rudolph Raspberry looked at his secretary, then back at Bart. "This is all new to me, Mr. Young. I'll have to ask you what your point is, and why it should concern this office."

"That's what I've come to explain," Bart said. "In the past, this office has been so plagued with corruption that I didn't dare risk bringing this story forward. But your reputation for honesty precedes you, and I am going to put my trust in you."

"Please do," Raspberry said.

"I would like to take you back over a century, to 1775. That year, Hugo O'Conor, Comandante Inspector of New Spain's Northern Frontier, campaigned against the Apache Indians in the Sacramento Mountains, located in what is now southern New Mexico Territory. A garrison captain named Nepomeceno Montoya saved O'Conor's life during the bloodiest battle of the campaign. In return, O'Conor recommended that the king of Spain grant a large tract of land to Nepomeceno, in those very mountains where he had fought so valiantly. The recommendation went up the ranks, through the viceroy of New Spain, and across the ocean to the king.

"In 1777, exactly one hundred years ago, gentlemen, King Carlos the Third signed the royal *cedula* granting Nepomeceno Montoya virtually all of the Sacramento Mountains. This grant of land was referred to as a barony, and thus Nepomeceno became the first baron of the Sacramentos. In addition, His Majesty had bestowed upon Nepomeceno the Star of the Order of Carlos the Third, and made him a Knight of the Golden Fleece and a member of the Military Order of Montesa."

The surveyor general and his secretary stared speechlessly. George raised one eyebrow in warning.

"I know that look, George," Bart said. "You're thinking that this is one of my jokes. You couldn't be more mistaken. I'm dead serious."

"Mr. Young," Raspberry said. "Once and for all, how does this fanciful legend concern this office?"

"Because it's not just a legend. Our investigations over the past seven years have proven the legend to be truthful in fact. Nepomeceno Montoya, the first baron of the Sacramentos, was Antonio's great-grandfather. That makes Antonio the fourth baron. And I—because I married Antonio's daughter Bitora, and because Spanish custom allows a husband to assume his wife's hereditary titles—will be the fifth baron of the Sacramentos.

He turned to George. "Actually, Bitora's older brothers and sisters got first crack at the title, but none of them cared to move into the wilderness to take possession of the barony." He shrugged and turned back to Raspberry. "So, you're looking at the future fifth baron of the Sacramentos. But I'm getting ahead of myself. Let me return to Nepomeceno Montoya, the first baron."

"If you must," Raspberry said, smirking incredulously.

"Nepomeceno was a bit eccentric. He was consumed with paranoia, convinced that his enemies—jealous army officers—were plotting to destroy his title to the barony. So he scattered the grant documents throughout New Spain and New Mexico, hiding them in obscure files in old missions, forts, and archives. These documents included Hugh O'Conor's original petition to the viceroy, the viceroy's letter to the king, the king's *cedula*, reports and orders from every level of government. Together, they proved Nepomeceno's title to his barony.

"It seems the first baron didn't even trust his own children with his barony. At least not all of them. He told only one son about the grant. This son, Miguel Montoya, became the second baron of the Sacramentos, and inherited the barony by means of a secret codicil. The second baron passed it on to his son, the third baron, Estanislado Montoya. Estanislado passed the barony down to his favorite son, Antonio, again by means of a secret codicil."

"Let me see if I understand correctly," the surveyor general said, interrupting. "Your father-in-law, Antonio Montoya, claims to be the fourth baron of the Sacramentos, yet cannot prove it because the old documents establishing his title have been lost? Scattered across the Territory of New Mexico and the Republic of Old Mexico?"

"That," Bart said, snapping his fingers, "is where the situation stood when I came to New Mexico, seven years ago, and agreed to help Antonio find the lost documents. For years, our search proved fruitless. I wrote to archivists and records keepers all over Mexico, and found nothing. It seemed Nepomeceno had hidden the documents so effectively that they couldn't be traced in any way. Until—"

"Until what?" George Baird demanded. "Get to the point, Bart!"

Bart grinned. He had his listeners right where he wanted them. "I wrote a letter to the National Library of Mexico, desperate for information on Nepomeceno. To my surprise, the head librarian wrote back, informing me that he had in his collection a handwritten manuscript authored by Nepomeceno Montoya himself. A book of riddles!"

"Riddles!" Raspberry put his hands on his head. "Sir, this entire story has become a riddle!"

"A real-life riddle," Bart replied, "which I will solve for you in a moment. You see, Antonio went to Mexico City to copy his great-grandfather's book of riddles. He brought the copy back here to Santa Fe where we could study it. It consisted of puzzles, conundrums, mathematical brain teasers—riddles of every description. At first we thought it just another example of Nepomeceno's eccentricity. Then, we began to see its genius.

"After deciphering all the riddles, my wife, Bitora, noticed a pattern. Often, the answer to a riddle would be the name of a Mexican city. Such a riddle was always followed by three mathematical problems. I'll give you an example:

"One riddle was of the sort commonly used to vex school children. It said that the Viceroy of New Spain was leaving the city of Mexico, traveling north, in a coach that would travel at a certain speed. If it traveled at that speed for a certain amount of time, would the Viceroy reach Durango, Chihuahua, or Santa Fe? The answer was Santa Fe.

"Now, after this riddle, we found three mathematical puzzles. The answers to these three problems were sixty-two, seven, and thirty-one. The moment I saw those three numbers after the name of Santa Fe, it struck a familiar chord with me. You see, in the archives, we still organize our documents by the old Spanish system: in numbered cases, drawers, and files. Any document can be located by its three numbers. Nepomeceno's book of riddles was trying to tell me something: Santa Fe archives, case sixty-two, drawer seven, file thirty-one!

"Antonio and I rushed to the archives and looked in the appropriate file. There, mixed in with the documents that were supposed to be there—I believe they were militia rosters, or some such thing—we found several documents pertaining to the barony of the Sacramentos. One was a sketch map drawn by an alcalde in 1781 that outlined the boundaries of the barony!"

"The book of riddles was a book of codes?" Raspberry asked.

"Exactly!" Bart said. "We wrote down all the answers to the riddles on a piece of paper. We came up with combinations like Guadalajara, seventeen, ninety-three, fifty-two. Or Mexico City, eighty-nine, ten, forty. Antonio had to go to Mexico, Texas, Arizona, and California in order to find all the documents, but they were all just where Nepomeceno had hidden them, a hundred years ago. He found them all: The *cedula* signed by King Carlos the Third: the Act of Possession conducted by the alcalde on the actual soil of the barony of the Sacramentos; everything! Where he couldn't talk the archivists out of the documents, he had official copies made and notarized."

Bart stood and covered the distance to Raspberry's desk in one stride of his gangly legs. "And, here, gentlemen," he said, patting the top of the crate he had carried in, "are the documents that will prove to this office, and to the Congress of the United States of America, that the Most Excellent Señor Don Antonio Geronimo Montoya de Cordoba y Chaves de Oca, fourth baron of the Sacramentos, knight of the Golden Fleece, caballero of the Chamber of His Majesty, member of the Military Order of Montesa, is the true and rightful owner of some one million acres situated in and around the Sacramento Mountains in southern New Mexico!" He grasped his lapels and stood in triumph before his listeners, defying his knees to tremble.

"You can't be serious," George said. "Do you mean to say that you are submitting to this office a lost Spanish land grant?"

Bart laughed. "How would such a thing be possible, George? This grant is not lost, it has been found! Open the crate and see the documents for yourself."

George looked at Raspberry and shrugged.

The new surveyor general stood excitedly and fumbled with the brass latches on the crate. He lifted the lid, flipping it back. Reaching into the crate, he removed a weathered leaf of parchment, handling it delicately. "What the devil is this?" he asked, baffled by the old pen script.

"This," Bart declared, "is the royal *cedula*, signed by King Carlos the Third one hundred years ago, entitling Nepomeceno Montoya to two hundred fifty square leagues in the Sacramento Mountains." He removed another wrinkled sheet from the crate. "And this is an order by the royal supreme court, directing the governor of New Mexico to make the grant." Another sheet of old paper fell on top of the first two. "Here we have the alcalde's report stating that no existing claims conflict with the proposed grant. And this one is the codicil to the will of the first baron of the Sacramentos, giving his son exclusive title to the barony. Now, here's an interesting document. . . ."

As Bart piled the sheaves of parchment higher, Raspberry stared with wonder, at a loss as to what he should make of it all. Finally he turned to his secretary. "Am I to take this matter seriously, George?"

Baird blew the dust from an old directive. "I don't think I've ever seen a grant so well documented," he said. "These papers are definitely genuine. A lost Spanish grant. Leave it to Bart Young."

"Handle those with care," Bart warned. "They're a hundred years old, you know."

Seventeen

❦

Bart came up the street at a trot, his eyes fixed on the adobe at the end of the row. The little house had insufficient space for the four people who lived there—Antonio, Bart, Bitora, and the baby, Nepomeceno—but it was only temporary.

"What are you doing here at this hour?" Bitora asked when he burst in.

He found her lying on a mattress on the floor, holding her giggling baby above her. He took the child away from her and pretended to gnaw at its ear like a hungry dog. The baby laughed with surprise and joy to see his father.

"Raspberry wants to see me and Antonio," Bart said, dangling his son upside down by the heels. "No, not you, Nepo, just me and Grandpa. Honey, have you realized that Nepo will be the sixth baron of the Sacramentos?"

Antonio was reading his paper at the window. "What does Raspberry want?"

"He's had the grant papers a week now. I suspect he's going to tell us he'll recommend confirmation to Congress." He handed little Nepo back to Bitora.

Antonio folded his newspaper. "Then we must not keep him waiting. I am anxious to settle my barony." He rose with the air of a grandee and reached for his sombrero.

Bart kissed his wife and baby and left with his father-in-law. When they were safely away from the house, they looked at each other uncertainly.

"What does it really mean?" Antonio said.

"I don't know. But, remember. If they challenge our title, you have the right to get madder than hell. You are baron of the Sacramentos, Knight of the Golden Fleece, Caballero of—"

"I know," Antonio said. "Caballero of the Chamber of His Majesty, Member of the Military Order of Montesa." He smiled. "I know it well." He had recited his hereditary titles a thousand times over the past three years.

It began after Bart's honeymoon with Bitora. By that time, he and Antonio had been secretly plotting for months. They would not even let Bitora in on their scheme, for doing so would make her an accessory to fraud.

When their plans were complete to the last detail, Antonio had called the family together at Vicente's house and told them the legend of the barony of the Sacramentos, adding that Bartolome would now help him locate the long-lost grant papers. Vicente and Francisco scoffed. Tomasa and

Gregoria hung their heads in shame, believing their father had lost his mind.

Bitora, on the other hand, joined in the search. She went to the archives every night with Bart and Antonio, making it impossible for them to produce any forgeries.

"You must give me a grandchild," Antonio finally told Bart. "That will give Bitora something else to worry about and allow us to get on with our work."

"I've been trying," Bart said resolutely.

After she got pregnant, Bart refused to let Bitora come to the archives, insisting she must get her rest while carrying his child. That gave him and Antonio the privacy they needed to practice the art of forgery.

First, they had to find parchment that would resemble the ancient documents. Antonio turned up some likely material in the back of one of his warehouses, but there was not enough. They finally had to buy new stock from various Santa Fe trading houses, intending to antique it after applying the forgeries.

Next, they had to figure out how to fade the ink to the proper value, and make it soak through the paper as in some older documents. They diluted it with water and alcohol, exposed it to sunlight, painted it with acids, finally arriving at a combination of techniques that would make it appear a century old.

Bart used an old quill pen to apply the ink, working for months at matching the flourishes of long-dead Spanish scribes. He forged the signatures of alcaldes, governors, viceroys, and kings. He spent nights working on a single page, and

when he got home, Bitora would chide him for
spending so much time away.

"When I have the baby, I know where you are
going to be," she complained. "In those cursed
archives!"

While Bart fabricated documents, Antonio traveled from Texas to California, Santa Fe to Mexico
City. He charmed archivists and records keepers
everywhere with his tales of the lost grant. In
Mexico City, he found the actual will of his great-
grandfather Nepomeceno. The will, of course, said
nothing about the barony. That was why Bart had
struck upon the idea of the secret codicils—
additions to the wills.

Antonio smuggled Nepomeceno's will out of the
Mexican archives so Bart could learn the first "baron's" signature and place it on the forged codicil.
Months later, he went back to Mexico City and returned the will without it having been missed.

After twenty-one months, the forgeries were
completed. The next several weeks were spent
staining them with various vegetable juices, drying
them in the sun, folding and pressing them between heavy books, fading them with acids, packing them in dust.

Bart fabricated wax seals for some of the forgeries. He made plaster casts of authentic seals he
found in the archives, then damaged the originals
so that his copies could not be traced to them. He
had to mix the wax by hand to achieve the correct
hues: the king's blue, and the Inquisition's red.

They had decided that the king of Spain would
grant Nepomeceno two-hundred fifty square
leagues. But the problem in fixing the boundaries
was that there were not going to be any old Span-

ish survey markers around the Sacramentos, since
the barony never really existed. To solve this problem, they decided to use one natural landmark as
a corner of the barony, and figure the boundaries
from that corner.

Studying the few available maps of the area,
they chose the confluence of the Rio Bonito and the
Rio Ruidoso as the northeastern corner of the barony. From this corner the boundary ran twenty
leagues to the southeastern corner, whence it
turned westward and ran twelve and a half
leagues to the southwestern corner, whence it
turned northward and ran twenty leagues to the
northwestern corner, whence it turned eastward
and returned to the confluence of the two rivers.

The huge rectangle closed in every peak and virtually every foothill associated with the Sacramento Range. When Bart converted the old
Spanish dimensions, he found the barony measur-
ing about thirty-three miles east and west by fifty-
three miles north and south—over seventeen
hundred square miles.

Finally, one late night in the archives, the tricksters spread the documents on the floor to look at
them. They included scores of orders, reports,
wills, codicils, land patents, petitions, maps, and
royal edicts. Bart knew what the surveyor general
required of a grant to recommend approval to
Congress. His perfect forgeries would leave no
doubt. Every line and flourish had been calculated
to convince. The Spanish was flawless, checked
and rechecked by Antonio.

After admiring and scrutinizing the documents,
the forgers gathered them and stashed them in a
locked drawer in Bart's office—except for the book

of riddles. This all-important forgery would have to be planted in Mexico.

Antonio departed for Mexico City, the book of riddles hidden in his bag. Arriving, he disguised himself as an old peasant and donated the book of riddles to the national library, saying his father had given it to him as a boy.

Weeks later, Bart wrote the Mexican library, requesting information on Nepomeceno, and was informed about the book of riddles. Antonio then made another trip south to copy the book, though he knew very well what it contained.

Bitora found the book of riddles absorbing, as Bart had hoped she would. She tore through the mathematical problems like lightning, and soon noticed that they came in sets of three. Bart and Antonio shrugged when she first told them. Then, several days later, Bitora realized that each set of three was preceded by a riddle answered by the name of a Mexican city.

"By golly!" Bart said. "I think you've stumbled onto something!"

That was when Bart and Antonio ran to the archives in the middle of the night and returned with the first set of documents pertaining to the lost barony of the Sacramentos.

Bitora was ecstatic. The fact that she had discovered the code in the book of riddles made her as much a part of the barony as her father or her husband. If she hadn't had an infant to take care of, she would have gone with Antonio to Mexico, Texas, Arizona, and California, to find the other documents referred to in the book of riddles. But Antonio had to accomplish that task on his own since he was not, of course, going to find documents, but to plant them.

In Guadalajara he planted three of the most important documents—the royal *cedula*, the alcalde's act of possession, and the viceroy's directive to the governor—in case number seventeen, drawer number ninety-three, and file number fifty-two, slipping them in with some obscure probate proceedings. When he brought these documents to the attention of the archivist, whom he had befriended during earlier visits, the man swallowed his story about the coded book of riddles without hesitation and let Antonio borrow the documents from the archives, requiring only his signature as security.

After a few months of traveling, Antonio returned to Santa Fe in triumph with his documents. Bitora wanted to present the evidence immediately to the surveyor general. But Bart cautioned her against telling anyone, explaining they would wait another several months to see if New Mexico would get a new surveyor general after the elections. He had reservations about handing the material over to R. T. Fincher, seeing as how Fincher and Vernon Regis were such good friends.

When he heard that Fincher was out, and a new man—Rudolph Raspberry—was coming in, Bart knew the time had arrived to launch the grand jest on Regis.

Now he was walking to the Office of the Surveyor General with his partner and father-in-law, hoping against hope that he hadn't made some silly mistake or failed to take some detail into account. He didn't see himself taking very well to prison life. But the risk was worth it. This was the only way to keep Antonio from hanging for the murders of Regis and Sebastiana. Besides, he was going to gain quite an expanse of land if it worked, to the detriment of no one but Vernon Regis.

". . . Grandee of Spain," Antonio mumbled, as they strode down the street, "bearer of the Cross of the Order of Carlos the Third, fourth baron of the Sacramentos . . ."

George Baird greeted them with a smile when they reached the Office of the Surveyor General. "Welcome, Baron," he said to Antonio.

Bart knew immediately that all was well.

"Please sit down, gentlemen," Raspberry said as the men entered his office. "I've presented your documents to several experts, and all agree that they are of the most genuine nature. Not that I doubted you, of course, but these things must be investigated fairly."

"Then I assume that you will be recommending approval to Congress," Bart said.

Raspberry frowned and stroked his chin. "It's not quite that simple. Congress is becoming more reluctant to approve these large grants. Changes are in order. That's why I was sent here. Congress now requires a survey before considering any new grant, to determine exactly how large the thing is beforehand. And in your particular case, there are other disturbing considerations."

"Like what?" Bart asked.

"George," Raspberry said, nodding at his secretary.

Baird unrolled a plat map on Raspberry's desk and put his finger on the Sacramento Mountains. "According to the boundary descriptions on the old act of possession, your barony encompasses the whole of the Sacramento Mountain Range. The biggest problem with that is that the government ceded about half that area to the Mescalero Indians four years ago."

"Congress is very unlikely to confirm a grant that takes land away from the Indians," Raspberry added. "Especially the Mescaleros. They are just now settling down to reservation life."

"We've already thought of that," Bart said. "We'll honor the government's cession of land to the Mescaleros and issue them a quit-claim deed to their reservation."

George's mouth dropped open. "But, that will amount to about half of your barony. Roughly half a million acres."

Antonio shrugged. "As Señor Raspberry has said, Congress will not confirm my grant if I take land from the Indians. Will I have half of my barony, or none of it?"

"Besides," Bart said, "we believe the Indians will benefit us. We'll be in a perfect position to win the government contracts to supply their rations of beef and grain. Lucien Maxwell made a lot of money off the Indians who lived on his grant, and as you know, both Antonio and I were good friends of Maxwell before he died."

"He never should have sold his grant," Antonio interrupted, shaking his head. "He survived only five years without it."

Bart put his hand on his father-in-law's shoulder. "Maxwell also used the Indians as guardsmen on his grant. The Mescaleros could serve us in the same capacity."

Raspberry exchanged a look with Baird. "So much for that problem," the surveyor general said. "But there are others." He gestured toward his secretary.

George continued: "There are several claims already taken up in the Sacramento Mountains. Congress is going to be reluctant to displace settlers."

"We don't intend to deprive anyone of home or livelihood," Bart replied. "There are only a few farms down there along the rivers. We'll quit-claim them all. They can't amount to more than a few thousand acres."

"Actually," George said, "it adds up to quite a bit more than that if you figure in Vernon Regis's holdings. He's been buying ranch, timber, and mining claims down there for the past several years. He owns quite a lot of valuable property in the Sacramentos."

"We will deal as fairly with Señor Regis as he has dealt with us in the past," Antonio said, poker-faced.

"Gossip places Mr. Regis's fairness in question," Raspberry said. "I understand the two of you had a disagreement over a piece of land a few years ago."

Antonio waved the suggestion away. "That was exaggerated in the newspapers. We had a contract. What could be more fair?"

"So, you'll quit-claim Vernon's land in the Sacramentos?" Baird asked.

Bart smiled. "We'll give him the opportunity to lease from us at fair prices. That's more than we're required to do, given the obvious validity of our title."

Raspberry grunted his approval. "Very well, gentlemen. I will include the intelligence from this interview in my report to Congress. I thank you for stopping by."

Bart rose with Antonio. "One more thing you might want to mention in that report," he said. "Neither Antonio nor I speculates in land. We're not going to sell the barony. We intend to reside permanently on it and colonize it with good, honest, hard-working settlers. Now that Antonio has finally obtained his legendary lost grant to the Sacramentos, he would no sooner give it up than he would surrender his hereditary titles."

"Titles?" George asked.

"Baron of the Sacramentos," Antonio began, jutting his chin, "Grandee of Spain, Knight of the Golden Fleece, Caballero of the Chamber of His Majesty . . ."

Baird walked the two men to the door of the office, and Bart took him by the arm and pulled him out into the street.

"George, does Regis know about our grant yet?"

"Word's getting around. I suspect he'll know soon if he doesn't already."

"Where are you keeping our documents?"

George jutted his thumb toward his office. "In our files."

"One burning lantern thrown through your window would destroy everything Antonio and I have worked for. Some of those documents are irreplaceable originals."

Baird smirked. "You're overdramatizing a little, aren't you?"

"Maybe. But you know how Vernon works. I'd

feel better if those documents were stashed somewhere else for safekeeping. Hide them in the archives. He'd have to burn down the whole Palace
of the Governors to get at them there. I know it's
extra trouble, but I'll compensate you for it. And,
for your own safety, I won't mention to anybody
that you know where the documents are being
held."

George laughed. "Now you're really over-
doing it!"

"Am I? Do you know who Domingo Archiveque
is? Rumor among the Spanish-speaking population
has it that he cuts people up for Vernon." He
stabbed the secretary with an imaginary knife.

Baird grew wide-eyed.

"It's best to take precautions, George. I'll pay
you fifty dollars a week to guard the documents
for us."

George swallowed hard. "If you insist."

Bart and Antonio shook hands with George, and
headed up the street.

"What now?" Antonio asked as they walked
back toward the plaza.

Bart interlaced his fingers and bent them backward, cracking his knuckles. He tipped his hat
back and took in the blue New Mexico sky, inhal-
ing a breath so fresh and dry that it almost made
him dizzy. "First, I quit my job at the archives.
Then, I suggest we take up residence on our
barony."

"So soon? What about our confirmation from
Congress?"

Bart hissed. "The more settled we are on our
grant, the more likely they are to take us seriously.

Besides, did Lucien Maxwell wait for Congressional approval before settling his grant in 'forty-eight?"

"No, he did not," said the fourth baron of the Sacramentos.

"Then neither will we," replied the fifth.

Eighteen

∽≈≈∼

I wish I could go," Francisco said, "but I must stay in Santa Fe to look after the freighting and the trading houses."

"And for me it is the legislature," Vicente added.

Bart shook the hand of each brother-in-law. "I understand. And thank you both for relinquishing the title of baron. As the older brothers, you were in line before me to inherit it."

Francisco put his hand on Bart's shoulder and tried to mask the ridicule in his voice. "You make a much more convincing baron, Bartolome."

Bart assumed a posture of high nobility, but in fact, he knew Francisco was embarrassed by the entire idea of the barony and doubted his father would ever gain legal title to the land. Vicente held the same view, as did the husbands of Tomasa and Gregoria. None intended to move to the Sacramento Mountains and risk losing his scalp to

Apaches just for the dubious honor of styling himself a baron. The only members of the Montoya family to make the move would be Antonio, Bart, Bitora, and little Nepo.

It was June when the grandees began loading their wagons. Antonio had recruited two hundred farmers, shepherds, vaqueros, masons, carpenters, and general laborers, many of them from the old Montoya grant. He had promised them homes and farms on the barony. He had purchased herds of goats, sheep, cattle, and horses with which to stock his grazing lands.

Every adult male in the party had been armed with a Winchester rifle. There was the possibility of trouble with Indians—and the near certainty of reprisal from Regis.

As Bart and Antonio supervised the loading of the last wagon in front of Francisco's house, a buggy approached with a pair of passengers. Bart saw the oversized head bobbing on its shrunken neck with every bump in the road. He had been expecting Vernon Regis. Sebastiana's presence, on the other hand, took him off guard.

The speculator stopped his buggy horse with a jerk of the reins and unfolded his stork's legs as he got out. Sebastiana turned sideways on the black-leather seat and crossed her legs casually, revealing quite a length of hosiery.

Regis chuckled as he watched the men load the last wagon. "Look who we have here—the baron of Bad Jokes, and the lord of Lord-Knows-What. I can't believe you're actually going through with this scam."

Bart answered without looking at him. "You'll

believe it when you get our first bill for lease payments, which, by the way, are already overdue."

A dry laugh rattled from Regis's throat. "You're out of your mind if you think you and that old man can extort one cent from me."

Bart turned his palms to the bright blue sky. "You have your choice. Pay us for the use of our land, or we'll chase you off of it with your tail between your legs. And if you choose to lease from us, this time *my* lawyer will draw up the papers."

"Go to hell, Young. You don't know what you're up against."

"If you wait until after we get Congressional confirmation, the lease fees will double," Bart warned.

Regis shook his head slowly as a grin stretched across his face. "You've got guts, Young. It's just a shame you don't have the brains to go with them." He turned back to his buggy. "I hope that pretty little wife and that baby of yours get to the Sacramentos all right. I'd hate to see something happen to them."

Bart smiled. "Do you know what our settlers call you, Vernon? *Cabeza de Calabaza.* It means 'pumpkin head.' I don't think you're that smart, though."

Regis turned to Antonio, who had been glaring silently and listening to the conversation. "By the way, Montoya. Sebastiana sends her warmest regards." He gestured toward the buggy.

Antonio spit on the ground as the speculator left, laughing. Bitora came from the house, carrying Nepo, to watch the buggy turn in the street. She had been listening at the gate. "Why did that ugly devil have to be the one to take up our land before us? It is like a curse. Everywhere we turn, he is there."

Bart glanced at Antonio. "It is some coincidence, isn't it? Serves him right, though. Now we can get back at him for taking the Montoya grant. Funny how things work out, isn't it?"

Wicked laughter growled from Antonio's throat.

"What do you find so amusing?" Bitora asked. "Didn't you hear him threaten your grandson?"

"I am thinking about how he will curse us when he gets back to the hacienda he stole from me to find it empty. When he sees that every servant in the house is coming with us today, he will probably order Sebastiana to cook his dinner, then beat her when he finds that she does not know how."

After Regis left, Bart inspected the string of thirteen *carretas* in the back of the immigrant train. Each cart was made solely of wooden members mortised together and bound with rawhide. The wheels were huge disks carved from big cottonwoods, sometimes one piece, sometimes three pieces doweled together. When in motion, they moaned and howled around the heavy cottonwood axles for want of grease. A long beam served as a tongue, an ox yoke lashed crossways to its end. The yoke itself was little more than a hand-hewn cottonwood beam, devoid of oxbows. It was lashed with rawhide to the horns of the beasts. Some of the *carretas* carried as many spare axles and wheels as cargo, and Bart assumed breakdowns would be frequent.

In addition to the *carretas*, the train included eleven American freight wagons and two strings of burros, not to mention the herds of cattle, sheep, and goats. The immigrants carried food for two

months and every kind of tool necessary for building a new colony.

After siesta, the drivers cracked their whips over
the backs of mules and oxen, and the train took its
first lurch toward the Sacramentos. The music of
the *carretas* filled the streets of Santa Fe like
gobbling turkeys, yodeling ghosts, and screaming
stallions breeding hollering nightmares.

The would-be barons rode at the head of the column on their finest mounts as the train passed the
Santa Fe plaza. Bart saw a reporter taking notes,
and sat a little straighter in the saddle. He had
taken to styling himself "Don Bartolome Cedric
Montoya-Young," often followed by one or more
of his heraldic titles. He relished every word of
publicity the barony had brought him.

Bitora and Nepo rode on the tailgate of the lead
wagon. The baroness swung her feet and played
with her son as the cumbersome vehicle bounced
under her. Santa Fe's adobes shrank away in the
distance as the wagons rolled down the valley
toward Albuquerque.

Bart held his horse back on the last swell that
gave a view of the venerable city. He let Bitora's
wagon come up beside him. "Take a last look at
old Santa Fe, honey. Don't know when we'll get
back up this way."

He was looking over his shoulder, twisting in
the saddle, when he heard a pop in the canvas
cover of the wagon beside his head. Glancing,
he saw a hole in the material. An instant later he
heard gunfire. Three more bullets peppered the
wagon sheet, slamming into the articles inside.

Bitora rolled like an acrobat into the wagon, protecting Nepo in the cradle of her arms.

"There!" Antonio shouted. The old *rico* pointed and charged toward a ridge some two hundred yards away.

Bart spurred his own mount and followed his father-in-law. He drew the Winchester from the saddle scabbard and gave his horse rein to run its fastest over the rocky ground. Mounting the hill, he smelled the faint odor of black powder smoke and knew Antonio must have seen the muzzle blasts. Then he spotted a lone horseman galloping across the arroyo to the east.

Both barons fired from the saddle, though the target was a hundred yards out of range. Bart gritted his teeth, trying to wish his bullets home, but the rider crossed the arroyo unscathed and vanished along the outskirts of a village.

Bart panted. It had felt good to return the fire of the ambusher, but the attack still had him rattled. "Damn," he said. "That could have hit Bitora. Or Nepo." He looked uncertainly back toward the wagon train.

Antonio seized him by the elbow and shook him. "What did you think it would be like? Another joke? When you take land, it is always a war. When I settled the Montoya grant, more than forty years ago, it was war with the Apaches. Now it is war with Vernon Regis. And it will be war for a long time. Are you prepared for it?"

Bart yanked his arm away. "Does a cactus have stickers?" he said, glaring at his father-in-law. "I've been waiting years for this."

Antonio smiled and stroked his whiskers into place. "*Sí*, amigo. You are ready." He swept his arm grandiloquently toward his son-in-law. "You are Don Bartolome Montoya-Young, baron of Bad Jokes. Come, we must get back to the wagons."

Bart reached for a cartridge from his belt and began reloading the rifle. He glanced once more toward the arroyo where the attacker had disappeared. "After you, Sir Lord of Lord-Knows-What."

Nineteen

❦

The cottonwood axles groaned like braying mules as the wagon train pulled up near the Mescalero village on the Rio Bonito. The *carretas* had long since lost their charm for Bart Young. A day had seldom gone by that didn't require stopping the train to change a wheel or an axle.

Men went to work tending the animals while the women set up the camps. The weeks had taken much out of the immigrants, but now there was a new energy up and down the train. The barony was only a couple of days distant. Bart could see the summit of Sierra Blanca up the valley to the southwest. It stood like a boundary marker to his barony, for his forgeries had placed it just inside the northern borderline.

Bart and Antonio marched to the Indian village strung out along the Rio Bonito. Over the trees that flanked the streets, they could see the flagpole of

Fort Stanton, but they had no business with the army. In Spanish, they asked a Mescalero boy to fetch the chief. They got two chiefs instead of one. The young one introduced himself as Estrella. The old one was called Ojo Blanco.

They wore shirts, pants, vests, moccasins, earrings, necklaces of elk teeth and bear claws. Estrella had a sash around his waist; Ojo Blanco wore a peculiar headpiece with no brim that looked like a Turkish fez with a feather on top instead of a tassle.

Bart made the introductions in Spanish. "We have come to negotiate a treaty with you," he said.

The chiefs looked at each other. "Come to my lodge and smoke with us, then," Estrella finally replied. "We have no food to share, but I have some tobacco."

"We have food," Antonio said. "I invite you to a feast at our camp tonight."

"First," Estrella said, "you will smoke with us." He walked to a nearby tepee, leading the older chief and the two visitors past a tripod made of lances hung with a painted shield and bows cased in deerskin.

They sat on holey blankets inside the hide tent, watching in silence as the chief's young wife fanned a fire. When the woman had gone, Estrella filled a pipe with tobacco, lit it, drew a breath through it, and passed it to Bart.

"Who are you to make a treaty with the Mescalero?" he asked suspiciously.

"We are the owners of your reservation," Antonio replied.

Bart almost choked on the tobacco smoke as he passed the pipe to Ojo Blanco. He considered

Antonio's approach a little too bold for comfort. The Mescaleros had lived more or less peaceably on their reservation for the past few years, but many braves in camp still felt their battle scars.

"The United States had no right to give this land to you," Antonio continued, taking the pipe from Ojo Blanco. He pulled a measure of smoke through it, and passed it to Estrella. Breaking a twig from a chunk of firewood, he peeled back the corner of the blanket he was sitting on and began drawing in the dirt with his twig.

"The Sacramento Mountains lie here," he explained, drawing in several peaks. He traced a rectangle around the mountain range. "All this land belongs to me." At the northern end of the barony, he drew a square. "This is your reservation. As you see, it belongs to me."

"We have papers," Estrella said, the scowl deepening on his face.

"So do we," Antonio answered. "And our papers are much older than yours, and signed by a king."

The chief held his pipe and glowered at Antonio for several seconds in silence. "You say you come here to make a treaty. Instead, you tell us you own our reservation."

"We have a deal for you," Bart said, removing a folded sheet of paper from his pocket, handing it to Chief Estrella. "With this deed we will give you the land the government says is your reservation. We will also grant you hunting rights on our land to the south. These things we will give you, if you will do something for us in return."

Each chief looked at the deed for a long moment, though neither of them could read—Ojo

Blanco held it upside down. They were skeptical, and wary of tricks, but Bart's offer to double their hunting territory obviously intrigued them.

"What do you want from us?" Estrella finally said.

"We need your braves to help us guard our boundaries," Bart explained. "Our enemies will try to take our land from us. They've already shot at us three times during our trip here. If you will help us, we will work and hunt together, like good neighbors."

The chiefs sat in silence and passed the pipe until Estrella replied, "We will come to your camp tonight and tell you what we have decided."

Antonio nodded. "Come when you smell the meat cooking."

Before he could rise, Ojo Blanco put his hand on Antonio's shoulder. "I know you," he said. "You have come to our mountains before."

Antonio smiled and nodded.

"I told you then that if you came back here, I would kill you."

"That was long ago," Antonio said. "Much has changed. Now I can make things better for you and your people—and for myself."

Bart was squinting at the old chief. He recalled now that Antonio had told him about a young Indian brave named Ojo Blanco with whom he had had a Mexican standoff in the Sacramentos, decades before. How the chief had recognized Antonio after all the years passed, he could only guess.

As the men rose from their blankets, Ojo Blanco smiled, revealing his only three teeth. "It is too late to kill you now, anyway," he said to Antonio. "We have already smoked the pipe together. It would be the same as killing a brother."

The flap of the tepee suddenly flew open. An army uniform stepped in, followed by another. Two corporals pointed their army carbines at the visitors and ordered them out of the lodge.

When Bart stepped into the twilight, he spotted the familiar face of a cavalry captain standing outside. The officer wore an almost invisible yellow mustache and stood with his hands on his hips, scowling.

"What are you men doing here with my Indians?" the captain said. He had both brims of his campaign hat buttoned up against the sides of its crown, as if he were wearing a wedge on his head.

"Delton!" Bart replied, spreading his arms as if to embrace the captain. "I see you've made rank since we last met." He smelled a touch of whiskey on the officer's breath. The face was still fair, but the youthful blush of Semple's cheeks had weathered away.

Semple pushed Bart from him. "Who are you? Why didn't you report to me? I'm the Indian agent here. You have to get my permission to meet with the Indians."

"Delton, don't you remember me? We fought Comanches together on the stage to Maxwell's Ranch."

Semple's eyes shifted. "Young," he said, with a note of disgust in his voice. "I've read about your scheme to take over these mountains. I can't believe you're actually going to try to get away with it."

"I can't believe your scalp isn't dangling from a Mescalero lance by now. How have you been?"

"Never mind. Just leave these Indians alone. They don't need your influence."

"What they need is a quit-claim deed to this reservation. Antonio and I have just given them one. We're making a treaty with them."

"What treaty?" Semple shouted. "What deed? Let me see it!" He took the deed from Estrella. "My God, it's in Spanish!" He tore the document into four pieces and let them flutter away on the breeze. "You have no authority here. Get out!"

Antonio stepped in front of Semple as he tried to walk away. "*You* have no authority to give me orders, Captain. I suggest that you do not destroy any more of my deeds."

"Corporal," Semple said, trying to step around Antonio, "seize this man."

Both corporals postured uncertainly with their carbines, pointing them at their own captain as well as at Antonio.

The *rico* finally stepped out of Semple's way. In Spanish, he repeated his invitation to the Indians to eat at his camp that night. Then he left, gesturing at Bart to follow.

"What did you say to them?" Semple demanded. "Come back here!"

The two barons would not obey.

Semple looked across the parade ground from the front door of his quarters on officers' row. The morning sun was striking the trees along the Rio Bonito and the grassy hills beyond. As he sipped his coffee, he tried to figure out why something seemed to be missing. He burned his lips when the answer struck him. He could no longer see the tops of tepees over the trees.

He shouted at the first two enlisted men he saw and marched them toward the Indian village. Where the evening before some eight-hundred Mescaleros had languished, he now found nothing but ashes from cook fires. Every man, woman, child, horse, mule, burro, and dog had vanished overnight.

The captain then marched for the wagon train camped upstream. He found Bart saddling his horse as the immigrants doused their own cook fires and hitched draft animals. "Young!" he shouted. "Where have my Indians gone?"

"They're not your Indians, Delton. You're not God."

"Where are they?"

"I invited them to go hunting on our barony. I suppose they accepted my invitation."

"Damn you, Young. They're supposed to be confined to the reservation. They're not allowed to hunt on the public domain."

"They're not hunting public domain. They're hunting private domain. Mine and Antonio's. They said they'd be back by next ration day."

Semple fumed. "I don't want them hunting. I want them farming."

"You can't make a bird dog out of a burro, Lieutenant."

"That's captain," Semple said, pointing to his bars. "And if they get hungry enough, they'll learn to farm."

"They might. Then again, they might fall back on something they already know how to do. Like scalping soldiers or raiding settlements. A man's got to eat."

"They get plenty to eat on ration day."

"You'd never know it by the way they stuffed themselves at our camp last night."

"That's because they haven't learned discipline yet. They eat everything I issue them in two days, then starve until the next ration day."

"Well, then, why don't you issue them more? Damn, Delton. Don't you have a lick of common sense? You don't want them to hunt, but then you won't give them enough food to get by on without hunting. You want them to farm, but you won't show them how. How in the world did you ever become an Indian agent?"

"Not by choice. I'd rather fight them, but I have my orders, and I'll carry them out to the best of my ability—and that does not involve fattening the heathens on government rations. The last agent here—a civilian—did just that, and couldn't get a lick of work out of them."

"From the looks of things, nothing's changed since you took over, except now they're skinny. If you want them to work, give them something they like to do."

"Such as?"

"Hell, I don't know, Del. I just met them yesterday."

"Exactly. You don't know what you're talking about. These people are savages. It's my job to civilize them. I have to crush their barbaric customs, and you're making my job more difficult."

"What customs do they have that could possibly be more barbaric then the United States Army's?"

Semple's pale lips twisted. "When I came here they were brewing a drink called *tulapai* that they made by chewing maize kernels, then spitting them into a pot to cook and ferment. And they would get stinking drunk from it."

"I smelled whiskey on your breath last night, Captain. Does that make you a savage?"

"A few years ago, they burned one of their own women at the stake as a witch! Tell me *that* isn't barbaric!"

"Our own people did the same thing in Salem, less than two hundred years ago. We're not that far ahead of them."

Semple's fists clenched in frustration. "Their customs and taboos are ridiculous."

"What taboos?" Bart said.

The captain's mouth writhed in an attempt to form words. "They go to extravagant lengths to avoid their mother-in-laws!" he finally blurted.

"Then they're more civilized than we are. We generally have to put up with ours. And, by the way, Lieutenant, the plural is mothers-in-law, not mother-in-laws."

"Captain!" Semple shouted, tapping his bars again.

As Bart continued to aggravate the officer, Antonio rode to the head of the wagon train. "The wagons are ready, Bartolome," he said.

"Good," Bart said, springing into his saddle. "Adios, Captain. I have a million acres to remove from the public domain today. Come see us when we get settled in. Bring your mother-in-law!"

Semple glared at the train of freight wagons and ox carts as it began to move. "Stay away from my Indians, Young! I'm warning you!"

The laughter of the so-called baron brought a fever to the soldier's skin.

Twenty

❦

Domingo Archiveque arrived at Dog Canyon an hour after nightfall on a lathered horse. He left the animal hitched in front of the ranch house gallery, not even bothering to loosen the saddle cinch. His spurs rang like tambourines as they raked the wooden steps, and the meaty bottom of his fist pounded on the door.

"Who's there?" Vernon Regis called from inside.

"Domingo."

"Come in."

Archiveque entered, the pale light of the pink lantern globe confusing his senses for a moment. Then he saw Sebastiana wrapped around Regis, the sheen of her satin dressing gown clashing with the floral pattern of the sofa.

Regis pushed her aside for the moment, and pointed to the bar. "It's about time you got here. Pour yourself a drink."

The gunman splashed the finest brandy he could find into a shot glass.

"Did they scare?" Regis asked, reaching for Sebastiana's thigh.

"No," Archiveque said, avoiding the woman's eyes. He knew she would be looking at him. "I fired at them from three different places south of Santa Fe, but they kept going. They camped near Fort Stanton last night."

The speculator shrugged. "It's just as well. Let them get way the hell out in the hills where nobody will ever know what hit them. Can you hire men around here?"

Archiveque nodded. "I can find maybe ten men in Socorro and El Paso."

Regis nodded. "You can stay out in the guest house tonight. There's some beef in the kitchen. Help yourself."

Archiveque threw back the brandy, allowing himself to glance at Sebastiana. Her lashes languished over her eyes, but he saw her dark pupils staring back. He took the bottle of brandy with him, his spurs ringing as he walked behind the sofa, through the dining room, and into the kitchen.

As he ate the beef and buttered bread, he could hear Regis grunting in the parlor and knew Sebastiana was pleasuring him with a few of her many wiles. He put his hand over his right spur, to keep it from jingling, and unbuckled it. He raked his fork across his plate a few times to make it sound as if he were still eating, then unbuckled the left spur. He slurped his brandy and clinked the glass against the plate as he got up. Moving silently through the dark dining room, he went to the parlor door, and peered through the crack he had left on purpose.

In the pink light he saw the back of Regis's head above the sofa back. Sebastiana was on top of him, facing him, holding him by the ears, rising and falling as if riding a rough horse at a trot. The speculator's breath rattled from his lungs in short gasps.

Sebastiana saw Domingo watching from the kitchen and smiled at him. She licked her lips. She reined her horse in from its trot, and settled low in the seat. Pushing herself away from Regis's face at arm's length, she looked blankly into the speculator's eyes as she reached for the belt of her dressing gown. Untying it, she let the satin fall away from her shoulders. She grabbed the ears again and plunged the ugly face between her breasts.

She rode on at a trot, returning Archiveque's stare from the kitchen. Domingo gestured toward the guest house with his head, and she nodded. When she put her tongue in the speculator's ear, he almost bucked her over the back of the couch like a bronc.

Domingo went back to the kitchen table, clinked the dishes a few times, and put his spurs on silently. Grabbing the bottle of brandy, he clopped loudly across the kitchen floor and slammed the door as he went outside.

Regis felt her leave his bed and waited to hear the back door click. He sighed. It was a shame Sebastiana couldn't be satisfied with one man. He would probably never find another whore to pleasure him like she could. But he had already warned her, even going so far as to blacken her eyes the night before they had left Santa Fe, when he had caught her with one of the servants.

Domingo should have known better, too. He was the one who had carved a large S, for Sebastiana, on the back of the offending servant, a permanent reminder for a night's indiscretion.

Regis got out of bed and dressed in the dark. He did not hurry. He had plenty of time. Sebastiana liked to make it last. He found his gun belt on the bureau and strapped it on, feeling the chambers for cartridges. He put a cigar and a few matches in his pocket before he left his room.

Taking an unlit lantern from the kitchen, he slipped silently through the back door and walked down the steps. He heard a bull bellowing a challenge somewhere up Dog Canyon, and stopped to listen to the night.

The precipitous western face of the Sacramentos loomed above his ranch house, a black veil over the eastern stars. He knew that somewhere across the mountains, where gentler slopes rose to the summit, Bart Young and Antonio Montoya were camped with their wagon train. The thought threw a crick into his neck.

He was just now getting established in this mountain country, after three years of development. He had bought Dog Canyon as his ranch headquarters, built his rambling frame ranch house, and hired cowboys to work his herds. He had bought timberland in the mountains, brought in lumberjacks to cut the trees, and bullwhackers to haul them. He had begun building his sawmill on the Tularosa River. Most importantly, he had blasted wagon roads up to his gold mine in La Luz Canyon, hauled in his stamp mill, and was now getting ore out at an encouraging pace.

He had counted on taking his first profits from the Sacramentos in three years—until Bart Young and old man Montoya had filed their ridiculous claim with the Office of the Surveyor General.

It was so outlandish that he almost had to admire them for it. The book of riddles was the most irksome part. He knew Young liked riddles. But the new surveyor general wouldn't know any better. Nor would Congress. Already, the population at large was fascinated with the story of the lost barony. But Regis didn't give a damn about public sentiment. He was going to wipe his shoes on Bart Young.

The guest house was dark, but he knew Sebastiana was in there. His anger made him strangely giddy. From the first night she had slipped into his room at the Montoya hacienda six years ago, he had known it would come to this. She was an odd woman.

He stepped quietly onto the guest house porch and lit the lantern. The board and batten walls were thin. He could hear the bed springs squeaking. Turning the lantern wick up, he kicked the door in and pulled his revolver from the holster as he rushed in.

Sebastiana gasped. Archiveque leaped out of bed and tried to grab his gun belt.

"I wouldn't, Domingo!" the speculator said, cocking his pistol.

The Mexican gunman stopped short of his weapons. Regis walked into the bedroom and put the lantern on a chest of drawers, its light bathing the two naked bodies. Sebastiana got out of bed and reached for her dressing gown, but Regis pulled it away from her. He grabbed her by the hair and shoved her into Archiveque.

"No need to dress for me," the speculator said. "Domingo will deal with you in a minute. But, first, I'll deal with him." The pointed nails on the ends of his spindly fingers scratched at the stubble on his chin. "Let me think. What will it be?"

Sebastiana glanced at Archiveque and began to shiver.

"I know," Regis said. "Domingo, get your knife." He waved the revolver recklessly. "Go ahead, get it!"

Archiveque obeyed, drawing the knife carefully from his gun belt. Unlike Sebastiana, he remained in perfect control of his faculties. He did not attempt to cover himself with his arms, the way she did. He knew how Regis fed on fear.

"Now, Domingo, what do I usually have you do when I want you to warn somebody?"

Archiveque turned the knife handle in his hand. "Cut them."

"That's right. Now, I want you to warn yourself against fooling around with my women. So, take off an ear."

Archiveque stared blankly. "Señor?" he said.

"You heard me. Cut off your ear. And feel lucky I'm not making you cut off something you're more partial to."

Sebastiana's knees buckled, and she staggered back and fell onto the bed.

The speculator took a menacing step toward his henchman with the revolver. "The one at the end of your scar. Do it!"

Domingo took the ear in one hand, and put the knife blade on top of it. The cold steel made him flinch. It was honed like a razor. He found a new grip on the knife handle. He heard Sebastiana start to cry. He felt himself begin to shudder, but then gritted his teeth and got control of himself.

Slowly, he took the knife away from his face and glared down the barrel of his boss's revolver. He lowered the blade to his side. He had almost forgotten who this Anglo was. He had no stomach for killing. Why else would he hire it done? And Regis had forgotten who Domingo Archiveque was. He was not afraid. He parted his lips in a smile as his grip relaxed on the knife. "You will not shoot me," he said, almost daring the speculator with the tone of his voice.

"No?" Regis replied. He changed the angle of his weapon and fired a shot that hit Sebastiana in the temple, bathing the headboard with gore and fragments of her skull. Her body jerked once, then slithered off the bed to the floor.

Archiveque was looking back down the muzzle of the revolver before he realized the woman was dead. A warm drop of blood had splattered against his naked side and cooled, prompting him to wipe it away with his palm. The smell of powder twisted his stomach.

"The ear," Regis offered.

Domingo felt numb as he put the knife back in place. He distanced himself, feeling as if he were watching through Regis's eyes. The scorching pain and the sound of the blade cutting the skin and cartilage so near his eardrum brought his senses back to the horrible reality. He averted his eyes from the hot river of blood he felt flowing down his chest.

"Drop the knife," Regis said, his eyes bulging. He picked up Sebastiana's robe and threw it at the Mexican. "Here. You don't want to bleed to death."

Archiveque dropped the knife—and his ear—and held the robe to his wound as he sank onto the bed. He heard the brandy bottle rattle against the shot glass.

"Drink!" Regis said, grinning down at the gunman. He shoved the glass at Domingo, continuing to cover him with the revolver. "I said drink, dammit."

Archiveque felt dizzy and ill as he put the glass to his mouth. Then a cigar poked him between the lips.

"Smoke!" Regis ordered, lighting a match on the cross-hatched steel of the pistol hammer.

The cigar smoke stuck in Archiveque's throat like a clod.

"You can use my liquor," Regis said. "You can use my tobacco. You can use my very home. But, by God, don't you *ever* use my women!"

The Mexican trembled so that brandy sloshed on to his fist.

Finally, Regis put the revolver in its holster. "I want that whore buried by dawn, and this place cleaned up. Understand?"

As Archiveque nodded, each movement of his head pumped the clod of tobacco smoke higher in his throat. He looked down and saw his own ear lying on a blood-speckled floor. He spit the cigar out, stumbled through the door Regis had kicked in, and vomited off the porch.

The speculator's sledlike shoes scuffed the steps as he walked casually past the prostrate gunman. "Now, see what you've done, Domingo?" he said. "What a waste of good beefsteak."

Twenty-one

~∞~

The road led southeast from Fort Stanton, then turned into the Sacramentos. The two barons at the head of the emigrant train wanted to follow the road up into the cool elevations of their domain, but they had to establish a stronghold in the lowlands before riding through the tall timber in the high country.

They turned off the road and continued along the eastern foothills of their mountains, with only trails to guide them. What Bart found strange was that he couldn't see his mountains. He had expected to see them raking the sky when he was this near. But on the eastern slope the mountains rose so gradually that they seemed nonexistent. Each hill hid a slightly larger hill to the west of it, but nowhere did he see his mountains jutting as in his dreams. It was a little disconcerting, but he trusted Antonio when he said they were there, and higher than he could imagine.

By the middle of the second day out of Fort Stanton, Bart knew he must have crossed the Mescalero reservation onto his own land. He had taken possession of his barony at last.

At sundown, they struck the Penasco River, and the next day he and Antonio explored upstream, finding a few remote farms where settlers— Mexicans for the most part—raised irrigated crops. Antonio told the story of the lost barony and handed out quit-claim deeds, winning instant friends.

The Penasco Valley wound among the foothills of the Sacramentos, narrowing between canyon bluffs in places, widening into expansive stretches of bottomland elsewhere. The barons decided to establish their headquarters at a place where the valley broadened out enough to make room for a village, fields, and pastures.

Bart led a timber expedition into the mountains to cut pines. He even swung an axe himself a couple of hours a day for the exercise. The trail from Santa Fe had toughened him, but he knew he was going to have to get tougher yet if he wanted to hold on to his barony.

The pines he found weren't really very tall, and they were spaced far apart. Still, it was good land for stock, and he continued to believe in Antonio's description of the thick forests higher up. He wanted badly to ride to the summit of the Sacramentos, but there was too much work to do now.

Oxen hauled the harvested pines down to the town site, where Antonio had established a regular factory for adobe bricks. His people would need tens of thousands of them to build their homes and the presidio.

"What are we going to call the place?" Bart asked as they laid out the settlement.

"The town we will call Montoya, New Mexico," the fourth baron said. "The presidio we will call Fort Young."

Chief Estrella stopped by on his return to Fort Stanton for ration day. He thanked Bart and Antonio for letting his braves hunt on the barony. He also performed his first function as chief of the baronial guards by reporting on the activities around Regis's gold mine in La Luz Canyon on the western slope. Several Mexican gunmen had arrived at the high mining camp, their leader a tough-looking man with a scar on one side of his face, and a bandaged ear.

Bart thanked the chief, lent him a fresh horse, and asked him to keep his guards circulating throughout the mountains. "One more thing," Bart said as the chief mounted. "I'd like you to carry a letter to Fort Stanton for me and post it."

Estrella agreed, and left with the envelope addressed to Randy Hendricks tucked into the balloon sleeve of his Mexican-style shirt.

Randy had disappointed Bart a few years before, when he refused to help take the Montoya grant away from Vernon Regis. But Bart was willing to give his old friend another chance. Besides, he knew no one else in Washington, and he needed a lobbyist to help push his confirmation through Congress. He was offering thousands of dollars, plus a bonus to be paid after confirmation. If Randy accepted, he was to come to Santa Fe, all expenses paid by the Montoya family, to review the grant documents. Then he would tour the barony before returning to Washington.

The walls of the presidio climbed daily with new layers of adobe brick. It was to be part palace, part fort. The parapets would stand four feet thick. The ceiling beams would be whole timbers, peeled of bark. Two stories would surround a central plaza. It would be large enough to afford protection for the entire village in case of attack by Regis men, hostile Indians, outlaws, or border renegades.

Antonio and Bart had worked for days on the plans for the presidio, sketching them on paper. Then Bitora had come behind them and changed everything. Her designs were practical, however, so they had let most of her changes stand. Their fort would include a kitchen to feed an army, a huge dining hall, two parlors, a music room, bedrooms, guest rooms, servants' quarters, barracks, blacksmith and carpenter shops, a powder magazine, a laundry, a trading post, stables, and a billiards hall. Like the old Montoya hacienda in Santa Fe County, it would have no windows to the outside, and two gates would secure it from the world.

The walls were ten bricks high when Chief Estrella rode into the valley with urgent intelligence. "They are coming," he told Antonio and Bart. "From the mine."

"How many?" Antonio asked.

The young chief held up his ten fingers.

"Guns?"

The chief nodded. "They are coming for a fight. The one with the big scar on his face is leading them."

"How far away?"

"They will be here tonight."

"Maybe we should plan a reception," Bart said.

"A wonderful idea, Bartolome. A surprise reception."

Bitora led the evacuation of the village site between sundown and moonrise, taking the women and children in groups of twenty to their hiding place in the piñon brakes over the hill. Crying babies caused her biggest problems. Otherwise, she accomplished the evacuation with little trouble. Her noncombatants were settled in among the piñons an hour before the moon rose.

Antonio sent ten men to guard the women and children, then positioned the rest around the rim of the valley, overlooking the village site. He and Bart took up stations flanking the trail they expected Archiveque to ride in on. They waited an hour for the moon to rise, then waited two hours more.

Bart began wondering if the attack would come tonight or at dawn. Or at all. He was well hidden in a clump of alligator juniper, his Winchester repeater across his knees. He was getting drowsy when he heard stones rattle on the trail above him.

Moonlight made the attackers look almost friendly as they rode down toward the village among the scrubby evergreens. Bart tried hard to watch their every move through the branches of the juniper he hid in. He eased his rifle slowly to his shoulder, his heart pounding as though he were trying to find a big bull elk in his sights.

The half moon caught the scar line on Archiveque's cheek. Bart counted as his thumb pulled the hammer back. Ten men, just as Estrella had reported. He held the trigger until the hammer was all the way back, then eased his finger off the trigger, preventing any part of the gunlock from clicking.

His left eye closed as the hooves became louder. He was looking down his rifle sights, waiting for Archiveque's men to ride by. They were going to pass not more than ten yards from his position.

His pulse throbbed in his ears as the attackers approached, but his hands were steady. Archiveque stood in his stirrups as he approached the overlook. The moment he rode in line with Bart's rifle sights, he stopped, raising a hand to his men. Bart found the ugly scar in his irons.

Unless he wanted to count the Comanche who had fallen under the stagecoach that had brought him to New Mexico, Bart could not say he had killed a man. Domingo Archiveque, however, was a good place to start. He felt his trigger finger curl a little as he held his bead. He heard the henchman's voice, followed by the sound of ten guns sliding from their scabbards. Three men soaked rag-wrapped torches with coal oil. Another struck a match.

One squeeze would drop Archiveque from the saddle right here and now. Bart felt a surge of excitement, and thought he heard a sound like distant thunder in the back of his head. He decided for a mere moment that he would do it. Then he remembered Antonio's plan, and his grip eased on the trigger. There would be nine others after Archiveque. It was better to wait.

"*Vamanos!*" Archiveque said, his voice striking through the moonlit night like a hammer on an anvil. He led his mob in the plunge down the valley slope, and rent the air with the first of the Indian yelps.

The torches shrank into the distance as Bart repositioned himself for the new angle of fire. He heard the bleating of terrified animals as two riders veered into a goat herd. The first gunshot punctured the darkness, and a wagon sheet in the valley took flame from a torch, helping to illuminate the attackers.

When Archiveque's men realized the village had been evacuated, their yells died and they turned their mounts back to the hills. Antonio chose that moment to fire the first shot of the surprise reception.

A ring of riflemen hurled a hundred slugs down at the ten invaders. Two of the torch carriers fell from their saddles, and the third threw his flaming branch aside. The other invaders scattered in confusion or fired ineffectually at the hills.

Archiveque attempted to lead two charges out of the valley, but lost another three men to hidden rifles. In desperation, he turned toward the walls of the unfinished presidio for cover. As he led his men into the plaza, a dozen farmers rose from their hiding places and raked the hired guns with deadly accuracy. Three men dropped. One of them screamed in pain in the presidio plaza, until another bullet silenced him.

Archiveque escaped the fort with only one of his men, and the two invaders retreated on the same trail that had led them into disaster. As they rode toward him, Bart located the scar-faced gunman in his sights, and squeezed his trigger. The muzzle blast blinded him for an instant; then he saw Archiveque rolling from his fallen horse.

Bart tried to aim for a second shot, but his initial blasts had speckled everything he looked at with spots. He shook his head and blinked hard, trying to clear his vision. He could make out only enough in the moonlight to see Archiveque climbing on behind the other surviving raider.

Bart ducked a smoking cartridge that flew from the chamber of his Winchester as the pair of raiders rode double toward him. He waited as the dancing spots melted away. He would let the raiders get closer. Then, if someone hadn't picked them off already, he would put a bullet through Archiveque himself.

A few shots were still ringing across the valley, but it seemed most of the riflemen had paused to reload. As he paced the two raiders with his rifle barrel, he tried to remember how many rounds he had fired. Certainly not enough to empty his magazine. They were within a hundred yards now, whipping the winded horse out of the valley. Then a lull came in the firing, and Bart saw the man in front of Archiveque fall inexplicably from his horse. The lone survivor shifted into the saddle, bent to catch a dangling bridle rein, and gouged the pony with his spurs.

Bart's finger drew the trigger back, but the hammer dropped on nothing, like a dead man falling into a bottomless grave. Archiveque was going to make it. As the mob leader reached the overlook, Bart saw his face turn back to the valley. The moon caught his smile.

Before he knew what was happening, Bart felt himself leaping from his cover. He sprinted for the trail to intercept Archiveque. The raider's head turned toward him as he leaped. He felt like an eagle as he vaulted, spreading his arms. He saw Archiveque reach for his sidearm, then slammed into the Mexican as the horse ran out from under them both. Archiveque took the impact from the waiting ground, and Bart wrestled the pistol from his grip. Archiveque lay on the ground gasping for wind. Bart cocked the old Colt, knelt, and put the barrel against the scarred face.

Antonio and a few village farmers scrambled to his side.

"Kill him," Antonio said.

Bart heard stray shots in the valley and knew the farmers were finishing off the wounded raiders. Archiveque turned his head and looked beyond the pistol barrel with complete detachment in his eyes.

"My Lord, Domingo!" Bart said. "What happened to your ear?"

"Kill him," Antonio repeated.

Bart shifted the revolver in his grasp. "No, I don't believe I will," he said. He pulled the panting gunman to his feet, keeping the cocked pistol against his throat. "Domingo, I want you to take a message back to Dog Canyon for me. Tell Regis we intend to seize his ranch and timber interests for payments past due. Tell him he can keep the gold mine, as long as he starts paying us royalties on it. If he doesn't, we'll close the roads and take over the mine ourselves. Tell him he's just a filthy trespasser to us, and we'd just as soon gut shoot him and leave him lay. You got all that?"

Archiveque nodded.

"Well, don't just stand there, boy. Go catch your horse and get the hell off of our barony."

Archiveque turned away.

"And, Domingo," Bart said, stopping the hired gun. "Next time, I'll take Antonio's advice."

They heard his spurs jingle into the darkness. Antonio ordered the farmers who had gathered around to escort the women and children back to the village site. When they had gone, he turned to Bart.

"I was worried about you," he said. "You can never predict how a man is going to act in a fight. I think you lost your senses, leaping on Archiveque like that, but it was a courageous thing to watch, and the men are already talking about it."

Bart shrugged with modesty.

"However . . ." Antonio motioned for Bart to follow him down the slope, toward the dead man who had rescued Archiveque. "The only reason Archiveque did not stick you with his knife is because he left it here." He nudged the corpse with his boot.

In the moonlight, Bart saw the knife handle jutting from rib cage of the dead man. "He killed the fellow who rescued him?"

"Of course he did. The horse was running too slow. I have heard that he killed his own mother. Why, then, would he spare this man? Promise me something, Bartolome. The next time you have Domingo Archiveque in your sights, kill him."

Bart studied the glistening current of blood trailing from the knife wound of the dead man. "By golly, I believe I will," he said.

Twenty-two

∽⌒∾

By October, the settlers had almost finished building Fort Young. The women were coating the walls with a mixture of mud and straw when Chief Estrella delivered the first mail from Fort Stanton.

Two important dispatches required Bart to make a hasty trip back to Santa Fe. One was from Vernon Regis. He wanted to negotiate. The other was from Vicente, concerning Randy Hendricks. The redheaded lawyer was on his way to New Mexico.

Bart hated leaving just as his fort was about to become habitable, but the future of the barony rested with the powers in Santa Fe and Washington. He saddled a good horse to ride over the mountains to La Luz, where he could catch the Mesilla-to-Las Vegas stage.

He took Hilario and a guard of five Mescaleros,

but he wasn't expecting any trouble. It was his first trip over the summit of the Sacramentos, and he was enthralled to at last find the dense forests Antonio had told him of.

Every bend in the trail filled him with wonder. He spooked a herd of elk from one meadow, and found two bear cubs hiding in a tree near the Sacramento Divide. He couldn't believe he owned it all. It had started as a prank, a way to get even with Regis. But now there was much more to it.

Nothing to feel guilty about, he thought. *You've deprived no one but Regis of anything. You handed out quit-claim deeds to the farmers who came here before you and doubled the hunting territory of the Mescaleros. You must serve these mountains. Then you will be a true baron.*

Suddenly, Bart jumped from his horse and marched out into a small trailside clearing. Chief Estrella watched in shock as the baron began pulling at weeds and throwing rocks into the forest.

"Long live the king, and may God preserve him!" Bart shouted. "Long live the king, and may God preserve him! Long live the king and may God preserve him!"

"Don Bartolome!" Hilario scolded. "What is wrong with you? You are making the Indians nervous."

Bart came back to his mount, grinning and panting. "It's the ancient Spanish Act of Possession. You're supposed to do that when you take possession of your grant."

"I thought you were going crazy. Look at Estrella. He is still not sure."

"Sorry, Chief," Bart said, returning to his saddle,

"but I always wanted to do that." He sighed and looked around him. "We're like *conquistadores*, Hilario. You and me, conquering these mountains for God and king."

"I am jut a servant," Hilario insisted. "And I have no king."

The party continued on and reached a pass along the divide before sundown. As Bart admired the newly revealed scenery to the west, a large flock of band-tailed pigeons chose his pass to cross the range. Their wings whistled just a few feet over his head for a second; then they were gone, flying over Fort Young and the village of Montoya before he could catch his breath.

Before dark, he led a side trip to the nearest peak. It sloped gently to a crest wooded heavily with evergreens. A labyrinth of small interconnected clearings, fringed with white-trunked aspens, led to the top where wildflowers dotted a field of knee-high grass. From the summit he saw the sun sink beyond the next range of mountains, far to the west. He remained there, gazing out over his domain, until the first star came out. He named the peak Star Mountain, and Chief Estrella was highly pleased, thinking it had been named for him.

The night was cold, but Bart found the clime invigorating after the long summer below. He decided he would build a grand lodge on Star Mountain. Maybe next year. It would be his summer retreat and autumn hunting lodge.

The next morning, Bart, Hilario, and the Mescaleros struck the old La Luz-to-Fort Stanton Road that ran northeast across the Sacramentos. It had been there over twenty years, since the establishment of Fort Stanton in 1855. It would lead them to the little Mexican town of La Luz, where Bart could catch the stage. But when they reached the mining road Regis had blasted into La Luz Canyon, Bart decided to investigate.

He came to a collection of ramshackle buildings on a bluff, and heard a muffled blast from the mine. The town had one crooked street of rocks and mud. The shacks were built of bark-covered planks the sawmill blades had cut from the big pines when squaring the timbers for lumber production.

Bart and Hilario decided to visit a shanty labeled "Regisville Saloon," but the Indians refused to go in. They wouldn't even dismount and seemed extremely uneasy in the village.

Inside the saloon, Bart found five dirty men bandaged with blood-soaked linens lying on cots. "Good Lord!" he said to the bartender. "What on earth happened here?"

The bartender leaned on his broom. "Not *on* earth, stranger. Within it. A shaft caved in two days ago. Three men killed. These boys hurt bad enough to lay up." He looked at Hilario. "Your man will have to go. We don't allow Mexicans or Indians in this camp, unless they work for Mr. Regis."

Bart felt his baronial ire flare. "You'd better get used to it, mister. I own these mountains, and I have many friends among Mexicans and Indians. If you'll look out your front door, you'll see five Mescaleros waiting for me outside."

The bartender cracked the door to look. He gasped, shutting the door again. "Who the hell are you?" he asked, examining the revolver on Bart's hip.

"Don Bartolome Cedric Montoya-Young, fifth baron of the Sacramentos."

One of the injured men chuckled. "You're that bullshit baron that's supposed to own these mountains."

"There's no supposition about it. My father-in-law and I are currently in possession of this range."

"Is it true you've got a fort on the Penasco?" the bartender said. "We heard there was a battle there."

Bart nodded. "With our militia and our Mescalero Guard, we all but wiped out a band of hired renegades." He drew his revolver and put it on the bar. "Now, my friend and I will have a whiskey."

Hilario grinned as the bartender poured the drinks.

"Why are these men quartered here?" Bart asked, taking his glass. "Doesn't this sorry excuse for a town have an infirmary?"

"This is it," the bartender said, shrugging.

Bart turned to the injured men. "How did the cave-in happen?"

"The shafts ain't shored up right," said a man with a broken leg. "Regis don't put enough timber in 'em."

Bart shook his head. "That will change. How much do you men get paid to lay up here?"

They looked at each other. The man with a broken leg started laughing. "What do you mean, Baron? Men don't earn nothin' layin' up."

"Our relief fund feeds them," the bartender said. "This 'sorry excuse for a town' takes care of its own."

Bart threw back his whiskey, then said, "Take your time mending, gentlemen. When I get back from Santa Fe, I'll have your wages in full for your time spent convalescing."

The bartender laughed as he took up his broom again. "If you manage that, Baron. We'll name this town after you."

"Bullshit, New Mexico," an injured man suggested, wheezing.

Bart frowned. "Come on, Hilario," he said. "We'd better get going."

He rode back to the La Luz Road and headed downhill with his Indian guard. As they neared the lower reaches of the pine forests, the deep shade suddenly gave way to stark sunlight. The scene reminded him of a photograph he had once seen of a Civil War battlefield. A clear-cut one mile wide flanked the road, exposing the sun-scorched forest floor. Thousands of the stumps jutted like poorly placed gravestones. Eroding soil had left dead roots bare. Bart heard the sounds of axes coming from over a ridge.

"Hilario," he said, "remind me to ask Randy Hendricks about hiring a forester from back East. I don't like what this does to my mountains."

The Mescaleros refused to ride any closer to La Luz, so Bart and Hilario went on alone. They made their guns ready, but found no Regis men to deal with. Bart was beginning to think that Regis was sincere about negotiating.

The Mesilla-to-Las Vegas stage arrived in the

afternoon. Three men and a woman were in the coach when Bart and Hilario climbed in.

"Howdy," he said. "Allow me to introduce myself. I am Bartolome Cedric Montoya-Young, fifth baron of the Sacramentos, knight of the Golden Fleece, caballero of the Chamber of His Majesty ..."

Twenty-three

~∾~

"Is Randy here yet?" Bart asked Francisco over a late breakfast. He had arrived in the night, and slept well into the morning.

"He should be here this week. Have you heard about the surveyor general's office?"

"No, what about it?"

"It burned about two weeks ago, in the middle of the night. Raspberry told me the papers for the barony were out of the office when it caught fire."

"I planned it that way," Bart mumbled, his mouth full of tortillas and eggs and hot peppers. "I'll bet anything Vernon Regis is behind the fire."

Francisco shrugged. "When will we start seeing profits from the barony?"

"Maybe today," Bart said. "Regis wants to negotiate terms." He reached for his jacket hanging on the back of his chair, and pulled a letter from its pocket. "Here's your father's list of supplies for the fall. We need more cash, too."

"Chihuahua!" Francisco said, banging his fist on the table. "That damn barony is supposed to be making us money, not taking it."

"We have to make a few improvements. We'll be the richest men in the territory when the investments start to come together."

Grudgingly, Francisco took the letter and began reading his father's demands. He didn't speak to Bart again all morning.

When Bart rode to the Santa Fe plaza before noon, he noticed a few people pointing at him. Celebrity agreed with him. He even went so far as to hitch his coat tail behind the grip of his side arm for show. He tied his horse at Regis's office, and the speculator's assistant announced him immediately.

"Come in, Bart," Regis said, an illegible expression on his oversized face.

Bart wasted no time with small talk. "Let's start with your ranch in Dog Canyon," he said, plopping into a chair. "I want you out of there immediately, and I'm going to take over your ranch house and herds for payments past due."

"I've already abandoned the ranch," Regis said. "As for the house, and the herds, you can't have them."

"I will have them," Bart said. "They are on my land."

"I'm afraid they're not negotiable. You see, a band of rustlers attacked my ranch, burned my ranch house, and stole all of my cattle." He smiled.

Bart shook his head with disgust. "As long as you're out of Dog Canyon."

"I am. At least for now."

"And forever, if you enjoy what little good health you have."

Regis laughed at the ceiling. "Threats sound ridiculous coming from a jester like you. I suggest you abandon them."

Bart stood and started pacing. "You will also cease your timbering operations. I don't like the way you're stripping my mountains."

The speculator sighed with disinterest. "The market's no good, anyway. You'll find out there's little profit in timbering. My interest is in the mines." He opened his desk drawer. "I have a little something drawn up for you."

Bart yanked his revolver from its holster as Regis reached into the open drawer.

"Easy, Bart," the speculator said, shaking with laughter. "Damn, you've gotten antagonistic."

"As anyone is apt to when they're shot at. Get your hand out of that drawer."

"You don't mind if I remove your royalty check while I'm at it, do you?"

"My what?"

"Your mining royalties projected through the end of the year." He eased the check from the drawer, placed it on the desk in front of Bart, and closed the drawer.

Bart slipped his Colt into the holster and picked up the check. "Ten thousand," he grunted. He sat back down and pondered the amount. "This isn't like you, Vernon. What's your plan?"

"To ruin you, of course."

"By paying me royalties? I can abide that kind of ruination."

"I figure it won't be long until somebody reveals

your entire scheme as a monumental hoax. Then, I'm going to stretch your guts clear across New Mexico for extorting money from me, and people will call me a hero for doing it. But for now, paying the royalties is cheaper than hiring the guns to take on your so-called militia and your Indian guard."

Bart folded the check into his pocket. "You'll pay more next year, but this will do for now, provided you agree to a few concessions."

"Like what?"

"Hire another shift of men at the mine and put them on eight hours a day instead of twelve. Hire a qualified mining engineer to improve the safety standards of that death trap you call a mine. Pay the men you've already injured their wages while they convalesce, and provide the wives of the dead ones with pensions."

Regis lost his temper in an instant and swatted a stack of papers from his desk. "What do you care about those goddamn miners?"

The outburst amused Bart. "I want them on my side, just like the Indians and the settlers down there. Do you agree, or will I have to blockade your ore wagons?"

Regis gritted his teeth and got control of himself. "You're costing me a fortune, Bart."

"Pen the orders to your mine boss right now. I'll deliver them myself." He gloated. "They're going to name the mining village after me. How does Youngstown sound to you? Much better ring to it than Regisville, don't you think?"

Twenty-four

❦

Three days after he deposited the mining royalties in the Bank of New Mexico, Bart greeted Randy Hendricks at the stagecoach station on the plaza. He was wearing his most baronial costume: pants tucked into polished stovepipe boots, shiny gold watch chain swaying from his vest pocket, broad felt hat, its brim flapping on the cool norther.

"Randy! By God, it's good to see you!"

The lawyer stepped from the stagecoach scratching his head of red hair. "I haven't been called Randy since law school. I go by Jay Randolph Hendricks now." Grudgingly, he shook his former classmate's hand.

"And I go by Baron Bartolome Cedric Montoya-Young, but you can still call me Bart. I haven't outgrown my britches." He slapped the dust from Randy's back and helped him with his bags.

Randy grunted and rubbed his rear end. "Whatever possessed you to take up residence in this godforsaken country? When I found out the railroads don't even come to New Mexico, I almost turned around and went home."

"The railroads are coming," Bart assured him, "probably next year. The next trip you make will be in the comfort of a Pullman coach."

The old classmates headed directly for the archives so Randy could see the grant papers.

"Shouldn't the papers be filed with the surveyor general?" the lawyer asked.

"Normally. But I'm paying Raspberry's secretary to hide the documents in the archives. Good thing, too. Somebody already tried to destroy them by burning down the surveyor general's office."

"I can't make heads or tails of these documents," Hendricks complained after examining a few files. "You know I don't read Spanish."

"I just wanted you to see them, so you'd know they're authentic. I'll introduce you to some land grant experts who can attest to their authenticity."

Bart spent several days setting up interviews between Randy and the local title experts, who all swore they had never seen a Spanish land grant so well documented. The story of the barony had them transfixed, and Randy had to hear the details of it several times.

Francisco and Vicente complained about the amount of money Bart spent showing his old law school chum around Santa Fe—feeding him in the most expensive restaurants, buying him drinks in every influential saloon, purchasing souvenir moccasins and hats and weapons in the trading posts.

After the last land grant expert had been consulted, Bart took Randy to the Paisano Club for drinks and free lunch. They sat at a table in the middle of the barroom to consume their beers and sandwiches.

"Tomorrow we'll take the stage down to La Luz," Bart said, "and you can see the barony first hand. Meet Antonio and Bitora. Stay a month or so. I'll take you hunting. Wait till you see my fort, Randy. You've never seen the likes of it."

"Why do I need to do all that?"

"You want to see that the barony actually exists, don't you?" He reached across the table as Randy took a bite. "Here, let me help you hold on to that sandwich," he said, as he squeezed his lobbyist's fingers through the bread and into the mustard and meat.

"Dammit, Bart," the lawyer said, spraying bread crumbs from his mouth. "When are you going to grow out of these stupid pranks?"

Some men nearby were laughing. They had been eyeing Bart since he came in, hoping to see him pull one of the little jokes he was famous for.

"I can't help myself," Bart said, tipping his hat to the men in the saloon. "I'm the baron of Bad Jokes. It's a hereditary title."

"Well, I'm sick and tired of your bad jokes. And I'm sick and tired of the Territory of New Mexico. The only stagecoach I want to ride is the one that takes me back to civilization."

"What about the barony?"

"I don't need to see it," Randy said, wiping his fingers on his napkin. "What matters to Congress is paper title. Which reminds me, you'll need a survey of your so-called barony. The Lands Committee won't even consider any of these Spanish land grants anymore unless they know exactly how big the parcels are."

"What do you mean, 'so-called barony'?" Bart demanded.

The lawyer smirked. "I knew you before you came out here, remember? You're no more a baron than I am."

"Spanish custom allows a husband to assume his wife's hereditary titles. My father-in-law is a baron and a grandee of Spain, and so am I."

"Titular precepts in Spain are no different than they are elsewhere. So if you really knew anything about Spanish custom, Bart, you'd know that you can't inherit your father-in-law's title until he's dead."

Bart flicked the idea aside like a crumb from the barroom table. "You're talking like a lawyer again. Those technicalities don't carry much weight out here in the territories. Antonio has assured me that I will be the fifth baron. It's already in his will. So I figured I might as well go ahead and get used to calling myself Baron Bartolome."

Randy just shook his head. "What about the survey?"

Bart tried not to show his consternation. Randy had become a real pain. "I've already contracted the surveyors," he said. "They're going with me back to the barony. Although it baffles me why the size of the grant should make any difference to Congress. If we have legal titles to the land, it should make no difference how much land."

"Politics," Randy replied. "Those congressmen have to answer to the folks back home. They don't understand how one man can claim a million acres of public domain. Public sentiment has a lot to do with it."

"That's exactly my point! There's more to it than paper title, Randy. There's public sentiment. And I have the public on my side. I'm a hero—a Robin Hood passing out quit-claim deeds to my new neighbors when I could be running them out of their homes. The public is fascinated with the barony of the Sacramentos. It's like buried treasure, or a lost mine. Use it!"

"All right, I see your argument. Just don't push my fingers through my sandwich again."

"Why would I do that? It wouldn't be funny a second time."

As Randy drank from his mug, Bart reached across the table and lifted the bottom of the glass, sloshing beer up his old friend's nostrils. The saloon erupted with laughter at Jay Randolph Hendricks's expense.

Twenty-five

❧

Randy had waited for three hours to see Senator Miles Armour, Republican from Pennsylvania, chairman of the Senate Lands Committee. Finally, the senator's aide called him in.

"Jay Randolph Hendricks," the lobbyist said, reaching over Armour's desk for a handshake.

The senator looked through his wire-rimmed spectacles at his docket. "Oh, yes," he said, his tired eyelids lifting. "The Montoya-Young grant in New Mexico. I read your dossier on the matter, Mr. Hendricks. What a fascinating tale."

"Yes, sir."

"And you represent these modern-day barons who claim this ancient grant entitles them to a million acres?"

"According to the survey, which Mr. Young orchestrated himself, the barony now encloses roughly six hundred thousand acres," Randy said.

"They deeded about half of the grant to the Mescaleros after I suggested that taking tribal lands might be an impediment to Congressional approval."

"Wise counsel," Armour said. "Well, there's no need for you to take up any more of my time. I suspect you're going to try to convince me to get the grant approved."

"Not necessarily," Randy said.

The senator looked over the top of his lenses. "You are the lobbyist for this Bart Young, aren't you?"

"Yes, sir," Randy said. "And in that capacity I feel obligated to tell you that I have seen the many documents pertaining to the grant with my own eyes, and they do appear to be quite genuine. I have also met with several impartial experts on Spanish land grants, all of whom insist that the barony is valid. And, as you know, Rudolph Raspberry, surveyor general of the Territory of New Mexico, is recommending approval, and he is a gentleman of unquestionable integrity, and a good Republican. However . . ."

Armour removed his spectacles and put an earpiece in his mouth. "Yes?"

"As a citizen, and a member of the Republican party, I feel obligated to report to you on some other aspects of the case."

"Please do," the senator suggested.

"The night before I left Santa Fe, I had a secret meeting with a man named Vernon Regis, a very influential land speculator in the Territory of New Mexico, a former Union officer from Missouri, a Republican, and a good contact in the West."

The senator nodded. "What was the nature of this secret meeting?"

Randy pulled his chair a little closer to Armour's desk and spoke in a hushed tone. "Regis believes Young manufactured the documents giving him claim to his barony."

Armour pinched the bridge of his nose and squinted. "Mr. Hendricks, you are the most confusing lobbyist I have had in my office in a long time. Are you suggesting that your own client may be a fraud?"

"There's no solid evidence of any such thing," Randy insisted. "Only Regis's word. But as I mentioned, he carries a great deal of influence. And, I did some checking into Mr. Young's background, and I found some rather disturbing things. He once attended Tulane University, though he didn't graduate. He was known as a habitual prankster who talked a great deal about Spanish land grants. He was also remembered for a certain facility he had with a pen. Some of his former classmates recalled that he forged signatures of their professors or their parents for them to get them out of awkward situations."

Slowly, Miles Armour put his glasses back on. "Mr. Hendricks, are you working for Vernon Regis as well as Bart Young?"

"Regis offered, but I refused. That would be an obvious conflict of interest."

"But you seem to be painting your own client as a fraud. Do you suspect that the documents for this barony of Young's may have been forged?"

"No, sir. Their appearance is quite genuine, and the experts have accepted them without question. However, if this news about Young's college forgeries gets out, your committee might stand quite a bit of ridicule if it recommended confirmation of the grant to the Senate."

"Do I take it, then, that you are advising the Senate *not* to confirm this barony of the Sacramentos as a valid land grant?"

Randy chuckled and scratched his scalp. "I wouldn't be much of a lobbyist if I suggested that, sir. Besides, Young has the public sentiment right now. I understand the *New York Times* has dispatched a reporter to New Mexico to interview him. You wouldn't make yourself popular if you ruined him."

"Then just what the devil *are* you suggesting?"

"That you delay action."

The senator slumped over his desk and glared at Randy. "Young man, I am a member of the United States Senate. I have to work within the multifarious manifestations of the federal government. *Of course* I am going to delay action! I delay action on *everything*! What kind of advice is that?"

"I mean, to delay indefinitely. If Vernon Regis loses his influence in New Mexico, or turns out to be nothing more than a disgruntled land speculator, then recommend confirmation of Young's grant. If, on the other hand, this news about Young's career as an amateur forger gets out, you can advise Congress against confirmation, or dismiss the case altogether, without embarrassment."

Armour turned in his swivel chair and stared through his window at the Capitol grounds, cloaked in pure-white snow. "That seems to make sense, except for one thing. Just where does it all leave you?" He laced his fingers together and propped his feet on a windowsill.

"Young will continue to develop his grant, with or without confirmation. That's the way they do it out there in the territories. I've done my duty as a lobbyist, and my duty as a member of the Republican Party. After all, I don't plan to make a career of lobbying. I prefer public service."

Armour turned back to his guest and stared into the pale-green eyes. "You have been most enlightening, Mr. Hendricks. Your counsel is appreciated."

Randy rose, bid the senator a good day, and left with a grin on his face. Armour's aide stepped into his office to announce the next appointment.

"All right, Richard, send him in," Armour said. "And, Richard, send a note to Secretary Schurz over at Interior. There's a position for a legal researcher open at the Land Office. Recommend that Hendricks fellow who just left."

Twenty-six

❦

Bart felt himself trapped in the dream—the same dream that came to visit him every couple of moons. He knew what was going to happen, but he couldn't stop it. He saw himself putting the final touches on the forgeries: the comandante's petition, the alcalde's report, the Viceroy's order. Then came the royal *cedula*, and, though he tried to fight it, his hand signed the name of Bart Young instead of His Royal Majesty, King Carlos the Third.

He woke with a start and sat up in bed.

"What is it?" Bitora said, she was sitting in front of her mirror, brushing her long, shiny hair, the pale light of dawn reaching in for her from Fort Young's plaza. "Bartolome, was it the dream again?" She came to his side of the bed.

He saw his familiar room and felt relief engulf him. "Yes," he said. "It was terrible. Archiveque had a hundred men this time. And a howitzer cannon!"

Bitora caressed his face as she crawled onto the bed next to him. He put his arms around her and buried his face against her warm neck. He held her for a long time; then his hands began to wander.

"Not now," Bitora warned, pushing herself away with a reproachful smile. "I have to go feed the baby. You know she will sleep all day and cry all night if I don't wake her up."

Grudgingly, he let her go.

After she left, he got out of bed and looked at himself in the mirror. His thinning hair was standing on end. Backlighted by the glare from the plaza, the top of his head looked something like a clear-cut. Well, at least his mountains weren't losing timber as fast as he was losing hair. Not since he had hired the forester from New England to establish a sensible harvest regime.

As he trimmed his beard, then dressed himself, he wondered what Carlos would have cooking down in the kitchen. He stepped onto the balcony overlooking the plaza and filled his nostrils. A cool snap was in the air, bracing him with anticipation of hunts in the snow, and cold nights by the fire with Bitora.

As he descended the stair steps made of halved logs, a chorus of familiar yelps reached him. The Mescalero guards were coming, and they were excited about something. He looked toward the western watchtower.

"Don Bartolome!" the man on watch duty shouted. "The Indians have captured somebody!"

Open the gates!" Bart shouted.

Antonio stepped from the kitchen with a cup of

coffee as two of the fort's workmen threw the heavy squared-timber bar from the west entrance and swung the gates open. Chief Estrella and four Mescalero braves rode into the fort, holding an old man in buckskins at gunpoint. The prisoner's hands were bound tightly behind him, his ankles lashed to his stirrups. His face consisted of the oldest looking batch of human skin Bart had ever seen, webbed with creases. Hair trailed in greasy gray strands from the back of his hat. He twisted relentlessly in the saddle, trying to loosen his bindings, his eyes raking the Indians with hatred as he used up every cuss word Bart had ever heard.

"Capitan," Estrella said. "We caught him hunting."

Bart looked at Antonio, who, leaning casually against a pine post, made a gesture indicating that he wanted nothing to do with the problem. "Stranger," Bart said to the old man, "I'll have them cut you loose if you'll settle down."

The prisoner forced himself to cease his struggles but sat quivering with rage in the saddle. Bart gave the order, and one of the Indians cut the rawhide bindings, jumping clear in case the old man intended to kick.

"Who are you?" Bart asked.

"Tolliver. They called me Uncle Dan, back to Tennessee."

Bart noticed, as the old man rubbed his wrists, that he was still hunched over unnaturally, as if being tied up had permanently disfigured him. "Why can't you straighten up?" he asked.

Through the folds of wrinkled flesh, the beady eyes shifted. "Fell down a mountain when I was young. Broke both shoulders."

"How long have you been hunting in my mountains?"

"Your mountains grow in hell. Anyway, I don't track years much."

"Years? Were you here before we built Fort Young?"

"Before the army built Fort Stanton."

"That would be more than twenty years ago. Why didn't you come down and introduce yourself if you were here before us?"

"Because I don't give a damn for you, that's why. Now, tell your Indians to stand aside before I show fight."

"Wait a minute," Bart said, squinting at the old man. "You're not the one the Mescaleros call *El Cimarron*—the wild one." He looked at the Indian guard and found them nodding. "Son of a gun! I thought you were just a legend. I've listened to tall tales about you in their tepees."

"Tell 'em I want my rifle back," Uncle Dan insisted.

"They say you can fly away like an eagle when you're cornered."

"Ignorant bastards. I kick like a mule, and bite like a bear, but ain't a man alive flies." He looked up and saw Bitora on the balcony with her baby. He didn't look again, but removed his hat in honor of her presence. He hadn't seen a woman in civilized dress in decades.

"What's wrong, Uncle Dan? Don't you like being a legend?"

"I like bein' alone. Tell that red buck if he drops ol' Kaintuck, I'll wear his scalp."

Bart saw Estrella holding an old Kentucky rifle, its heavy octagonal barrel mounted in a stock of tiger-stripe maple. "Chief, give him his weapon back. Where's your cabin, Uncle Dan?"

"I sleep on the ground," he said, yanking "Kaintuck" from Estrella's grasp.

"Tell you what. I'll build you a cabin and give you a deed to any place you want to settle in the mountains. You don't bother the Indians, and I'll see that they don't bother you."

Uncle Dan put his hat on and reined his horse toward the open gate. "See that *you* don't bother me, either, or ol' Kaintuck'll do you like a Indian."

"Where do you want your cabin built?" Bart asked as the old man rode out.

"I don't."

"How about over Five Springs up Bear Canyon?"

"Suit yourself," the mountain man answered, nudging his horse to a lope.

When the old man had gone, Bart noticed something different about the Indians. "Why'd you boys cut your hair?"

Estrella looked downward, almost in shame. "Semple said he would cut our rations if we did not cut our hair. So, we cut our hair, and then he cut our rations anyway."

Bart looked at Antonio. The old *rico* raised his coffee cup as if toasting his son-in-law. "You are doing well, Bartolome. Why do you look at me?" He turned into the kitchen laughing.

Bart sighed. "Chief, how many problems are you going to bring me this morning?" He stared at the stone-faced Mescaleros for a few seconds. "Well, if Semple cut your rations, I guess you boys are hungry. Come on in the kitchen and fill yourselves while I think of a way to get you a new Indian agent."

The Mescaleros leaped from their ponies and left them loose in the plaza. Carlos had to split more wood before they were through with breakfast.

"I think I've got it figured out," Bart finally said as the Indians lounged in the kitchen, rubbing their full stomachs. "Now, the first thing you do, Chief, is go down the river and steal about twenty head of my cattle."

The two barons rode down to their Penasco Ranch with the Indians and showed them which steers to steal. Estrella and his men went at it as if it were really a raid, riding hard, practicing their battle cries, looking over their shoulders for pursuers. They herded the beeves upstream, past Fort Young, into a secluded bend of Penasco Canyon.

While Estrella rode to his reservation to bring back the tribe for the feast, Bart retired to his office and started writing letters. He wrote first to Captain Semple's commanding officer at Fort Stanton, Colonel Hampton, telling him that Semple's policies as Indian agent were starving the Mescaleros and driving them to thievery. He also requested a troop of cavalry soldiers to protect Fort Young.

Next he wrote to the Bureau of Indian Affairs, demanding compensation for the stolen cattle and lambasting Semple's lack of compassion. Finally, he demanded that the bureau remove Semple as agent and appoint a civilian to replace him.

"Why did you ask Colonel Hampton to send troops for our protection?" Antonio asked, the letter in his hand. "We are in no danger."

"First, it will give this Indian crisis a facade of

authenticity. Secondly, it will give us a chance to
personally harangue Colonel Hampton about Captain Semple's incompetence as an agent. And third,
I can sell the army a fortune in food for the troops
and grain for the horses while they quarter here."

Antonio nodded approvingly, shuffling to the
Bureau of Indian Affairs letter. "I will write a letter
to the bureau, too," he promised. "And I will include the signatures of the chiefs on my letter."

"And if that doesn't work, we'll get Randy
Hendricks to lobby the bureau for us. That will get
some action."

The Montoya villagers attended the Mescalero
feast in Penasco Canyon and contributed more
food—mutton, *cabrito*, corn, beans, tortillas, honey,
and *leche quemada*. Antonio spent most of his time
swapping old stories with Chief Ojo Blanco.

For days, the Mescaleros feasted and dried the
excess beef for future use. When a rider announced
the approach of the cavalry, the Indians scattered
across the mountains.

As Bart had predicted, Colonel Hampton had
left Semple at Fort Stanton while he came to
Montoya to investigate the reported Mescalero
raid. The barons insisted that the blame was
Semple's more than the Mescaleros'. Even Indians
had to eat. Hampton listened without response. He
was an old veteran of the Mexican War, the Civil
War, and numerous Indian campaigns—a tough
warrior, but an honest and fair-minded man.

"Semple's a good soldier," he finally said. "He
follows orders. But I would just as soon remove
the Mescalero agency from Fort Stanton. It would

prevent them from prostituting their squaws to my men."

Bart felt near victory. "When they have enough to eat, and some dignified work to earn their own keep, they won't have to prostitute their squaws."

As Bart had predicted, the barons procured government vouchers from Hampton before he left Fort Young. They would make a nice profit on grain for cavalry horses and grub for the soldiers.

"Gentlemen, I'm going to request that Captain Semple be relieved of his duties—with honors—as Indian agent," the colonel said as he climbed into his cavalry saddle. He looked at Antonio. "I have just the man in mind to recommend as his replacement. Maybe it's time for a civilian agent." He tipped his hat and waved his troops toward Fort Stanton.

Twenty-seven

❧

One evening in June 1879, Chief Estrella and two braves galloped into Fort Young with the mail from Fort Stanton, including a letter from the commissioner of Indian Affairs.

Bart was riding Nepo around the courtyard on his shoulders and carrying his baby daughter, Maria, in his arms when the Indians arrived. "Get down and stay awhile, Chief," he said. "This may be good news for you." He tore eagerly into the letter from Indian Affairs. He had been waiting months for the reply.

Estrella shook his head. "I am going back to the reservation. We have trouble there."

"What kind of trouble?"

"Victorio has come."

"Who?"

"Chief of the Mimbres Apaches."

"What's he doing here?"

"He doesn't want to stay on his reservation at San Carlos."

"Well, he can't stay on *your* reservation."

"He doesn't want to stay on any reservation at all."

Bart looked at the blank faces of the three Indians. "Antonio!" he shouted. "You better get out here!" He tucked the rest of the mail under his arm and unfolded the letter from Indian Affairs. "At least stay until I read this letter. It probably concerns you more than me." He scanned the first couple of paragraphs as he heard Antonio's boots striding across the plaza.

"What is it, Bartolome?" the old baron said.

Bart glanced up from his letter. "Some Mimbres Apaches under Chief Victorio have jumped their reservation and moved into the Sacramentos."

"How many?" Antonio said.

"Only thirteen," Estrella said, "but Victorio is trying to get Mescalero braves to follow him. Raiding."

"Did you hear that, Bartolome? We will have to send riders to the Penasco Ranch, and across the mountains to the Dog Canyon Ranch, as well. We have some sheepherders on the Sacramento River this summer, don't we? They will be easy targets if we don't warn them. Bartolome, are you listening?"

Bart was staring at the letter in his hands, his mouth hanging open, his eyes showing rare surprise. "They made *me* the new Indian agent," he said.

"Of course they did," Antonio said. "I recommended you. So did Colonel Hampton and Ojo Blanco."

"Didn't you think about asking me?"

"I know how tricky you are. You might have talked your way out of it."

"But, why would I want the job?"

"For your friends the Mescaleros. And for the barony. If the Mescaleros are happy, the barony is safe."

Bart's arms went limp and the letter hung in his grasp at his side. "Why now? There's an Indian war brewing. What am I supposed to do about it?"

"The army will go after Victorio," Antonio said. "Captain Semple will kill any Indian not camped at the agency. I suggest you establish your agency here, at Fort Young, and tell all the Mescaleros to come here for protection if they do not want to be mistaken for Mimbres."

Bart looked at Estrella.

"I will bring everyone from my camp," the chief said. "But Ojo Blanco has maybe a hundred others at Fort Stanton."

"Start for here at dawn," Bart said. "I'll ride to Fort Stanton and bring Ojo Blanco's band back myself."

The chief jerked his reins and thundered out of the fort's plaza, his two braves on his heels.

"I will go with you to Fort Stanton," Antonio said. "Ojo Blanco will listen to me."

"I don't know why in hell they didn't make *you* Indian agent," Bart said. "I wish I'd have thought of recommending you before you recommended me."

Antonio chuckled and held out his hand. "Congratulations. You are going to be a good agent."

* * *

They started for Fort Stanton the next morning before dawn, riding the longest-winded mustangs they had in the stables. It was fifty miles to the fort, and they intended to make the ride in one day.

At noon, they saw a faint dust plume in the distance, and knew Estrella's people were on the move. They veered from their trail to meet the chief, who was riding at the head of a large band. The scene struck Bart with dread: Horses, mules, and burros dragged travois; women carried papooses on their backs; dogs and children ran everywhere. He could not imagine moving everything he owned overnight. How was he going to administer to these people, so different from himself?

"Victorio left our camp last night when we started taking the lodges down," Estrella reported. "Seven of my warriors rode with him. I told them you are going to be our new agent, Capitan, but they said it is too late. They want to go raiding again, like in the old days."

"I can only help the ones who camp at Fort Young," Bart said.

The barons swapped their tired mounts for two Indian ponies, and continued toward Fort Stanton at a gallop. For two hours they rode through a mountain thunderstorm, then finally broke free of it.

They were crossing a meadow, less than an hour from the army post, when they saw half a dozen Indians approaching from the tree line.

"Recognize them?" Bart said, reining his mustang back to a walk. The horse blew like a bellows.

Antonio squinted and shook his head. "I cannot see their faces from here. But that pinto pony in the middle is one I have seen in Ojo Blanco's camp."

The rains had been plentiful on the Mescalero that summer. Grass was knee-high in the meadow, and green as new aspen leaves. A huge ponderosa pine stood alone in the middle of the meadow, and Bart rode into its shade to wait for the Indians. He sat casually in the saddle, trying to find a familiar face among the six warriors who loped toward him.

Then, without explanation, one of the braves flew from the back of his horse, his moccasined feet cartwheeling over his head. Bart heard the shot and the dull thud of a heavy rifle ball hitting flesh. He reached for his Winchester even before he understood what had happened.

The Indians milled around their fallen friend long enough for Antonio to find the black puff of smoke at the edge of the meadow. As Bart looked toward the place, he saw the unmistakable figure of Uncle Dan Tolliver galloping toward the lone pine, his long rifle in his hand.

The war cry from the five braves leaped into Bart's ears and crawled up and down his spine on scorpion legs. He drew his rifle, not certain what he would do with it, and levered a cartridge into the chamber. Two of the Indians charged Uncle Dan. The other three came directly toward him and Antonio.

Bart rode into the sunlight, holding his rifle over his head. "Whoa, boys!" he shouted. "Don't shoot!" He looked toward Uncle Dan. The old man was still coming, but had dropped to the off side of his saddle, clinging there like a Comanche raider, his horse shielding him from bullets.

Bart heard the grass hiss around him and heard the rifle reports. A pine branch split above him.

"Behind the tree, Bartolome!" Antonio shouted. "Take cover! They are trying to kill us!"

Bart wheeled his pony behind the pine and hit the ground with one rein in his hand. The tree trunk was wide, but not wide enough. "Why are they shooting at us?" he yelled. "They must think we're with that old bastard!" He looked toward Uncle Dan in time to see the long Kentucky rifle belch smoke over the saddle seat. Another brave twisted from his pony, and the old man kept coming.

"I don't know," Antonio said. "But I am going to show them I can shoot back." He leaned around the tree and let a few rounds go over the heads of the attacking braves.

Bart stepped into the open and added to the barrage. The three warriors parted, held their horses back, and returned the fire. Bart jumped back behind the cover of the lone pine as Uncle Dan arrived, leaping from his horse, holding his rifle in one hand, reaching for his powder horn with the other.

"What the hell is wrong with you, old man?" Bart shouted. "The Mescaleros aren't hostile!"

The old man smiled as he took a greased patch from the box on Kaintuck's stock. "Damn fool. You don't know coons from ringtail cats. Them ain't Mescalero, they's Mimbres."

Bart checked the four Indians for position and found them regrouping two hundred yards away, contemplating another attack. "How do you know?"

"I know," the mountain man said, ramming the

patched ball down the muzzle. He leaned his ram-
rod against the tree.

"But those are Mescalero ponies."

"Ponies is swappable. You're ridin' a Mescalero
horse yourself."

The shrill cry came across the meadow again,
and bullets started tearing into the lone pine. If
those were Mimbres Apaches, Bart figured he had
good reason to shoot for the kill. Victorio's renegades had no business here causing trouble among
his Mescaleros. He braced his Winchester against
the tree and worked the action as fast as it would
go, taking little time to aim. Antonio fired more
deliberately. Uncle Dan was merely aiming,
awaiting the perfect shot.

As the four Apaches rode by, firing their repeating rifles, Bart wheeled and shot from the hip, hitting an Indian pony in the neck. As the horse
collapsed, the Indian flew through the air and disappeared in the tall grass.

Old Kaintuck roared, and Bart turned to see another empty Apache saddle.

"Get any?" Tolliver asked.

Antonio shook his head as he pushed rounds
into the loading port of his rifle.

"I unhorsed one," Bart said, pointing.

The old mountain man leaned his long rifle
against the tree, handed his bridle reins to Bart,
and skulked into the grass. Dropping to his stomach, he vanished, the grass in front of him falling
like wheat before a mowing machine, revealing his
progress as he scrambled toward the dead horse.

"What's he going to do without a gun?" Bart
asked.

"Quién sabe?" Antonio replied. "Let him kill himself if he wants to."

One of the Apaches caught a loose horse and charged back toward the downed warrior, leading the extra mount. Bart tried to find him in his sights, but the Indian was riding fast and Bart's nerves were wound. His shots went wild. When the rescuer came near enough, the warrior Bart had unhorsed jumped up from the grass and ran for the extra horse. He vaulted into the empty saddle just as a shot from Antonio's rifle took the horse out from under him.

The Indians tried to mount double, but Dan Tolliver rose from the grass, not thirty feet away. A flash of reflected sunlight glinted from his hand, then flickered through the air like ball lightning. The steel blade hit the mounted Indian high in the shoulder and almost knocked him from the horse.

The Apache on the ground wheeled and pointed his rifle at Uncle Dan, but no report came. As the mountain man rushed the two Apaches with bare hands, the one on the ground jumped behind his rescuer, holding the knifed man in the saddle. He urged the pony on, but Dan Tolliver was there, clawing at the bridle with one hand and the Indians with the other.

"He's trying to get his knife so he can stab the poor bastard again!" Bart said, looking over his rifle sights for a clear shot.

The Indian riding double brought his rifle down on Dan's head like a club, then rode away with the knifed man in front of him. Bart followed them in his irons, and twice lined up a shot, but he couldn't see killing either man after they had shown such courage in rescuing each other.

Antonio had been watching the other mounted Indian catch the last loose horse. When the three surviving Apaches were all mounted separately, they sent a last barrage of shots toward the lone pine, then disappeared into the woods, the knifed man riding between the other two.

The two barons mounted and rode to check on Uncle Dan. They found him on his hands and knees, shaking his head.

"You all right?" Bart asked, dropping from the saddle to lift the old man to his feet.

"Did you get my knife?" he asked.

"Hell, no, I didn't get your knife. You left it stuck in that Apache."

"Damnation," he said, rubbing a bloody spot in his long gray hair. "My old Green River knife."

"What are you doing on the reservation, anyway?" Bart asked. "You don't have authorization to be here."

"You'd be dead if I wasn't here. Been followin' that bunch of Victorio's boys for two days, waitin' for a chance to get their scalps. You two spoilt it for me."

Bart shook his head in disgust and handed the old man his reins. "I want you to stay clear of the Mescalero from now on, you hear?"

"Go to hell. I was here before the damn reservation. Who are you to tell me where I go?"

"I'm the new Indian agent. You'll do as I say or I'll have the Indian police arrest you."

"What Indian police?"

"The ones I'm going to form to take care of trespassers like you. Why don't you stay up at that cabin I built for you at Bear Canyon?"

"Been usin' it."

"Good." Bart got back on his horse.

"Tore the damn floor out of it, dug me a fire pit, and used it for a smokehouse."

Antonio broke into laughter in spite of the glare Bart gave him.

"Just stay off this reservation," Bart warned, reining away.

"Wait, dammit!" Uncle Dan shouted. "I need a loan of a knife."

"What for?"

"Take them Mimbres scalps."

"Forget it," Bart said. He spurred his mustang, and headed for Fort Stanton, Antonio laughing behind him as they began to gallop.

Twenty-eight

꩜

Five minutes from Fort Stanton, Bart sensed the sky rumbling over the thundering of hooves. His pony slid on its hocks as he yanked back on the reins. Echos of gunfire were leap-frogging around the valley of the Rio Bonito.

The barons looked at each other. They heard stray shots now, piercing the air from the direction of the fort. The reports did not come with the regularity of a rifle drill. Bart and Antonio spurred their exhausted mounts on as the sun sank behind the western hills.

At Fort Stanton they found a couple of hundred soldiers herding Indians like cattle. The bugle blew mixed signals. The muzzle of a Mountain howitzer trailed smoke. They rode on, and at the edge of the village on the Rio Bonito, Bart saw the bodies—men, women, and children. A mother wailed as she dragged her wounded son, begging the soldiers for help, leaving a trail of blood.

Flecks of foam dropped from Bart's horse as he rode to the woman and jumped from the saddle beside the wounded boy. He wrapped his bandana around the shattered leg to stanch the flow of blood. In Spanish, he told the mother to lay the boy in the shade until the post surgeon could help.

"All Indians in the corral!" a private shouted. "Baron, you'd better get the hell out of the way. We're rounding up Indians."

"You're not rounding this one up. He's got a busted leg."

"Orders, baron. That squaw will have to drag him."

Bart drew his Colt and pointed it at the private. "Tell Colonel Hampton I want him here *now*."

"Colonel Hampton's at Fort Union."

"Where's the major?"

"Sick in bed."

Bart trembled with rage. "Captain Semple's in command?"

"Yes, sir," the private said, staring down the barrel of the Colt.

"Get him."

As the private galloped away, Bart carried the wounded boy to the shade and calmed his mother. He looked for Antonio, and saw him kneeling over a body on the riverbank. Ojo Blanco. Antonio crossed the old chief's arms over his chest. His eyes met Bart's, a fury in them such as Bart had seen only once before, in the courtyard of the old Montoya hacienda, the day Regis took Sebastiana in his arms.

Captain Semple rode back with the private.

"Young! This is army business. Stand aside, or you'll be arrested."

"This is the business of the Mescalero Indian agent. And that's me." He handed the letter from Indian Affairs to the officer.

"You?" Semple said, glancing down the letter. "I was told a civilian was coming. "But *you?*"

"What happened here?"

Semple handed the letter back to Bart. "Victorio killed two prospectors on Eagle Creek this morning. I had reason to believe some of his men were in Ojo Blanco's camp. When I ordered the Indians to turn over their weapons, some of them tried to sneak away up the river, so I had my men open fire."

Bart saw Antonio stalking toward the captain and knew trouble was coming.

"You stupid son of a bitch. You don't know coons from ringtail cats!"

"What?"

"Can't you tell the difference between a Mimbres and a Mescalero Apache?"

Semple's pale lips curled under his wispy yellow mustache. "I can tell a good Apache from a bad one." He pointed at the body of Ojo Blanco. "There lies a good one now."

Antonio grabbed the silver bars on the officer's collar and pulled him down from the saddle. Bart just watched as the *rico* pummeled Semple with his fist, his knees, and his boots once the captain had fallen.

"Private!" Semple called as he collapsed. "Arrest him!"

The private spurred his horse forward, grabbed Antonio by the arm, and pulled him away. Jumping from his mount, he pinned Antonio to the ground, putting the muzzle of his carbine against the old baron's chest.

As Semple struggled to find his feet, Bart drew his Colt, grabbed a handful of yellow hair, and held his gun barrel against the captain's head. "Tell that private to drop his carbine."

The officer and the enlisted man looked at each other.

"Tell him, or you'll leave your brains in this Indian camp," Bart warned, shaking the captain.

"Do as he says, private."

Reluctantly, the private dropped his carbine and stepped away from Antonio. The *rico* was slow getting up, and Bart knew he was getting too old for this sort of scuffle.

He shook the captain again, unable to check his anger. "This is what's going to happen, Semple," he said. "You're going to order an ambulance brought here to the village, and you're going to take every wounded Indian back to the infirmary where the post surgeon can work on them. Then you're going to order a burial detail to put these massacred citizens in the ground, one to a grave, each with a marker and the name of the person buried there on it. Finally, you're going to release the rest of those citizens from your damn stinking corrals and turn them over to me. I'm taking them to Fort Young. Do you think you can remember those orders to the letter?"

Semple nodded as Bart shoved him toward his horse. "Come on, private," the captain said, picking up his campaign hat. He mounted, but looked down at Bart before riding to the fort. "You've never seen what an Apache on the warpath can do to a good man in uniform, Young. This private here has seen it, haven't you, private?"

"Yes, sir. I've seen the guts of my friends stretched across the desert to cook in the sun."

The soldiers rode away, leaving the barons to hunt for survivors among the dead.

Bart saw the body of a dead Mescalero woman draped through the entrance hole of her tepee. "I wonder why, Captain," he muttered to himself.

Twenty-nine

❧

Little Nepo rode just in front of the pack mule that carried the antlers of the buck his father had killed. He had to look back at the trophy every few steps. He believed his father was the best hunter in the world, not even excepting Indians or mountain men. And, why not? His father had told him so, and his father was the fifth baron of the Sacramentos. Someday Nepo would be the sixth.

Nepo was eight, and on his first big hunt. His mother had tried to keep him from going, but his father had insisted. He was ready to get home to Fort Young—his toys were there, and it was warm—but he had enjoyed the hunt. The horses stepped high through the fresh snow. They knew their stables were near.

"Hey, Nepo!" his father shouted. "Come here. I want to show you something."

The boy reined his mount out of the pack line and joined his father under a small pine sapling.

"You see all the snow on these pine branches?" Bart said, when his son came to his side.

The boy looked up into the gray sky. "Yes, sir," he said.

"I want to show you what you can do with it. Call Carlos over here."

Nepo scanned the pack line for the cook. "Carlos!" he cried, squinting his eyes. "Come here!"

"*Qué pasa?*" Carlos said, riding under the branches of the small pine.

"Look what we found up in this tree, Carlos," Bart said. When the cook looked up, Bart shook the trunk of the sapling, bringing a cloud of frozen powder down on Carlos's face.

Nepo kicked in his stirrups as he laughed.

"You are going to teach that boy all of your bad habits!" Carlos scolded, shaking the snow from his face.

When they arrived back at Fort Young, Bitora was waiting in the plaza with Maria and Lucia. "You have a visitor," she said, handing her daughters to Bart one at a time so he could hug them. "In the saloon with Papa." She kissed him, then helped Nepo down from the saddle.

"Who is it?"

"That deputy sheriff. Yarborough."

Bart found Antonio entertaining Linden Yarborough over a game of billiards.

"How'd the hunt go, baron?" the deputy asked.

"Damn good," Bart said, shaking Yarborough's thick hand. He saw the lawman maybe twice a year and didn't know him well, but he had no reason to dislike him. Yarborough stood a few inches short of six feet, and was built stoutly. His broad face grew the thickest, curliest mat of whiskers in the county. Bart considered him a rather simple man, but he was hell on criminals. He had ridden with Sheriff Pat Garrett in the Lincoln County War and had helped capture Billy the Kid at Stinking Springs.

"What brings you to Fort Young?" Bart asked. "Chasing outlaws?"

"You might say so. I came to lay down the law to your Mexicans. I'm going to be the new justice of the peace for this precinct, and I intend to clean this place up and Americanize it. I was just telling Antonio that he's the only good Mexican in the county, as far as I'm concerned. Every other one I've ever known was either a thief or a killer."

Bart sauntered around behind the bar and poured himself a glass of whiskey. "Deputy, you live in Lincoln, right?"

Yarborough nodded as he rammed the cue ball with his stick.

"I don't suppose you live on the Mexican side of town."

"Hell, no."

"Got any Mexican deputies working with you?"

"Wouldn't have 'em."

"Mexican friends?"

The sheriff smirked.

"That explains it. You've got honest Mexican citizens everywhere around you, but the only ones you associate with are those you track down to haul into jail. Your opinion's slanted."

"You don't know what the hell you're talkin'

about," Yarborough said. "You don't have to keep the law in this county."

"I maintain perfect order on this barony, and I do it with the help of the Mexican citizens in Montoya."

Yarborough straightened slowly and put his cue stick on the table in the middle of the game. "You never got congressional approval for this grant did you, Young?"

Bart shrugged. "Congress works slow."

"As far as I'm concerned, your so-called grant ought to be opened up to settlement by Americans. I'm on my way up, Young. I don't plan to be a deputy forever. I've got connections in Santa Fe. If you don't want me to open your grant up to settlement, you better not stand in the way of me cleaning out that den of thieves you call Montoya."

Bart chortled in disbelief. "We haven't had a serious crime since we established the village."

"You've exported your share. I'll be holding court in Montoya the first Friday of every month," he said, taking his hat from a set of antlers on the wall. "Of course, I'll still be deputy sheriff as well as justice of the peace. I can arrest 'em and try 'em all in one breath if I want to. Too many Mexicans on your side of the county, Young. Time to get some of them out and get some Americans in."

"Just when did you become justice of the peace?" Bart demanded. "I didn't hear anything about it."

"The commissioners' court is going to appoint me at its next meeting. It's all arranged." He put on his coat and headed for the door. "I won't have Mexicans taking over this county. If you want to hold on to this grant of yours, I suggest you remember that."

Bart stood with his mouth open for several seconds after Yarborough walked out. He looked at Antonio, still standing across the pool table and holding his cue stick in both hands, scowling.

"Antonio," Bart said suddenly, "put that pool stick down." He walked around the table and tugged on the bottom of his father-in-law's vest.

"What are you doing, *idiota*?"

Bart stepped back, put his hand on his chin, and studied Antonio. "Go stand behind the bar."

"What?"

"Go on, do as I say." He led the old grandee around the end of the bar by the arm. "Slick your hair back on the right side."

"Stop acting like a fool. What are we going to do about that deputy?"

"Hmm . . ." Bart said, observing Antonio. "I don't know. I just don't know. It might work."

"What might work?"

"Stay right there. Don't move a hair." Bart ran out of the saloon, down the stairs, and across the plaza to the carpenter's shop. He found a heavy wooden mallet with a head the size of a peach can.

"What do you have that thing for?" Antonio said when Bart came back with the mallet. "Are you going to knock some sense into yourself?"

"Here, hold it," Bart said, handing the mallet to Antonio. He backed away to behold his old amigo across the billiards table. "Now, pound that thing on the bar three times, and shout, 'Order! Order! Order in the court!' "

Thirty

∽∾∽

A heavy snow made traveling difficult, but the barons got every healthy man in Montoya over the rolling plains to Lincoln for the next meeting of the commissioners' court. The Mexican population in Lincoln had been alerted, too, and met the procession from Montoya as it came in from the south. Other Mexican citizens streamed in from all over the county to join the movement.

They gathered outside the courthouse, and harangued the Anglo commissioners as they went to convene. When the meeting was called to order, Bart led in as many of his followers as would fit the cramped quarters.

"Mr. Young," the county judge stated, pounding his gavel. "This court is well aware of your penchant for practical jokes, but this disturbance is beyond decorum. Why have you brought this rabble here?"

"Why, to show our support for this august body, Your Honor," Bart said.

"Your support is noted. Now, please clear this room."

"And to get these citizens registered to vote," Bart continued. "And to inform this court that if it appoints Deputy Sheriff Linden Yarborough justice of the peace in my precinct—or any other precinct, for that matter—not a single Mexican in the county will vote for Your Honor or any of the commissioners come next election!"

A cheer rose from the Mexican contingent, and the judge banged his gavel ineffectually until Bart quieted the crowd.

"However," he continued, "if this court were to exercise its infinite wisdom by appointing the venerable Don Antonio Geronimo Montoya de Cordoba y Chaves de Oca justice of the peace instead of Linden Yarborough, Your Honor would be virtually assured of re-election!"

The judge pounded his gavel again until the voices died down. "Where is Deputy Yarborough? Why isn't he here to speak up for himself?"

"Strangely enough, Your Honor, he had to investigate an alleged shooting over at my Penasco River ranch—an incident that I fear may have been greatly exaggerated. But, you know Lin. He had to see for himself. He'd make a damn good sheriff!"

Again the county judge had to pound his gavel until Bart quieted the crowd. "This court is going into executive session to consider this matter," the judge declared. "I want all citizens and newspaper reporters out!"

* * *

Bart was unable to attend Antonio's first session of court at Fort Young. Pressing matters required his attention elsewhere on the barony. The graders for the Sacramento Railroad had reached the Regis mine and would work through the winter to get to Star Mountain, where Bart had wanted for years to build his grand log lodge house. With the money the railroad would bring him, he would be able to appoint it in high luxury.

It was his railroad. He had gone to Santa Fe to recruit investors, but he was president of the company and the largest stockholder. The narrow gauge spur from El Paso would enable him to better get his timber to market. Regis would also pay dividends getting his ore out of his mine.

When he got to Youngstown, where the railroad construction crews were quartering, a fancy coach in front of the Youngstown saloon caught Bart's eye. When he entered the saloon, he saw Vernon Regis sitting at the bar, his long, paper-skinned fingers wrapped around a jigger of whiskey.

"Hello, Baron," the speculator said.

As he glanced quickly around the barroom for Domingo Archiveque, Bart opened his coat so he could get to his side arm.

"He came alone, Bart," the bartender said.

Regis laughed. "You're a little nervous, aren't you . . . Baron?"

Bart hung his sheepskin coat on a hook. "I underestimated you once, Vernon. Never again." He felt like a regular mountain man when he compared his red-flannel shirt and hunting moccasins to the speculator's patent leather shoes and boiled collar. "What are you doing here?"

"Damn miners are threatening to go on strike again."

The old woodstove stood in a box of sand that had caught many a hot coal. Bart hooked his heel over the rim of the box as he warmed his hands. A gust whistled through the cracks between the warped pine boards.

"Doesn't surprise me. I encouraged them to strike months ago." He moved to the bar and sat two stools away from Regis. The bartender had a jigger of bourbon waiting for him. "Did you see the trestle my railroad engineer started across La Luz Canyon?"

"Yes. That's going to be quite some feat of engineering. Too bad you'll have to give it to the government."

"What's that supposed to mean?"

"It means you never did get your congressional confirmation."

"Congress works slow." Bart rubbed his cold hands together before picking up the shot glass. "I've got my lobbyist in Washington working on it."

"You mean that redheaded Hendricks fellow? Last time he reported to me, he said the debate over your claim would never get out of committee. I know as well as you do that he's working for the Land Office now. He doesn't have time to lobby for you."

This was a shock. Randy reporting to Regis? No, that was just a bluff. But, Randy *had* been neglecting the question of confirmation for the past couple of years. It was time to renew the campaign. "Randy Hendricks is not the only lobbyist in Washington," he said, scrambling to cover himself.

"He's the only one you ever hired."

Both men went back to drinking their whiskey.

"Where's old Antonio?" Regis asked.

"He's holding court across the mountains."

"I heard about that stunt you pulled with the county commissioners." Regis took a swallow. "You two bullshit barons are building your own little dynasty down there. What I can't figure out is why you ever agreed to serve as Indian agent. Can't be the salary."

"As long as I keep the Indians happy, they'll help me look after my barony."

"Happy? I heard you got fourteen of them massacred your first day as agent."

"That was also Delton Semple's last day as agent. He's the one that shot them down."

"*The* Delton Semple?" Regis said, craning his frail neck to look at Bart. "The Indian fighter? I don't remember him getting reprimanded for any massacre."

"The army promoted him to major and sent him out after Victorio."

Regis laughed and pounded his fist on the bar. "Now he's a bigger hero than you!"

Bart winced. "I was just happy to get shed of him. We haven't lost a single Indian to disease or murder since Semple left. I got the Bureau of Indian Affairs to increase rations, and nobody's been able to put in a lower bid than me to supply them. The Mescaleros and I have a great partnership.

"Chief Estrella has ten officers in his Indian police now. His band is building cabins on the reservation. I've got five braves learning how to farm over at Montoya, two learning the cow business at my Dog Canyon ranch—you remember the place, Vernon—and three more at my Penasco River ranch. One brave is working in that old sawmill you built on the Tularosa River, another three are earning wages in the grist mill we just built at Fort Young, about half a dozen are learning how to tend sheep on the reservation, and nine or ten have entered into the freighting business."

"If they'll work cheaper than these Irishmen, I'll hire them as scab workers in the mine," Regis said.

"Indians don't like working underground. And I wouldn't let them work for you, anyway. I wouldn't want to lose their trust."

Regis poured himself another drink and stared at the wall. A gust howled through the cracks and sounded as if it would tear the roof off of the saloon. Bart threw his whiskey back, slid from his barstool, and fetched his coat from its hook.

"I noticed your railroad crew is grading above town," Regis said. "How high's the road going to go?"

"All the way to the summit of Star Mountain. I'm going to build a lodge up there, and I want all my influential friends to be able to ride in style right to my front gate. It's going to be quite a mansion, Vernon. A summer retreat. Up there the dog days run about seventy-five degrees." He slipped his coat on and put his hand on the door handle.

"When you get it built, I hope you'll invite me to come see," Regis said.

Bart chuckled as he held the door open to let the frigid mountain air in. "Sure," he said. "The day you get frost-bit in hell."

Part III

⌒∾⌒

Thirty-one

❦

Bart heard the *Conquistador*'s steam whistle from the music suite of his Star Mountain Lodge. He usually went to the window to watch it chug up the tracks, belching smoke and spewing steam, but this morning he had other matters on his hands.

"I know you don't want to go, son," he said, "but you're going to be the sixth baron of the Sacramentos, and you have to finish your education."

"Why can't I just go to the Indian school at Montoya this year?" Nepo pleaded. He was fifteen now, and hated leaving the adventures and luxuries of the barony to go to school.

"Son, you know the reverend doesn't teach those Indians anything but reading, writing, and ciphering. No Latin, no Shakespeare, no history. Even the Indians have to go away to Carlisle if they want to learn more."

"But, Papa, I learn more here with you than I do at school."

The baron grinned appreciatively. "Nice try, Nepo, but you're going back to school. You need a city education if you want to get into a good college. Anyway, Albuquerque's not so bad, and you'll be back for the holidays."

Nepo clenched his fists and bunched his lips, but he knew it was useless. His father had always been strict about his education. He stalked out of the music room and stomped up the log stairway to his bedroom.

The Star Mountain lodge had turned out grander than even the baron had imagined: two stories high, covering an acre of ground, looking more like a hotel than a home. Bart claimed it was the largest log structure in the world, though he wasn't at all sure about that.

Bitora rose from the piano bench and marched to the door to watch her son go up the stairs. "He has been seeing some girl at Montoya," she said, her voice rasping her disapproval. "That's why he doesn't want to go back to school."

"Really? Mexican or Indian?"

"Indian?" Bitora hissed. "My son had better not be fooling around with any squaws!"

Bart sipped his morning coffee casually. "Why not? Why shouldn't the seventh baron be half Mescalero?"

"Because I am his mother, and I say he is not going to fool around with any Indian girls."

Bart chuckled. "Well, honey, he's going back to school, anyway, so I wouldn't worry about it. Just sit down there and play some more of that Beethoven you've been working on."

Reluctantly, Bitora returned to her piano bench.

Hilario entered the room with a bundle of envelopes. "Don Bartolome, the mail has come up with the *Conquistador*."

Bart put his cup on the coffee table. "Hand it over, and let's see what's new." He untied the string binding the envelopes together.

"*Mas café, Don Bartolome?*" Carlos asked, carrying the coffee pot into the room as the piano started playing.

"*Por favor, Carlos,*" the baron said, nodding at his cup. He shuffled through a few envelopes, opened one, read the contents, then said, "Francisco wants to know why the mill earnings are down this year. Doesn't he realize there's a drought on?" Bart tossed the letter on the sofa and shuffled more envelopes, flipping them aside like a card dealer, until one caught his interest. "Here's something from George Baird."

"Who?" Bitora said, pausing between chords on the piano.

"He used to work in the office of the surveyor general. He hid the grant papers for us, remember?" The baron read in silence for several seconds. "I'll be switched! Looks like we're finally going to get our grant confirmed. George says Congress has established a Court of Private Land Claims to settle the question of all the old Spanish and Mexican land titles. They're going to have headquarters in Santa Fe."

"What kind of court is that?" she asked suspiciously, turning away from the ivory keys.

"Says it's like no other court ever invented. Five justices will decide each case. He's got their names listed here. A bunch of fellows I've never heard of.

All of them from the States. Says the court will include a government lawyer to argue against each claimant. The lawyer's name is—" Bart's mouth dropped open, and he stared at the letter in silence.

"Who?" Bitora demanded.

"Jay Randolph Hendricks." His eyes drifted across the room.

"What does that mean?" she asked.

"What does it mean? My Lord, woman, what a stroke of luck for us! It means Randy's going to be arguing the government's case against us in the Court of Private Land Claims, but just how hard do you think he'll argue against his old pal?"

The boyish look on her husband's face made Bitora smile. "That's wonderful."

"Where's Antonio? He'll jump through the roof when I tell him."

"He's probably still in bed," Bitora said. "He's getting lazier every day."

"Well, he's old, honey. He's earned it. I'll go wake him up and tell him the good news."

He sprang from the sofa and bounded out of the room. Taking three stairs in each stride, he ascended to the second floor and trotted down the long hall to Antonio's wing, where the old don's bedroom, library, and office overlooked the slopes.

He knocked on the door as he opened it. "Antonio," he said, peering into the room. The velvet drapes were open, and the sun was beaming in on the old man's head, pressed neatly into the pillow. "Good news, Antonio," he said, walking to the bed. "We're finally going to get our grant confirmed." He sat on the mattress and felt Antonio's weight shift loosely toward him. "Antonio?" he said, putting his hand on his father-in-law's shoulder.

The old baron's body was as cool as a chunk of granite in a shady canyon. Bart shook him but knew Antonio would never wake again. The letter he had brought with him dropped unnoticed to the floor. He sighed and looked down at the lifeless face.

He had always known this moment would come, but somehow it seemed impossible. On their last ride together, just a week ago, the old man had pointed out the meadow on the mountain peak where he wanted to be buried.

"All right, I promise," Bart had said, "*if* I outlive you." But Antonio had seen the end of the road.

He could not think of going downstairs to tell Bitora. He would wait here. She would suspect something after awhile, and come up to investigate. For now he would have a few last minutes alone with the old man.

If he suffered tortures the rest of his days, he would still die wealthy for having known Antonio Montoya. Together, they had accomplished what perhaps no other men could have: pulled off the world's greatest hoax. A million acres of historic jest. It had been good for a few laughs.

"Ol' Antonio . . ." he said, pulling the covers up on his father-in-law's chest, as if to warm him. "Now you're going to miss it. We've finally got a chance to get our grant confirmed." He didn't really feel very sad. That would come later. "But, don't worry. I'll get it done by myself. I'll put our barony on the map."

Thirty-two

❧

Bart produced a whiskey bottle from the bar in Fort Young's billiards parlor. He poured three shot glasses, giving one to Jay Randolph Hendricks and another to his lawyer, Clarence Tankersly of Denver.

"You've seen the barony now, Randy. You've seen the documents. You've talked to the land-grant experts. How long do you think it will take to get me a trial date with the Court of Private Land Claims, and to get my patent?"

Randy nodded. "It's about time we got down to talking business."

For seven days, the men had toured the barony from Dog Canyon to Fort Young, from Star Mountain to the Mescalero. At Fort Stanton, the new commander, Colonel Delton Semple, had let them use the guest quarters.

"I'd do anything to help the government take

Young's land away from him," Semple had said to Hendricks.

"Why?" Tankersly had asked.

"He's turned the entire Mescalero nation into his own private army. The man's dangerous."

"For an army, they sure get a lot of farming, stock raising, timber cutting, and freighting done," Tankersly had argued.

Now they were back at Fort Young, and Randy was ready to negotiate. He turned his back to the baron to confer with Tankersly. "I've worked up a proposal. If you would agree to give up all but, say, a hundred thousand acres, we could reduce the amount of the claim, restore most of it to the public domain, and still leave your client with a sizeable piece of property."

"Absolutely not," Tankersly said. A brilliant court lawyer, he was a handsome young man with long waves of hair.

"You tell him, Clarence," Bart said. "That's the lamest idea I ever heard."

"I've got a better idea," Tankersly said. "The original grant was for roughly a million acres, right? But the baron deeded about half of it to the Mescaleros. So, why not have the court reduce the grant by half, and take away the Indian reservation and that little bit of land around it that Bart hardly uses anyway. That would look good on paper for you, and still leave the baron with almost everything he's using right now."

"Now, wait a minute, Clarence," Bart said. "I don't plan to give up one acre—"

"Not good enough," Randy said, interrupting the baron. "The cession of land to the Indians has received too much publicity. I'll have to reduce the grant by more than half. I won't let your client get away with any more than a quarter of a million acres."

"*You* won't let me get away with it?" Bart said, his anger building. But the lawyers ignored him, and continued to negotiate.

"Hendricks, you don't want to argue this case before the public. The baron's documents are too complete. You're better off taking the Indian reservation, and maybe another fifty thousand acres as a token of my client's willingness to deal with the court, but that's all you'll get."

Bart picked up the half-full whiskey bottle and hurled it across the room, shattering it on the adobe wall. "Damn you two arrogant little lawyers!" he bellowed. "Who in the hell do you think you are, trying this case in my saloon?

"Randy, I will not cede so much as a square inch of my barony to the government without a fight! I have killed men in defense of this property, and damn near been killed myself! You can argue yourself blue in the face, but you won't get an acre!

"And as for you, Clarence. How dare you negotiate away even an acre of my domain without consulting me first? If I didn't like you so much, I'd terminate your services right here and now for such a stunt! Now, brace yourself for a fight, and get me every clod of dirt I'm entitled to—and the Court of Private Land Claims can be damned!"

Tankersly stood and took Bart by the arm. "Excuse us," he said to Randy as he pulled the baron to the far end of the saloon. "I can get you an excellent deal tonight," the young lawyer whispered. "You'd hardly miss fifty thousand acres on a place as big as this. Your legal expenses would be minimal, and you could have your patent before spring."

"I'd miss fifty thousand acres like I'd miss my front teeth," Bart growled. "I won't give up one rock or blade of grass."

"Baron, I'm talking about getting a cinch on this case tonight. This Court of Private Land Claims is the strangest body the United States has ever created. We don't know what it's going to do. The justices are going to favor the side of the government that hired them for this court. They'll want to make an example out of you. You can't fight them."

"Clarence, you don't know what I can and cannot fight," Bart said, loud enough for Randy to hear. "Let me tell you one more time. The legal expenses are immaterial. The time is of no importance. The justices can make an example of somebody else. The barony is *everything*! Every square foot of it. Every rock, tree, cactus, and lizard will remain under my dominion. If you're not up to that, I'll get another lawyer. We're going to fight!"

"I wouldn't do that, Bart," Randy said, grinning at the other end of the saloon.

"And just why not?" the baron said stalking toward his old friend.

"I can tell you why not," Tankersly said, following his client. "You may not like this, Baron, but you hired me to give you legal advice, and, by God, that's what I'm going to do. If you fight this case in court, Hendricks will drag it out as long as he can. He'll use every delaying tactic in the book. He'll disrupt your family life and your ability to do business. He'll cost you a fortune. And then, who knows whether or not you'll win your case."

Bart looked at Randy and found the redhead nodding, grinning smugly. He sat down at the table with his old classmate. "Randy, we go back over twenty years. Why in hell are you doing this to me now?"

The lawyer scratched his crown convulsively, shaking his red curls like loose springs. "You never understood the legal system, did you, Bart? I am counsel for the United States government. I have to argue against you with everything I've got. *Especially* because you and I were once friends. I won't be accused of favoring you. To you, the barony is everything. To me, the law is everything."

"The law can go to hell. What about justice?"

"To ensure justice for the government, I have to take an adversarial point of view to your claim. The whole thing is your fault, Bart. If you hadn't brought me out here to lobby for your barony in the first place, then I wouldn't know a thing about Spanish land grants, I wouldn't have been appointed to this court, and I wouldn't have to live in this godforsaken country for the next several years of my life."

"If you don't want to live in New Mexico, you should have turned the appointment down. You don't think straight anymore. You don't understand what's right or wrong. You've only said one thing tonight that makes sense."

"What's that?"

"You and I were once friends. Once, but no more. I want you on the next train that leaves the Star Mountain depot; then you can go back to

Santa Fe and prepare yourself for the fight of your life in court."

Randy shrugged and pushed his whiskey glass away. "I'll get an early start in the morning." He rose and left the saloon without even saying good night.

"Now, you," Bart said, turning to his lawyer. "Are you ready to argue my case in court?"

Tankersly picked up his whiskey glass and poured its contents down his throat. "I'm advising you against it, but if that's what you want, I'll fight the Court of Private Land Claims until I'm as old as its damned justices are now."

Thirty-three

∽⚬∾

The baron provided his former friend with a hearty breakfast the next morning while his men hitched the carriage to take Randy from Fort Young to the Star Mountain depot. Bart and Tankersly stood in the plaza as Randy came from the dining room to get in the coach.

The crisp smell of the New Mexico morning grabbed Bart by the nose and put a smile on his face. He was shoving loads into the open cylinder of a Smith and Wesson revolver as Randy threw his bags into the coach.

"Is that for me?" the lawyer asked.

"Not the way I'd like to give it to you." He snapped the breech shut and put the loaded pistol in Randy's hand.

"What do I need that for?"

"Indian trouble. A radical bunch of ghost shirts have gone on the warpath. They've been stirred up ever since they heard about the Battle of Wounded Knee up north. A scout came in last night and warned me that they would be looking for scalps today."

"I don't even know how to use this thing," Randy complained.

"Double action. Just point it and pull the trigger."

"Your driver is armed. Why do I need a gun?"

"Just take it," Bart said. "Now, get in the coach and keep your head low."

Randy frowned as he climbed inside.

"And remember the code of the west, Randy."

"What code?"

"Save the last bullet for yourself."

"What for?"

"You'd rather die quick by your own hand than suffer slow in their's." He nodded at Hilario in the driver's seat, and the horses snapped tension into the rigging.

The carriage had just passed Burnt House Canyon when Randy heard the yelps. He thought geese were honking until the first gunshot rang out. A pang of fear leaped from his heart, and he glanced at the revolver on the seat across from him.

Sticking his head out the window, he saw a dozen Apaches giving chase. They were close enough for him to see their gaudy Mexican and American dress, accented with beads and feathers. He heard the driver whistle and shout Spanish at the horses.

Falling back into the coach, he stared at the Smith and Wesson. He hated New Mexico. He

remembered what Bart had said as he picked the
revolver up. Point it and pull the trigger. The war
cries of the Apaches had already engulfed the
coach, grating on Randy's nerves like a rasp. He
sank as far back into the seat as he could and
waited.

Suddenly, a dark face and a tomahawk appeared
in the window. Randy closed his eyes, pointed the
pistol, and fired. When he looked again, the face
was gone. His hopes mounted. Maybe the others
would go away, now that he had shot one.

But the hideous squalls only mounted, and a
shot splintered the ceiling of the coach. When the
next rider appeared at the window to the right,
Randy jerked the trigger of his weapon again and
saw the Indian roll from his mount. Glancing to
the left, he saw more braves. He shoved the
muzzle of the revolver through the window and
fired. Another warrior fell from his horse, but others came to take his place.

Save the last bullet for yourself, he remembered.
Certainly it wouldn't come to that. Surely this
wasn't really happening.

He killed a fourth Indian, but several others
reached the team and slowed the coach. Randy
heard the driver's shotgun erupt and saw two
more dead bodies pass by his window, but the carriage continued to slow.

As the coach came to a stop, the lawyer pointed
his revolver at the war party and fired his fifth
round. To his surprise, two warriors fell to the
ground. He could hear Indians crawling all over
the coach. A movement outside caught his attention, and he saw two warriors dragging the strug-
gling driver into the trees. A long, horrible yell

came from the shadows where they had disappeared, and Randy felt a core of nausea grip his stomach.

Sinking to the floor of the coach, he wondered what he would do. Jump from the coach and catch a loose Indian pony? No chance. Maybe rescue would come. Certainly it would. Where was the army? Where were the good Indians, the Mescalero guard Bart had told him about? The tortured scream of agony came from the forest again.

Randy put the muzzle of the pistol to his chest. The coach was rocking with Indians. He tried to make his finger tighten around the trigger, but it wouldn't. He didn't know if it was courage or cowardice that prevented him from using the last bullet on himself, but he couldn't do it. That was too final. There had to be some hope of rescue.

He gritted his teeth and cursed Bart Young for bringing him here. He took the revolver in one hand and waited for the next savage to try him. Maybe he could kill one in the coach, steal the dead man's weapon, and keep fighting.

The door flew open, revealing a young brave in the white cotton of a Mexican peasant, a red sash tied around his waist, and a knife in his hand. Randy leveled the pistol, almost point blank, and fired.

The brave looked down at a black spot that appeared on his white shirt, then looked back at Randy. "Are you Mr. Hendricks?" he asked, speaking perfect English as he tucked his knife into the red sash. It was John Seven Stars, a bright young brave whom Bart had sent to the Indian school at Carlisle, Pennsylvania.

Randy could find no words to answer.

"I have a message for you," John Seven Stars said, pulling a piece of paper from his sash. "From the baron." He tossed the folded missive down on the lawyer and vanished from the doorway.

Randy heard the wild yelps again, and saw riders passing by outside. Relieved, but infuriated, be clutched the message with shaking hands, and unfolded it.

Randy,
Did you save the last bullet for yourself? It's just tallow and charcoal mixed together, with hardly enough powder behind it to send it down the barrel. Ha, ha.

Disrespectfully,
Don Bartolome Cedric Montoya-Young, baron of the Sacramentos, caballero of His Majesty's Chamber, knight of the Golden Fleece, etc., etc.

His rage and embarrassment mounted until he saw the face of his coach driver appear over the top of the letter.

"Did you like all that screaming?" Hilario asked. He rolled his eyes back in his head and filled the coach with another gurgling yodel. "I bet you thought they were cutting my guts out or something like that, huh?" He jumped down from the coach step and climbed up to his driver's seat, laughing harder with every step.

Thirty-four

~∞~

It's the dangedest court you ever heard of," Clarence Tankersly said. He had just arrived at the Dog Canyon ranch from Mexico City, where the court had gone to gather testimony.

"So I've heard," the baron said, "but just what makes it so all-fired peculiar?"

The young lawyer threw his coat on a chair back and sank into the seat. "The government won't spend money to bring witnesses to the courtroom, so it sends the courtroom to the witnesses. One of the five justices will go wherever Randy Hendricks wants to gather testimony, and takes along an interpreter, a translator, a stenographer, and a photographer. It's a traveling courtroom. Of course, I have to go along, too, if I want to cross-examine the witnesses."

"Where all has Randy dragged you?" Bart asked as he adjusted the flue in the stovepipe.

"We were at the old San Xavier Mission in Tucson before we went to Mexico City. Before that it was Texas to California."

"Retracing Antonio's trail?"

Tankersly nodded. "Going to all the archives where your father-in-law found documents hidden, interrogating the archivists. He's trying to make them suggest that Antonio could have planted the documents instead of actually finding them there, but I've been able to head off any damaging testimony through my cross-examinations."

"Planting documents?" Bart said. The suggestion truly shocked him, though that was exactly what Antonio had done, with great success. "Why would Randy insinuate such a thing?"

"He's trying to make you look like a master forger, Baron. He's going to try to get your entire grant rejected. It's personal with him now."

"A forger!" The baron kicked a billet of stove wood, sending it rattling across the wooden floor of the ranch house parlor. "This is not a criminal case!"

"He doesn't have the evidence to get you arrested for forgery, of course, but he's trying to plant a seed of doubt in the minds of the justices. He won't get your barony away from you—I can almost guarantee you that—but if he can raise enough doubts, he might get the justices to reduce the acreage on some technicality."

"Reduce it! Can they do that?"

"I'm not sure what they can do, Baron. Yours is the first case to come to trial before this court. All Hendricks needs is a quorum. He has to convince three of the five justices that your grant is somehow irregular. The problem is, I don't know what all he has on you. In addition to his own investigation, the Secret Service of the Treasury Department has loaned him two detectives, and they're working for him."

Bart sank into a bentwood rocker and stretched his stocking feet toward the stove. The big toe on his right foot was throbbing where he had kicked the stove wood, but he didn't let on. "When do I get to testify?" he said.

"The court will convene April first in Santa Fe. The justices will review the ambulatory testimony first; then Hendricks and I will call and cross-examine additional witnesses. You'll be my star witness, of course. I'll save you till last."

The baron smiled, looking forward to making a fool of Randy Hendricks in court. It wouldn't be difficult. Randy had always been an easy target. "Clarence," he said, "Randy Hendricks, the Secret Service, and the Court of Private Land Claims can all be damned. This trial is going to make me a legend."

Thirty-five

The halls of the Court of Private Land Claims filled with Santa Fe citizens an hour before the court convened. When Bartolome Cedric Montoya-Young strode in with his lawyer, a cheer rose from the ranks. Rumor had it that the secret mission of the court was to take land away from native New Mexicans and that baron Bart Young, true champion of the people, was spending his fortune fighting the court.

Bart strode to his table wearing spurs and a huge Mexican sombrero. Clarence Tankersly came in behind him, dressed in conservative courtroom attire. Behind Clarence came a dozen servants carrying small boxes, each containing papers of the fabled Montoya-Young Grant—the *cedula* with the signature of King Carlos the Third, the book of riddles written by Nepomeceno Montoya, orders, reports, wills, and the secret codicils.

The chief justice almost broke his gavel quieting the crowd, but finally the trial got under way. Bart had trouble staying awake the first couple of days, as Jay Randolph Hendricks and Clarence Tankersly presented their ambulatory testimony to the justices.

"In summation," Randy suggested, at the end of the third day, "not one of the archivists anywhere in Texas, New Mexico, Arizona, California, or the Republic of Mexico could recall seeing any document pertaining to the alleged barony of the Sacramentos before Antonio Montoya showed up and produced them. The government intends to prove that the documents didn't even exist until Antonio Montoya planted them in the various archives. And where did the late Mr. Montoya procure these documents?" He swept his finger across the courtroom and pointed at Bart. "The government will prove beyond the shadow of a doubt that this man forged them! This man who calls himself baron of the Sacramentos! This fraud sitting here!"

The court spectators roared with indignation and rose to their feet. The chief justice pounded his gavel, but the rabble grew even more unruly and began pushing against the railings.

Finally, Bart rose, turned to the crowd, and held his hands in the air, imploring the spectators to return to their seats. When they had quieted themselves, he pointed at Randy. "Counsel seems to have missed his calling in the theater," he said.

When the laughter died, Clarence Tankersly summarized the ambulatory testimony for the claimant:

"Not one of the archivists so vigorously interrogated by counsel for the government even remotely suggested that the documents of the barony had been planted in their files. The reason the grant papers had never been discovered before Señor Montoya found them was because they had been so expertly hidden by Nepomeceno Montoya, first baron of the Sacramentos."

Tankersly put his fists on Randy Hendricks's table and glared down at the redheaded lawyer. "The fact that counsel for the government cannot grasp this genius should come as little surprise to the court."

The courtroom roared with laughter, and Randy's face turned red as his hair.

"Order!" the chief justice shouted, banging his gavel. "This court will now recess until the fifteenth. When we reconvene, counsel for the claimant will refrain from insulting the personal intelligence of counsel for the government!"

Live witnesses took the stand when the court came back in session. Francisco and Vincente Montoya were among the first. Randy made them both admit that before Bart Young came to New Mexico, they had never heard of the barony of the Sacramentos.

Randy shook his head as his fingernails circled through his curly red locks. Addressing Francisco, he asked, "Mr. Montoya, don't you think it rather odd that your father did not deed this valuable tract of land equally among his heirs, instead of giving it all to your youngest sister and her husband?"

"No," Francisco answered. "It was part of Nepomeceno's plan to deed the barony through the codicils to only one family member of each generation to prevent the barony from being divided. Its value to the entire family is much greater as a whole. My brother, my sisters, and I relinquished our rights to the inheritance because none of us cared to move into the mountains to take possession of the grant. Besides, we all agreed that our brother-in-law would, by his passion for the land, manage the barony far better than either I or my brother ever could."

The Montoya brothers had two things going for them. First, they honestly believed in the authenticity of the barony. Secondly, Tankersly had laboriously rehearsed their testimony with them.

When Bitora took the stand, Randy thought he could badger some kind of damaging testimony out of her. He knew her only as the demure hostess of the Star Mountain lodge, not as the young mother who had braved assaults by hired assassins to take possession of her inheritance.

"Mrs. Young," he said, "what was your role in this fraud against the state?"

"Objection!" Tankersly shouted, springing to his feet.

"Sustained."

Randy bowed his head before the court and scratched it. "I'll rephrase the question, Your Honor. What was your role in producing the documents to the alleged land grant?"

"I was the first to suggest that the book of riddles may have contained a code."

"Of course you were," Randy said. "Wouldn't it have looked much too convenient if Bart Young himself, or your father, had discovered the code?"

"Objection!" Tankersly shouted.

"I'll withdraw the question, Your Honor," Randy

said. He strode to the table holding the documentary evidence, and picked up Nepomeceno's book. "The book of riddles!" he shouted, smirking and waving the volume about carelessly. "Isn't it true, Mrs. Young, that your husband has always been rather fond of riddles?"

"Yes, I suppose so," she said.

"In fact, isn't it true that before you ever laid eyes on this book, your husband had recited some of the self-same riddles to you in person?"

Bitora looked away from the lawyer. "Only one or two. They are probably very old riddles. . . ."

"No further questions!"

The court recessed again for an Easter holiday and reconvened the first Monday in May. Clarence Tankersly brought an impressive parade of character witnesses from the barony to testify on Bart's behalf. Bart's railroad engineer, Youngstown's mining engineer, Dog Canyon's ranch foreman, the baronial forester, farmers, shepherds, and even Chief Estrella came to praise the baron's accomplishments.

"Mr. Young's actions are not those of some document-forging land-grabber," Tankersly insisted. "These are the responsible deeds of a true and rightful steward of the earth."

Next, the lawyer called in a string of land title experts, and each testified that the Montoya-Young grant was the most highly-authenticated he had ever seen. Paper, ink, style of writing, and Spanish grammar were all flawless. Signatures of individual Spanish officials stood up against the harshest scrutiny.

Randy Hendricks chose to cross-examine just one of these witnesses: George Baird.

"You were present at the original unveiling of the baronial documents in the office of the surveyor general, were you not?" he began.

"Yes," George said. "I was secretary to the surveyor general at the time."

"Did you file the documents in accordance with standard procedures of that office?"

"No. I hid them in the territorial archives."

"Why?"

"Bart asked me to. He said certain parties might try to destroy them. And in fact, the office of the surveyor general later caught fire in a very suspicious—"

"Just answer the question before you, Mr. Baird. How much did you receive for this service of hiding the documents?"

"Objection!" Tankersly shouted, leaping from his chair. "Your Honor, whether the documents were hidden or not has nothing whatever to do with their authenticity."

"Your Honor," Randy argued, "I intend to exhibit to this court that at least one of Mr. Young's so-called experts received payment from him for services relating to this case."

The justices whispered among themselves for a few seconds. "The court will allow the question," the chief justice finally said.

"Well, Mr. Baird . . ." Randy said, looking down his nose at the witness.

George sighed, and glanced at Bart. "The amount was so trivial that I don't even recall how much it was."

"But isn't it a fact that Mr. Young paid you cash

money for hiding the grant documents in the territorial archives? Answer yes or no."

"Yes."

"Might we also assume, then, that he paid you or the other experts for your endorsement of the grant papers?"

"Objection!" Tankersly shouted.

"Never mind," Randy said, grinning. "No further questions."

After the land grant experts had been examined and cross-examined, Randy called his star witness to the stand, one Vernon Regis. The old speculator hobbled grotesquely toward the bench. His health had been declining in recent years. Arthritis had struck his knees and he had a bad back, to say nothing of his stomach trouble.

"Mr. Regis," Randy said after the swearing-in, "how did Mr. Young get his job as custodian of the territorial archives?"

"He came to my office looking for work. I knew the position in the archives was about to vacate, so I recommended him."

"Did he specifically request the archivist job?"

"No, he did not. He didn't even know about it."

"But Mr. Young has long maintained that he came to New Mexico with explicit intentions of landing a job in the archives where he could search for the lost barony documents his father had told him about."

"Mr. Young is a liar."

The courtroom erupted with laughter and angry shouts from opposing factions. The chief justice had to threaten to clear the courtroom before the crowd would contain itself.

After the disturbance, Regis told his version of the sale of the old Montoya grant. He said Bart and Antonio, when they realized they had made a bad deal, had decided to get even by forging the papers for the barony that would displace Regis from the Sacramentos.

"When did you first suspect that the documents were forged?" Randy asked.

"When I procured a copy of the book of riddles from the surveyor general."

"Were you aware of Mr. Young's affinity for riddles?"

"I'll say I was. In fact, there isn't one riddle in that book that I didn't hear spoken from Young's own lips *before* he supposedly found the book in Mexico. He forged the entire thing himself!"

The baron backers rocked the courtroom with their jeers, and the justices took turns with the gavel.

"After the claimant took up residence on his so-called barony," Randy continued, "what happened to your land holdings in the Sacramento Mountains?"

"Young's gang of thugs chased me off of my ranch and my timber claims."

"What about your gold mine?" Randy asked.

"He let me keep that, but extorted mining royalties from me at gunpoint."

Bart found the testimony so absurd that the judges had to caution him for guffawing.

That afternoon, Tankersly called Regis back to the stand for cross-examination. He glared at the speculator for several seconds, then picked up the famous book of riddles from the exhibits.

"I have just one question to ask you, Mr. Regis,"

the young lawyer said. He thumbed through several tattered pages, scanning them in silence. "Ah,
here's a good one. How many eggs could the giant,
Goliath, eat on an empty stomach?"

Regis stared, dumbfounded.

"I object!" Randy cried. "That's not a question.
It's a riddle!"

"Your Honor," Tankersly insisted, "Mr. Regis testified this morning that he has both heard and read
every one of the riddles in this book. If that is so,
he should remember them. I simply wish to confirm the value of his testimony."

The chief justice rubbed his chin. "You may proceed," he said.

"Again, Mr. Regis. How many eggs—"

"I don't remember the riddles individually,"
Regis blurted.

"But you testified just a few hours ago that you
heard Bart Young tell every one of these riddles *before* he found the book in Mexico City. Is there
something wrong with your memory? Do you
want me to try another riddle?"

"No."

"Then we'll try this one again. How many eggs
could the giant, Goliath—"

"*Are you deaf?*" the speculator bellowed. "I've
told you I don't know the answer to that damned
riddle!"

"Why not?"

"I don't remember it!"

"Might we assume, then, that your memory also
fails you in regards to the way Mr. Young got his
job in the territorial archives?"

"No."

"Or the way he allegedly chased you off of your ranch and timber claims?"

"No."

"Or the way he allegedly extorted mining royalties from you at gunpoint?"

"No! No! No!"

"Mr. Regis, how many eggs could the giant, Goliath, eat on an empty stomach?"

"I don't know!"

"Why not?"

"Because I don't remember!"

"No further questions, Your Honor."

As the speculator's face writhed with indignation, the judges huddled, whispering, for almost a minute. Finally, the chief justice looked toward the witness stand. "You may step down," he said to Regis. "Mr. Tankersly," he added, "it would please the court to know the answer to that riddle."

Thirty-six

✧

Bart recognized a familiar face as he approached the courtroom. He tipped his sombrero to Linden Yarborough and noticed the U.S. marshal badge pinned to the weathered jacket.

"Well, if it ain't the baron of bullshit," Yarborough said. Since losing the appointment as justice-of-the-peace to Antonio, Yarborough's political ambitions had slid into oblivion. He had, however, become noted for his efficiency as a U.S. marshal, and carried what grudge he still held with hardened grace. Linden Yarborough was still hell on the criminal population, and had accepted the apprehension or obliteration of that element as his lot.

"Howdy, Lin," the baron replied, stopping to shake hands with the lawman. "You come to see the show?"

"No. I heard you were wrapping up your testimony today."

"So what?"

"That lawyer, Hendricks, says he'll prove you a fraud today. If he does, I'll have to put you under arrest."

Bart smiled. "You'll have the day off, then. In fact, meet me at the Paisano Club after court, and I'll stand treat for drinks." He slapped Yarborough on the shoulder and entered the courtroom.

The onlookers rose to applaud when Bart appeared. He doffed his sombrero as he strode confidently to his seat, then made a pistol of his right hand and fired a playful round at the newspaper reporters on the front row. Their columns had become megaphones for Bart's voice, and they had made great sport of Randy Hendricks's head-scratching antics.

Since destroying Regis's testimony, two weeks before, Tankersly had been brilliant, finding every chink in Randy's case. Randy had stooped to bringing the marshals to court in a show of false confidence.

The spectators did not hiss when Randy came in. They simply laughed. He marched sheepishly to his table, avoiding the eyes of Bart and Tankersly.

When the judges had taken their places and called the court to order, Randy called his former classmate to the stand for cross-examination.

"Mr. Young," he began. "For the past few days you have kept the spectators and newspaper reporters in these chambers spellbound with your fanciful stories of lost land grants, secret codicils, hidden documents, and coded books of riddles."

"Thank you," the baron said, "You know, I've

always considered myself something of a elo-
cutionist—"

"However!" Randy interrupted, "you seem to
have omitted two important aspects of your story."

"If that is true," Bart said, "I will beg the court's
pardon."

"Isn't it true, Mr. Young, that you are quite a
practical joker?"

"I have been dubbed the baron of Bad Jokes,
the count of Humbuggery, and the duke of Tom-
foolery."

"Isn't it also true that you are a practiced
forger?"

Bart bunched his eyebrows for a second. "Isn't it
true that you always ask your questions in the
negative because it is an old lawyer's trick de-
signed to elicit a confused response?"

"I object," Randy blurted, stomping his foot as
he turned to the black robes.

The chief justice covered his smile with his hand.
"Counsel, you have the floor. You are in no position to object. However, I will advise Mr. Young to
answer counsel's questions, even if they are
phrased negatively."

"In that case," the baron said, "absolutely yes, I
am not a forger."

Randy stood transfixed for several seconds, then
seemed to gather himself. He straightened his lapels, pulled his sweaty collar from his neck, and
threw a new bearing into his posture. Slowly, he
turned on Bart Young.

"Mr. Young," he said quietly, "Isn't it true that
you and I were classmates at Tulane University?"

Bart saw Tankersly about to object, but pinned
the lawyer in his seat with a glare. "Yes, it isn't al-

together untrue," he said, his eyelids sagging as he looked back at Randy.

"And isn't it true that you once forged documents for me?" Randy began ferociously scratching his favorite place above his right ear.

The courtroom murmured with confusion.

"As I recall, I signed your father's name on a check because you had spent your allowance on a harlot. Whose honor do you intend to impeach here? Mine or your own?"

The chief justice fired a warning shot with his gavel, but the crowd continued to hum.

Randy's fingernails had worked their way up to his crown. "Isn't it true," he shouted, "that you also forged diplomas and transcripts that you used in an attempt to lure me to New Mexico to help you with this preposterous scheme of yours?"

"Objection!" Tankersly yelled.

"Your honor, I intend to prove once and for all, despite the personal embarrassment to myself, that Mr. Young has a long history of forging documents to meet his every whim." His fingers were at his left temple now, his arm virtually wrapped around the back of his head.

"Objection overruled," the chief justice said, turning his ear to the witness stand.

"Well, isn't it true?" Randy demanded.

Bart looked with awe at the vibrating mop of red hair. "You know, Randy, I could recommend a really good brand of sheep-dip for that itch of yours." He paused to let the laughter roar through the chambers. "Why, I would even volunteer to help you soak your head in it!"

Laughter regenerated itself in orbits around the outer walls, twisting Randy's thoughts until he forgot his question. When the judges finally regained control and admonished Bart against personal remarks, Randy Hendricks made one last attempt to proceed.

"Isn't it true," he said, his voice quavering, "that this case is nothing more than a historic practical joke to you?" His voice rose. "That the barony of the Sacramentos never existed, and"—he drew a breath meant for shouting—"that your entire case—every leaf of every codicil, *cedula*, report, and order—is nothing but a monumental fraud!" He pounded his fists on the baronial documents like a madman.

Bart watched Randy with satisfaction as the lawyer stood wild-eyed and panting. When the murmurs died in the courtroom, he put his elbows on the railing of the witness stand to lean into the glare of his adversary. "Counsel," he said, "the only fraud that has been presented to this court is your case against me."

Thirty-seven

$\infty \multimap \infty$

A week later, Randy Hendricks still hadn't figured a dignified way out of the embarrassing defeat that was sure to visit him when the court reconvened. The justices had called for an adjournment of two weeks to let things settle down and allow the lawyers to prepare their closing statements. Bart and Bitora had gone back to their barony, trusting Clarence Tankersly to wrap the case up.

Counsel for the government sat like a drunk in his office chair, staring at the baronial documents. They were scattered all over the desk and the floor as if a whirlwind had passed through. Bart Young was no fraud and he knew it. Why had he ever taken that tack? Imagine a man forging all these documents so perfectly. Ridiculous.

He had treated this case as a personal score he had to settle, and it was the mistake of his career.

One that would follow him everywhere. There were suspicious coincidences involved with the case—like the book of riddles conveniently turning up in Mexico City about the time Bart and Antonio needed to find it—but there was no proof of forgery. Never had been. Vernon Regis was a liar. Bart Young was a baron.

Randy had come up with a new argument yesterday. He could claim that the barony was illegitimate since the documents had been improperly filed with the Spanish and Mexican authorities, hidden as they were. Why hadn't he thought of it before? That was a tricky angle, and the courts loved technicalities.

But it was too late for a new strategy now. His closing statement was next week. He needed more than an idea. He needed proof of forgery, and that proof didn't exist. He had let Bart beat him at his own game of law.

Jay Randolph Hendricks hated New Mexico.

As he sulked in his chair, his office door opened and Sam Kincheloe, Secret Service detective, came in with a bolt of blinding sunlight. "Morning, Mr. Hendricks," he said.

Randy squinted. "Morning, Kincheloe. I don't suppose you've turned up anything new on the Young case."

Kincheloe shook his head. "I heard about what happened in court. Too bad."

Randy sighed and rose from his chair. "What's that?"

"Something I thought would cheer you up. You may have lost the Montoya-Young trial, but your next case is a cinch." The detective waved Randy to the window. "This is one of the documents from the Smith-Gutierrez grant. Take a look at it."

Randy studied the document, but his mind was too worn out to find anything unusual. It was an old Spanish deed, much like the one pertaining to Bart's barony. Randy had no idea what it said without his translator at his elbow. "I don't see anything suspicious," he confessed.

"Neither did I, at first," Kincheloe said. "Then I started thinking: If we want to find out whether or not this document is counterfeit, why not examine it the way we examine counterfeit bills at the Treasury Department?"

"How's that?"

"Hold it up to the light."

Randy put the leaf of parchment against the window and felt the warm morning sun on his palm. "So what?" he said, the parchment glowing in a rich amber hue above him, like a pane of stained glass.

"Look right there," Kincheloe said, putting a manicured finger on the paper. "Do you see that light area in the grain?"

Randy's eyes widened. "It looks like the letter W."

"It's the watermark of a paper mill in Wisconsin. This document is supposed to be over a hundred years old, and yet the mill that produced this parchment has only been in operation eleven years." Kincheloe stood beaming with pride, his finger still pointing out the character in the paper.

Randy's mouth dropped open, and his mind started feeding on new ideas. He looked down on the Montoya-Young papers scattered all over his office. He backhanded Kincheloe hard on the shoulder. "Why didn't you tell me about this before?"

The detective retreated, letting the counterfeit document flutter down from the window. "It just occurred to me yesterday," he said, holding his shoulder where Randy had stung him. "What difference does it make? The Smith-Gutierrez case hasn't even gone to trial yet."

"Yes, but the Montoya-Young case has!" Randy shouted. He started gathering Bart's documents from the floor.

"But, those papers are genuine. You won't find any watermarks on them."

"You don't know that!" Randy said.

Kincheloe stared for a moment, then picked up a few old sheets of parchment at his feet.

"Give me those," Randy snapped. "I'll conduct the examinations. You go find one of the justices."

"What for?"

"If I find a watermark on one of Bart's documents, I want an immediate warrant for his arrest!"

It was almost midnight when Bart heard the whistle of the *Conquistador* blow somewhere down Star Mountain. He sat up in bed and listened, straining to hear. Finally the steam blast came again, and he knew something unusual was happening. The *Conquistador* had never approached the lodge in the middle of the night.

He slipped out of bed without waking Bitora, got dressed, and ran downstairs. Pulling on his coat by the door, he left the log mansion and trotted to the depot to meet the *Conquistador*. He heard it chugging up the mountain, saw its headlamp casting fragmented rays among the tree trunks.

As the engine neared the depot, Bart saw Clarence Tankersly jump from a passenger car. The young lawyer trotted to him in the moonlight and leaped onto the depot platform.

"Clarence, what have you done? Bought the railroad with all the legal fees I've been paying you?"

Tankersly shook his head as he caught enough breath to speak with. "Trouble's coming, Baron."

"What trouble?" he shouted over the hissing of the steam engine.

"A warrant has been issued for your arrest. Conspiracy to defraud the government. A U.S. marshal named Yarborough and a Secret Service detective named Kincheloe are coming with Randy Hendricks to get you tomorrow."

Bart felt a knot in his throat. "How can that be?"

Tankersly gritted his teeth and looked up at the moon's silver light on the pine needles. "Hendricks held one of your documents up to the light and found a watermark."

"A what?"

"He found the mark of an American paper mill on one of your old Spanish documents."

A pang of nausea hit Bart in the stomach. "Which one? Which document?" he demanded.

"I don't know. I didn't get a chance to see it, but it convinced the justices of the court that you are a fraud. You have some explaining to do, Bart. What does it mean?"

A watermark! Bart's mind race back to Santa Fe, fifteen years ago. The paper. Where had he gotten the stock for the forgeries? Some of it had been old, authentic parchment Antonio had found in the back of one of his warehouses. But there hadn't been enough. They had purchased some. Bought it at a Santa Fe trading house. Where had that stock come from? Missouri, probably. Of all the stupid mistakes! A watermark! The one thing he had failed to look for.

"Baron!" Clarence said. "What does it mean?"

Bart felt the sick tide of guilt rise in his stomach, but he glowered at his lawyer with a look of false anger. "It means Randy Hendricks is a lying little fart. You better get back to Santa Fe and have a look at this supposed watermark."

"I don't think so," Clarence said. "I'd better be here when the officers arrest you."

"You don't understand, Clarence. All hell's going to break loose in these mountains when word gets out that I'm wanted. I'll be lucky if Marshal Yarborough gets to me before Vernon Regis's gang of regulators—or the U.S. Army."

"The army?"

"Colonel Semple's been dying for an excuse to campaign against my Mescalero guard, and this is it. He'll say they're rising up to protect me, and he'll come to slaughter them and me both." He grabbed Tankersly by the arm and led him to the passenger car door that had pulled up to the depot. "Now, get back on that train, and get to the bottom of this watermark business." He shook his lawyer's hand and slapped him on the shoulder. "I have until dawn to prepare my barony for invasion!"

The baron left Tankersly bewildered on the platform.

Somewhere between the depot and the lodge, the sickening feeling of remorse passed, replaced

by the smell of pines and the bite of the cold wind
on his cheeks. How many men could claim their
own barony? He thought of Antonio. The *rico*
owed his last fifteen years of happiness to Bart's
pen. Hadn't it been worth it? He had to remind
himself that they were invading *his* barony. They
would have to play by his rules now. He would
plan his escape to Mexico, and his family's. Then,
if it killed him, he was going to have some fun.

Thirty-eight

❧❧❧

Bart saw smoke as he rode nearer to the top of the rise. The wind had stretched it to a faint haze, but he had learned to look for such sign in the sky. Then the stone chimneys rose over the hill, and the shingled roofline, the peeled timbers of the huge log lodge house, and the manicured gardens surrounding it.

Leaning over the saddle horn, he gave the stallion his head, and galloped down the slope. As he jumped the second rail fence of the great pasture, he saw Bitora coming from the doorway at a trot. He watched her carefully. This would be their last hour as baron and baroness of the Sacramentos.

"Bartolome!" she scolded. "Where have you been? Nobody will tell me anything, but I know something has gone wrong!"

"Nothing's wrong," the baron said. "I just came home for dinner."

"Don't lie!" she ordered. "I heard one of the servants say that they are coming to take us from the mountains."

"Who is?" Bart demanded, looking over his shoulders as if he would see some invaders.

"That is what I am asking you! They say the papers for the Montoya-Young grant are fake, that you forged them!"

Bart shook his head and laughed. "It's just more of Randy Hendricks's danged rumormongering."

"Look at me," she said, grabbing him tightly by the arm and turning him to face her. "I can always tell when you are lying. Now, tell me the truth. Do these mountains belong to us, or not?"

The baron tipped his hat back and looked her straight in the eyes. "As sure as you belong to me, and I belong to you. By everything that is holy and fair, these mountains were your father's, and now they are ours. And damn any soul who should ever try to take them from us."

She sighed with relief and hugged him, pressing her face against his chest. "You are telling the truth, aren't you?"

"What do you think I am, a liar?"

"I know you are a big liar when you are trying to play a trick on someone."

"Let's go eat dinner. I'm starving." He handed his reins to Hilario, who had sauntered out to take the stallion to the stables. "Have the coach hitched and waiting for us after dinner," he said to the servant.

"Where are we going?" Bitora asked.

"We'll go down and stay at Fort Young tonight, then we'll take a nice trip to Santa Fe and straighten out this latest nonsense about forged documents. Have the girls been fed?"

"Yes, but if we are going to Santa Fe, why don't we ride the train?"

"There's some kind of trouble on the tracks. The *Conquistador* can't get up. That's where I've been this morning. Taking care of business."

They walked beneath the mammoth pine transom and entered the lodge. Bart tossed his hat onto a brass hat tree as they passed through the front room with its mounted heads of deer, elk, and bighorn sheep hanging over the fireplace, its bearskin rugs on the floor.

After dinner, Bart went outside to find Hilario standing beside the coach, the team of four hitched.

"Did you empty the safe?" the baron asked.

"*Sí.*"

"How much was in it?"

"About twenty thousand dollars, I think."

"Where is it now?"

"Hidden in the luggage boot, where you told me to put it."

"Good man."

When Bitora finally came out with the girls, Carlos took her baggage from her and loaded it in the boot. Bart held the door open for Bitora and helped his daughters in. As soon as they were settled into their seats, he closed them inside, jumped onto the step and shouted at Hilario to whip the horses.

"What are you doing, you fool?" Bitora said, as the vehicle lurched forward. "Get in the coach. You are not going to ride out there."

"Kiss me," he said, clinging to the outside of the

vehicle, and sticking his head through the window opening.

The girls giggled.

"What?" demanded Bitora.

"Kiss me, or I won't do a thing you say."

She pressed her lips together in frustration, but then put them on his, knowing she must humor him. Bart grabbed the back of her neck and held her lips on his until a bump in the road shook them apart. Bitora reeled back into the coach, against her daughters, staring at her husband in amazement. "*Idiota*," she said, panting. "Get in the coach with us—now. And tell Hilario he is going the wrong way."

"No, he's not," the baron said. "We're not going to Fort Young, or to Santa Fe. I'm sending you on that trip you've been wanting to take to Mexico City. I'll meet you there and explain everything."

"What are you talking about?"

Bart looked back and saw Carlos riding from the lodge house, leading a fresh horses. "*Vaya con Dios, querida*," he said to his wife. "*Mi corazón vaya contigo.*" He jumped from the coach step, thinking how corny that would have sounded in English: *My heart goes with you.* He ran a few steps as he hit the ground, then stood to watch the coach drive away between the rows of firs and spruces.

Bitora was hanging out the window, shouting hysterically at Hilario to stop, but the coachman obeyed his orders from the baron. He wouldn't stop the horses until he changed teams at Caballero Canyon.

Carlos led the fresh mount to his employer. "I wish you wouldn't have made them leave like that, Don Bartolome." He took a gun belt holstered

with a Colt revolver from his shoulder and handed
it to Bart. "I don't like it."

"I didn't have a choice, Carlos," Bart replied,
buckling the belt around his waist. He drew the
weapon to check the loads. "You know Bitora
wouldn't have left me behind of her own free will
if she knew what was going on. I can't drag them
along where I'm going. Hilario will get them
across the border."

"Sí, but your wife is going to be very mad at
you, señor."

"I'll smooth the whole thing out with her in
Mexico City." He took the Marlin repeating rifle
the cook handed to him and opened the breech to
find brass in the chamber. "Carlos," he said, looking back at his huge lodge house, "I want you to
get everybody out of the lodge. You and the other
servants can take anything you want from it. Then
I want you to burn it to the ground."

"Con permiso?"

The conifers lining the road framed the log mansion beautifully, the spruces draped with strands
of greenish moss. "You heard me. I won't have
Colonel Semple and Vernon Regis and Randy
Hendricks sitting around my fireplace drinking
toasts to my downfall with my liquor."

"But, Don Bartolome . . ."

Bart slid the Marlin into his saddle scabbard. "I
don't like it any better than you do, Carlos. I might
as well be burning what little hair I have left right
off my head." He raised his hat to run his hand
over his nearly slick crown. "But it has to be done.
I've already sent men to blow up Fort Young, too.
I didn't build it to quarter Colonel Semple's troops
so they could invade my domain."

Carlos sighed heavily and looked back at the grand log lodge. "If you order it, Don Bartolome, I will do it."

"I do and you will." The baron took the reins of the horse from Carlos and climbed into the saddle. He urged his mount next to Carlos's. "I don't know when I'll see you again, amigo." He grasped the cook's hand and shook it. "Maybe a long time."

Bart smiled, cast a final gaze at the log palace on the mountaintop, and spurred his horse onto a trail branching off of the Caballero Canyon Road.

Thirty-nine

✧

Dan Tolliver's cabin stood cold and dark, while an open fire blazed nearby. Uncle Dan never used the cabin, except maybe as a place to hang game where bears and wolves couldn't get it, or to shelter his horses when the weather turned stormy.

Bart reined his mount in at the edge of the clearing and cupped his hands around his mouth. "Uncle Dan!" he yelled. A man had to be careful riding into Dan's camp. "It's Bart!"

"What do you want?"

The voice came quietly, but it made both Bart and his horse flinch. He turned around to see old Dan rise from a clump of scrub oak beside the trail, holding his ancient Kentucky rifle. "How'd you sneak up behind me so quiet?"

"Didn't have to. You rode right by me. Didn't you notice your horse smellin' me?"

"No," Bart admitted. "How'd you know I was coming?"

"Seen you comin' a hour back. Knowed when you'd git here. Kilt a deer and waited for you. What do you want here?"

Bart noticed the dried blood of the deer on Dan's knuckles and remembered hearing the rifle shot. "I was wondering if I might stay in your cabin tonight."

"Won't crowd me. I sleep on the ground." The old man stalked out of the bushes and onto the trail. He looked beyond Bart to the southwest. "Your little gals got off the mountain," he said.

The baron's heart ached to think of his family heading for Mexico without him. "Did you see them?"

"No, but I seen some lawmen what told me they let 'em go. Didn't have a warrant for 'em. Just you." His eyes narrowed. "I always knowed they'd come to get you. Be glad when you go. Get the hell off my mountain."

"What kind of lawmen were they?"

"That Marshal Yarborough, and some other feller I never heard tell of. Rode like he was saddle sore."

"Detective Kincheloe of the Secret Service," Bart said. "Any others?"

"They had that redheaded lawyer with 'em."

His insides went cold as an anvil when he thought of Randy Hendricks invading his mountains. "Where did you see them?"

"Caballero Canyon Road."

"They'll probably camp on Alamo Peak tonight, and split up to find me in the morning."

"That marshal'll likely git you. Might git out if

you go down the Sacramento River, over to Shakehand Springs, then run for the Guadalupes."

The old man was reading his mind. Uncle Dan was the only white man who knew his barony better than he did. Bart patted the flap of his saddlebag. "I brought you some coffee and whiskey."

Uncle Dan marched toward his camp, hunching so far forward that he looked as if he would fall on his face.

Bart brewed the coffee and laced it heavily with bourbon. Dan fried venison in bear fat, boiled some beans, and roasted a few ears of corn over the coals.

The stars came out as they ate, and the darkness from the forest crept into the meadow until it enveloped them like a cocoon. The mountain man took his time eating. He had an annoying habit of sniffing his food for several seconds before every bite, like a wolf smelling a carcass for poison.

They were picking their teeth with wood splinters when they sensed a distant rumble, first from the mountain, then through the air. Uncle Dan dropped his toothpick from his mouth, reached habitually for his old musket, and clutched the breast of his deerskins, blackened where he so often wiped the grease from his fingers.

"Easy, Uncle Dan," Bart said. He had never seen the likes of fear in the old man's eyes. "That'll be Fort Young. I had the men blow it up so the army couldn't quarter there."

Uncle Dan panted and put his rifle aside. "And may God damn you to hell for doin' it! I thought the world was shakin' again."

"Huh?"

"Back to Tennessee, when I was a pup. Damnedest shake-up ever you felt. Knocked down trees. Cracked the ground. Made lakes where weren't none there before. They told me the Mississippi run back'ards and blowed water spouts up in the air like the Yellowstone country. Scared me so bad I went to soilin' my britches again, right when my ma thought she had me broke of it. Ain't nothin' come worse enough to scare me since."

"The New Madrid earthquake," Bart said, more to himself than to Dan. "That was in 1811, wasn't it?"

"Hell, I don't know."

"How old are you, Uncle Dan?"

The mountain man shrugged. "Old."

"If you remember the New Madrid earthquake, you'd have to be ... over eighty."

"Feels like a hunnerd."

"When did you come West?"

"Never tracked years much. I was married four years when I left Tennessee. I 'member that much."

"You had a wife?"

"What else would a man marry?"

"What happened to her?"

Dan spit in the fire and listened with satisfaction to the sizzle. "I like to hunt. Come in one mornin' with some meat—been after it a few days—and she went to naggin' about me never workin' none. Told me if I liked huntin' so much, I'd shoot that chicken hawk that was killin' her settin' hens. I picked up ol' Kaintuck again, and went out after that hawk." He slurped his coffee and stared into the darkness as if he saw something there.

"And what happened?" Bart asked, following the old man's gaze.

Uncle Dan put his coffee cup aside and wrapped

his gnarled fingers around the breech of his rifle. "That hawk flew west." He stood suddenly and kicked the wood from the fire, scattering embers.

"What are you doing?" Bart said, dodging coals.

"Man's a damn fool to set by a fire at night in Indian country." He stomped out the last flames.

"The Mescaleros aren't hostile."

"They'll have your scalp one day. Them reds'll rise back up some half moon and kill every white man breathin'. Them ghost shirts are bulletproof. You mind what I say."

Bart began to feel uneasy about staying with Uncle Dan overnight.

"Yeah, that hawk flew west," said the voice in the dark. "I come out here with it and found me these young mountains."

"Nice of you to name them in my honor," Bart said. "Young Mountains. Has a nice ring to it."

"I wouldn't name a clod after you. When I say young, I mean not old. Them mountains back to Tennessee, them was old mountains. Now, these ones out here is still young."

"I didn't realize you knew anything about geology," Bart said.

"To hell with all them -ologies. Man's a fool can't tell a old mountain from a young one just lookin'. Them old ones back to Tennessee, they're all slump shouldered and beat down—carved up by the weather, like me. Mist cloudin' around 'em like a old man's breath in the cold.

"Now, these here mountains, they stand straight and upright, like I was when I first found 'em. Young, high, and mighty. Give a damn about fire and blizzard. Shoulders like somebody chiseled 'em fresh." He sniffed and spit in the dark. "Hell, they'll be young yet when I'm a thousand years dead."

Bart remained silent. He knew the old hermit was talking mostly to himself. As he warmed his fingers around his coffee cup, he realized that something about the night was making him feel uneasy. He listened, and his eyes swept the tree-tops against the stars until he located the strange flicker of orange far up the mountain to the north. Carlos had followed his orders. The Star Mountain lodge was burning.

This was no way to spend his last evening on his barony—with a man who had never wanted him here in the first place. For all he knew, Uncle Dan might shoot him in the dark to collect the bounty. *Whoa, Bart,* he thought. *Don't let the old codger rattle you. He's more talk than anything else.*

A sorrowful moan suddenly rose from the darkness nearby, and Bart heard Uncle Dan scramble in the dark.

"Goddamn Indian wolf call," he whispered hoarsely.

Bart heard the percussion lock catch on ol' Kaintuck. "That'll be Chief Estrella. I told him to meet me here."

"You brung a Indian to my camp?"

The wolf call wailed from the darkness again and Bart started collecting wood to stoke the fire.

"Don't light the fire!"

"It's just Estrella. I've been expecting him." He fanned the coals with his hat until a tiny flame leaped onto the kindling.

Old Dan cussed and hid in Bart's shadow, ready to shoulder his long rifle.

"*Venga,* Estrella," Bart shouted, waving the chief into camp.

The chief materialized from the dark carrying a Winchester rifle decorated with brass tacks hammered into the stock and feathers tied to the barrel. The ends of the woman's *rebozo* he wore like a sash around his waist hung to his moccasins.

"What have the scouts found out, Chief?"

Estrella squatted by the fire and put his rifle butt on the ground, but remained vigilant of Uncle Dan. "Colonel Semple is riding to Fort Young with a column of handpicked soldiers."

"You'd better keep your people out of his way, or he's liable to slaughter you."

"I will. You must ride south, Baron."

"That's what I had in mind. Anybody else coming after me?"

"Red Hair is camped on Alamo Peak with two officers."

Bart turned to Uncle Dan. "What did I tell you, Dan? Randy's predictable as sunrise. I guess Vernon Regis and ol' scar face haven't showed up yet."

"No sign of them," Estrella said.

"If I know Vernon, they'll be coming on the *Conquistador* tomorrow. He never was one to ride. Want some coffee, Chief?"

Estrella shook his head and rose. The mountain man rose with him like an image in a mirror. Estrella backed away from the fire a few steps, then looked at Bart and tossed his head as a parting gesture.

"*Adios,*" the baron said, watching the chief back away into the darkness. Another friend he would never see again.

Just as the night swallowed Estrella, Bart saw him turn his back to the camp. At the same instant, he caught a glimpse of ol' Kaintuck's long barrel swinging upward. He lunged for the muzzle, swatting it aside as it erupted inches from his face.

The powder flash took his sight momentarily, and the ringing in his ears muffled all sound, but he didn't let on to the mountain man that he was deaf and blind. "Damn it, Uncle Dan! What the hell do you mean?"

"You fouled my bead!" the old man growled, as if it were an indiscretion beyond sin.

Bart turned to the darkness where Estrella had disappeared and raised his hands. "Don't shoot, Chief. Just ride." He heard no answer. "Chief? You all right?" The wolf call moaned from the darkness, followed by the pounding of hooves on the trail.

He turned to Uncle Dan, who was pouring black powder from his horn down Kaintuck's muzzle. "What makes you hate Indians so damn much?" he demanded.

The old eyes rose and glared at him as the knotty fingers opened the brass lid of the patch box carved into Kaintuck's maple stock. "I hate you, too." He walked away from the fire and disappeared.

Bart knew about how long it would take Dan to finish reloading the long rifle in the dark, and he was in the cabin, with the door bolted, before the time elapsed. He was able to calm his nerves inside and spread his blankets on the floor. As he lay his head back and stared at the darkness, he cursed Dan Tolliver for ruining his last night on his barony.

* * *

When he stepped out of the cabin before dawn, he found Uncle Dan waiting for him. The mountain man had put Bart's saddle on one of his own horses.

"Take Peso," Dan said. "He's got bottom, and he's rested. Meet me at Shakehand Springs before sundown and I'll have another fresh mount waitin' for you. You can make a run for the Guadalupes." He handed the reins to Bart.

"Why would you do that for me? You just told me last night that you hated me."

"I hate everybody. This here's the best way to git you and all them damn lawmen off my mountains. It'll be nice and quiet when they chase you south to Mexico. I don't reckon you'll be comin' back."

"No," Bart said. He slipped his boot into the stirrup and mounted Peso. "I don't reckon I will."

Forty

∽◦∾

What the hell have we stopped for?"
Vernon Regis bellowed from his Pullman car. He
was sitting on a velour settee, his waxy white fingers interlaced like stripped willow branches
woven into a basket. "Domingo, go see what's
wrong!"

The Mexican gunman stared at Regis blankly for
several seconds. His five hired guns wouldn't respect him much for hopping to orders like a servant boy. Finally, he stepped from the Pullman,
leaving the door open.

"Goddammit!" Regis yelled. "The damn smoke's
coming in! Close the door!"

Archiveque's five gunmen stared at the old Anglo without concern.

"*La puerta, la puerta!*" the land speculator
shouted, squinting against the cinders floating into
the coach. He could hear the boiler letting off

steam as one of the gunmen got up slowly to close the door.

Archiveque returned, letting a last puff of smoke into the car as he entered. "The engine fell off the tracks," he said.

"What do you mean, fell off?"

"That's what they said." Archiveque shrugged and sat down.

Regis had to get up then, no matter how badly it hurt his stove-up knees and back. He paced to the rear of the car, his arms and legs swinging like those of a misguided marionette. He knew exactly what the delay meant. Bart Young had chosen this site well. The canyon was so steep here that Domingo and his cutthroats couldn't unload their horses from the stock cars. They would have to back the stock cars down to a place where the horses could jump out. Then Archiveque and his gunmen would have to ride into the mountains to find Bart. He would resist them, of course, and they would have to kill him. Regis wasn't about to let the courts have the baron. He had waited years for this.

"Domingo!" he shouted. "Come with me!" His stomach was burning like fire as it always did at times of stress. He lowered himself laboriously down the iron steps on his bad knees, and hobbled toward the steam engine, which was hissing like a monster ahead in the mouth of the Devil's Canyon tunnel.

The engineer and his fireman were walking back to Regis's Pullman car from the mouth of the tunnel, feeling the morning sun on their backs.

"What's the problem?" Regis shouted.

"Somebody lifted the tracks inside the tunnel

where we couldn't see," the engineer replied. "Lucky the grade is steep here, and we weren't going very fast. The engine just drove off the end of the rails and sat there."

"Young," the speculator growled. "How long will it take to get going again?"

"Mr. Regis, we aren't going anywhere. We'll have to hike up to Youngstown and get a repair crew down here. Lord knows how we'll get the engine back on the track."

"You hike anywhere you want. We don't need the damn engine to coast downhill. We'll just uncouple the cars and coast down the grade until we find a place where we can let the horses off."

"Suit yourself," the engineer said.

"Domingo, get up there and ride the brake."

Archiveque climbed the rungs on the back of the stock car with amazing agility for a man of his spread—he was over forty now, and rather fat. The shaft of the brake wheel ran up the rear end of the car, next to the ladder rungs, and the wheel itself came to the gunman's waist when he stood on top.

One of the Mexicans uncoupled the forward stock car. When the three loose cars started rolling, Archiveque had to put all his weight and strength into the wheel to lock the brakes.

"All right, get back in the Pullman," Regis said. "*Venga, venga!*" he prodded, waving at the gunmen, who had stepped out to see what was going on. "You sons of bitches don't understand a word I say, do you?"

Bart looked at his watch. Everything was on schedule. His railroad crew had been ordered to blow up the La Luz Canyon trestle in fifteen minutes.

The explosion would serve two purposes. First, it would strand Vernon on the tracks between the derailed engine and the demolished bridge. Vernon would have to ride out, and that would dang near kill him. There wasn't even a road within five miles where he could order his coach to meet him.

Secondly, Regis would have to build his own trestle if he wanted to continue using the narrow gauge to work his mine. Bart wasn't about to leave behind anything his enemies could profit from.

From around the bend, he watched the Pullman and the two stock cars coast down to the mouth of Devil's Canyon. Domingo and his men found a place to let their horses out there, and rode into the mountains. Vernon would wait for them in the Pullman.

Bart chuckled as he mounted Peso. He tried to rein the stallion toward Shakehand Springs, but couldn't do it. He just had to see the look on Vernon's face. The speculator was going to be mad as hell.

He made sure Archiveque's men were well up La Luz Canyon before approaching the stranded railroad cars. Just as he was ready to ride out of the trees for a social call, he heard the door of the Pullman open.

Regis laboriously lowered himself down the steps, both hands on the rail. He hobbled toward the lead stock car, paused to piss beside the tracks, then began trying to climb the rungs that led to the brake wheel on top of the first car.

Bart had underestimated Regis again. The speculator was going to stand on top of the car, ease the brake off, and coast the three cars down the mountain, riding the brake all the way. He never dreamed the old stove-up bastard would try such a stunt.

He couldn't let him do it, of course. The railroad crew was going to blow the La Luz Canyon trestle to splinters any minute now, and Regis would plunge to his death if he didn't get the brake clamped down in time.

As the speculator reached the second rung of the ladder, Bart came up with a great idea. He left Peso tied at the edge of the trees and sneaked down to the front of the first stock car as Regis was climbing up the back.

He climbed quietly up the side of the car, stepping in the spaces between the boards left to give the animals fresh air. He slung one arm over the top of the car and pulled himself up. He could hear Regis heaving on the ladder at the other end, damn near killing himself just climbing a few rungs. Bart rolled onto the top of the car as he saw the long clammy fingers of his old rival reach over the far edge of the stock car roof.

When the speculator climbed high enough to see over the top of the car, he looked up in midgrunt and saw the unexpected image of a man sitting cross-legged on top of the car, facing him. His heart surged, and his reflexes almost jolted him off the ladder.

"Howdy, Vernon," Bart said, listening to the echoes of his own laughter bounce across La Luz Canyon.

Regis wrapped his left arm around the shaft leading up to the brake wheel. He rested his forehead against the top of the car, and panted. His free hand reached into his coat. "Goddamn you, Young," he said.

"What are you doing?"

The speculator found the grip of his pistol in his shoulder holster. "Getting the hell off of this god-forsaken mountain."

"I wouldn't do that if I was you," the baron replied. "You're stuck here. I sent a crew to . . ."

He saw gunmetal rise above the car in Regis's hand and reached for his own Colt, but it was too late. The blast covered him with darkness, and he felt himself rolling backward, then falling. A painful blow to the shoulder revived him, and a crosstie slammed into his back, taking his wind. Gasping, his eyes focused on the coupling that had hit him in the shoulder, the sky beyond it. He reached for his revolver, expecting Regis to start shooting down on him from the top of the car at any second.

He managed to get his Colt drawn and cocked. He put his hand on top of his balding head and found the warm, slick feel of blood where Regis's bullet had creased him. As he tried to catch his breath, sit up, and watch the top of the car all at once, a screech of metal on metal gripped his nerves and gave him strength.

Bart heard footsteps on the roof as the stock car rolled slowly away. A gun barrel appeared over the top edge of the car, followed by the water-melon head of the speculator. The baron flinched as he pulled his trigger. His eyes opened just in time to see Regis's revolver hit the steel rail beside him, its grip spattered with blood. He heard the speculator scrambling on top of the car.

Bart managed to stand up. He was getting air to

his lungs now, but he couldn't find enough of it to shout. He stumbled to the side of the tracks until he could see the speculator crawling awkwardly on top of the car, holding his bleeding right hand under his left arm. Bart fired a shot in the air to get Vernon's attention, but the speculator only shrank down on the roof as the cars sped away downhill.

Heaving for oxygen, the baron sprinted to the tree line to get his horse. Just as he unwrapped the reins from the pine branch, a clap of thunder shook the whole mountain. The stallion reared and jerked him from his feet, but he held one rein. Above the echoes of the dynamite blast, he could hear the creaking timbers of the trestle falling into La Luz Canyon.

He leaped into the saddle, jabbed his spurs into horseflesh. Old Uncle Dan was right. Peso could run. He galloped like a racehorse on the downhill grade, closing the distance to the runaway cars.

When Regis heard the blast, he figured out what Bart had been trying to tell him just before he shot. He gripped the brake wheel with his good hand and pulled himself uncertainly to his feet, the car lurching dangerously under him, building speed. Putting both hands on the iron rim of the wheel, he tried to turn it, but the right hand had been shattered by Bart's bullet and was useless. It had taken all his strength with both hands to loosen the brake in the first place. His left hand alone could not move the wheel, though his hooklike fingers pulled with everything he had.

Ahead, a cloud of dust was rising from the blast and the collapsing bridge. Regis looked over the side of the car. The gravel roadbed rushed by in a blur. He would bust himself to pieces if he had to jump. A movement pulled his eyes backward. Young was coming. The damn fool was going to try to rescue him.

Bart knew the stretch of road well. Once around the next curve, there was still a quarter mile to the trestle. Plenty of time to catch the car, climb aboard, and apply the brakes. The stallion seemed to sense a race, stretching every stride as he gained on the car.

The stock car was just two lengths ahead, but still building speed as it rounded the curve. Bart glanced at the dust cloud from the trestle, then threw his concentration back to the three-car runaway. Still time. He could almost number the crossties. He would stop the cars a hundred yards shy of the gulch. He hadn't killed anybody yet. If he let Regis go over the edge, it would just make things worse for him.

The side boards of the car were almost within his grasp. He began to lean left, settling his weight in one stirrup for the leap. Three feet, two feet . . . He gathered himself for the jump.

The sky shook again, louder than before, and the stallion shied from the car, planting his hooves. Bart saw timbers sailing end-over-end across the gulch as he fell forward onto the neck of the horse and grabbed a handful of mane. Again, he held his rein as he hit the ground.

"Jump! Vernon, jump!" he yelled as he sprang back into the saddle. He saw the speculator peer over the edge of the rushing car. The speed was too great. Regis could not find the courage. His broad white face turned back to Bart as he rushed away, and the bloody fingers reached for nothing, like the splayed tines of a deer antler.

Bart was fifty yards from the gulch when the cars left the crippled trestle and plunged downward. He saw the outline of the speculator drift away from the stock car, one arm flailing like a broken wing. He heard the scream. Then another blast, and a new cloud of dust grew to the size of a thunderhead in a second, engulfing the railroad cars and the speculator in midair.

Flinders fell around him as he felt the pain in his shoulder where the stock car coupling had broken his fall. He raked his shirtsleeve over the top of his head to sop the blood from the bullet wound. One thing for sure. Regis would be mad as hell when he hit bottom. He never could take a joke.

Forty-one

ꞇꞁꞇ

Now the baron knew he had trouble. The explosions alone may not have attracted much attention—his enemies surely knew by now that he was destroying his baronial monuments—but the gunfire before the explosions would make them wonder. Bart knew Domingo Archiveque, Randy Hendricks, and the two federal officers had all been within earshot of the shootout.

He spurred Peso back up the railroad grade and mounted a steep trail that would lead him over Star Mountain. If he happened to pick up any pursuers on his way southeast to Shakehand Springs, he had a trail of surprises planned for them.

He came to the edge of a clearing, and was about to swing down from the saddle and loosen the cinch so Peso could breathe, when a rifle shot ripped through the tree limbs behind him. He spurred the stallion across the meadow, riding low over the saddle horn, looking for the source of the shot. He heard more muzzle blasts and saw the six Mexicans riding hard to catch him as he made it safely into the trees.

Archiveque's men wouldn't be easy to outrun, but Bart knew the terrain, and they didn't. If he could just get over the summit and past the lodge house before them, he could beat them.

He put Uncle Dan's stallion to the test, and the animal answered, covering ground like a thoroughbred, thundering onto a long stretch of straight trail. Bart looked back to see the Mexicans holding their ground, maybe gaining. He drew his Colt and slung a couple of shots their way to slow them down.

When he came over the last high roll before the summit, the sight of the smoking logs reeled him. They had taken everything from him. Never again would he sit in his parlor and listen to Bitora play her piano as he sipped his brandy and watched the sun set beyond the San Andres Range. It was over, and he was being hunted like an animal on his own barony. Maybe he should have skipped the social call on Vernon Regis. He could have been halfway to Shakehand Springs by now.

He scolded himself: *Now, Baron, you're not whipped yet. Pull yourself together.*

He thundered past the charred remains of his little passenger depot at the end of the tracks, and rode through the smoke of his own lodge house. He paused, looking over his shoulder. He wanted to make sure Domingo followed him on the right trail. When the gunman appeared, Bart got his attention with a pistol shot, then reined Peso down the trail, into the forest.

He could hear the rumble of pursuing hooves as he anticipated every turn in the trail he had memorized yesterday. About a mile from the lodge house, he rounded a crook and saw the place he had been looking for—a bright spot in the forest where the sun shone down through a stand of young aspens, spaced far enough apart that he could see through them easily. With rehearsed precision, he reined his mount off the trail, running between the two trees he had marked so certainly in his memory. He slowed the stallion, then stopped at the edge of the dense evergreens, turning to watch. A thousand aspen leaves fluttered as if in warning.

Only three rounds in the revolver, he reminded himself, but the rifle magazine was full. Within seconds, Archiveque appeared on the trail with his five gunmen. The Mexican saw Bart waiting, pistol drawn, and jerked his reins back. But the horse suddenly dropped from under him, sending him flying through the trees.

Bart's spirits leaped as he saw the first four horses trip and fall over each other. Two other riders tried to avoid the pile, reining their mounts off the trail, but they stopped in midair, their saddles running out from under them. The ropes stretched across the trail at ankle level had brought the horses down exactly as Bart had planned. And the ones suspended at chest level had unhorsed the other riders better than he could have dreamed.

He fired his three pistol rounds into the woods to scatter the frightened animals, then watched Domingo roll to his feet as he holstered his pistol and reached for the Marlin. He could have ridden safely for cover, but he knew he had Domingo beat. His rifle came up as the Mexican reached for his hip. He saw the scarred face over his irons and remembered Antonio's advice: The next time you see Domingo Archiveque in your sights . . .

The blast jerked the one-eared head back on its thick neck. Then Bart was gone, listening with satisfaction to the scattered horses of the gang crashing downhill through the pines.

The shootout with Archiveque would bring more trouble, of course. He might as well have been telegraphing his location all over the mountains with all the shooting he had been doing.

His instincts were telling him to ride now for everything he was worth to Shakehand Springs. But for now he had to stop. The pony would die running at this rate. He came to a rise in the trail, jumped down, and loosened the cinch. Peso was puffing like a locomotive. He began to reload his weapons.

He wasn't worried about Semple's army. Troops moved too slowly in formation. The investigator from the Secret Service concerned him even less. Mountain trailing was not his specialty.

Marshal Yarborough worried him, though. What he lacked in brains, he made up for in trail savvy. This was going to be the narrowest escape in the history of the old Southwest.

Forty-two

❧❧❧

It had been less than forty-eight hours since Clarence Tankersly had come to warn him, and now the fifth baron of the Sacramentos was trying to think like a U.S. marshal, riding hard for Shakehand Springs. He hadn't seen Yarborough, but he knew the lawman would be closing in.

His strategy had to be apparent to them: Run for the Guadalupes and follow the mountains through Texas and into Old Mexico. What the marshal didn't know was that Bart had a fresh mount waiting at Shakehand Springs, courtesy of Uncle Dan Tolliver. That would put some distance between him and his pursuers. He would be halfway to Mexico by the time they got to a telegraph office.

He was riding near the east rim of the Sacramento River valley, staying off the ridges where he would be easily seen. He would have to cross the ridge soon to get to Shakehand Springs, and he knew just the place to do it.

About a mile ahead, the dirt trail turned to rock for a long stretch. When he hit the rock, he would rein his stallion up and over the ridge. Yarborough would lose his trail on the rocks, and that would slow him down.

This southern extreme of his barony was the least familiar to Bart, but he had been here just a year ago, thinking about establishing a new ranch on the Sacramento River. He had visited Shakehand Springs then. It was the only water hole he knew of between here and the Guadalupes.

He stopped when Peso's hooves first rattled on stone, and looked at the mountain slopes over his shoulder, looming above him now. He was leaving forever. Already he had left the firs and spruces. Here the ponderosa pines were not quite so tall, not nearly as thick, and interspersed with scrubby piñons. His barony was slipping away from him.

He saw nothing of Yarborough in the trees above, so he spurred Peso up the steep rock slope, toward the ridge. He wasted no time getting over the divide and back into cover, but he did glimpse the Organ Mountains, far to the southwest, and the Guadalupes to the southeast. He remembered his trip here last year. He had looked south from this ridge in the night and had seen the lights of El Paso, seventy miles away.

Four miles to Shakehand Springs.

As he loped the exhausted buckskin around a rocky point, a uniformed man on horseback suddenly appeared a hundred yards ahead of him. He jerked his reins, and the stallion's hooves clattered

against the rocky ground. The soldier looked up
from the trail he had been studying.

For several moments they stared. Each man had
surprised the daylights out of the other. The baron
risked no move until he saw the soldier clawing at
his holster.

Nothing to do now but charge. Gouging the stallion hard with his spurs, Bart drew his revolver
and began firing over the head of the soldier. He
gave the Mescalero war cry so well that the soldier's horse shied from the trail. The baron used
every round in his Colt, and was near enough with
the last shot to see fear in the soldier's eyes.

The bluff had worked; the scout ran for cover.
Would he follow? No, too scared. He would go
back for help. Soldiers fought in bodies. But who
was he? Probably a scout Semple had sent out.
How far away was Semple? Near enough to have
heard the shots? Yarborough had certainly heard—
and now had a new bearing. The gunshots would
draw him like a homing pigeon.

Looking back to make sure the scout wasn't following, a flash of metal up the canyon caught
Bart's eye. He had to rein the stallion in to make it
out. Not one, but two—no, several glints of sunlight on metal. He squinted the dust from his eyes.
A whole column of cavalry rode single file down
the slope at a trot, coming to save its scout.

Semple must have guessed that Shakehand
Springs was the place to cut the deposed baron's
trail to freedom. Still, his lead was five minutes.
Maybe six or seven. Enough time to switch his
saddle to a new horse and run for the Guadalupes.
He could see them, almost due east from here,
dark mounds of timbered land rising above the

desert, twenty or thirty miles away. It was going to
be a punishing ride.

The sun remained just high enough to cast its
light on Shakehand Springs when the baron first
caught sight of the water near the base of the bluff.
It was a small, clear pool on a rock-and-sand bed,
surrounded by a few trees. And there was Uncle
Dan, straddling a horse at the edge of the piñon
brakes! The spare mount? In the shade, probably.
The old man knew how to keep a horse fresh for a
hard ride.

Peso was frothing. Since dawn, he had covered
more ground than any horse should have to in a
day. He was too tired to even drink when he carried the baron up next to the old mountain man.

"Where's the horse?" Bart asked, peering into
the piñons and alligator junipers growing near the
springs. "The cavalry and Marshal Yarborough are
biting my tail!" The only answer he heard was the
sound of the old musket's lock catching. When he
turned back to Uncle Dan, he was looking down
the long octagonal barrel.

"Don't try your luck, Baron, or ol' Kaintuck'll
take a hunk out of you."

"What the hell is this, old man? You were supposed to bring me a fresh horse! Son of a bitch,
you brought Semple, didn't you?"

Uncle Dan merely smirked as he turned his face
toward the piñon brakes, keeping his eyes locked
on the baron. "Lawyer!" he shouted, his voice full
of gravel.

Faintly, Bart could hear the weaponry of the
horse soldiers rattling not far enough up the
canyon. Then he saw the shock of red hair coming
down from the piñons above the springs.

"I brung you a fresh hoss, all right," Dan Tolliver drawled. "Didn't say who'd be ridin' it."

Bart's breath caught on a heartbeat and came up his throat hot as chimney smoke. Uncle Dan had sold him out. He thought about the revolver. He had spent all six rounds on the scout up the canyon. He would have to reach for the Marlin rifle in the saddle scabbard, but ol' Kaintuck had him covered, just five feet away.

"Bart," Randy said, pausing to look up the canyon, "we'd better talk."

"Like hell," Bart replied. He could already feel the checkered grip of the rifle against his right palm. He leaned to the off side of his horse as he drew the Marlin, but ol' Kaintuck followed.

The rifle ball hit his left shoulder like the blunt end of an axe, twisting him in the saddle. The stars he saw parted in time to reveal Uncle Dan wielding his long rifle overhead. The right hand worked alone with the Marlin, cocking the hammer, raising the muzzle, pulling the trigger.

He barely clung to the saddle as Peso lurched away from the other two horses. Uncle Dan and Randy hit the ground at the same time. The mountain man dead, the lawyer merely thrown. That was Randy yelling. Two horses were running.

He collected his wits and looked down at a bloody left sleeve. The arm wouldn't work. He managed to get his saddle squarely back under him, but couldn't find the reins. He remembered: Uncle Dan trained his mounts like buffalo horses, to respond to knee signals. He turned Peso to face the lawyer.

Locking his fingers in the loop of the rifle's lever,

the baron slung its muzzle downward, pivoting the action open with one hand, sending a fresh round to the chamber. A wisp of gun smoke stung his nostrils like smelling salts. He glimpsed blue uniforms moving in the canyon above him, three minutes away.

Randy had clawed his way to the body of the dead mountain man. He looked up at his former friend, disbelief in his eyes. "My God, Bart, what have you done? What in God's name are you doing this for?"

"What did you think I would do? Go to prison without a fight?" He lifted the rifle and tried to find the lawyer in the wavering sights.

"My God, don't shoot me, Bart!" Randy yelled, jumping to his feet. "It was just a joke! For Christ's sake, Bart, it was only a joke!"

Bart narrowed his eyes and lowered the rifle. "What?" he said, wincing against the pain in his shoulder.

"The watermark was on a document from some other case. I just told the judge it was one of yours. He didn't know the difference. He can't read Spanish. It was a joke. I was going to have the marshal bring you to Santa Fe in leg irons and handcuffs; then I was going to tell the judge I had accidentally mixed up the papers. I was going to recommend that your grant be confirmed. We were going to have a big laugh over it, Bart."

"A laugh?" the baron growled. "We were going to have a *laugh*?" He could hear the colonel shouting orders now, forming the men into a skirmish line.

Randy smirked and shrugged. "I had to get you

back for that Indian attack you pulled on me. I had to save face in Santa Fe somehow. As God is my witness, I never dreamed the army and Regis's gang of thugs would come after you. I never dreamed you'd blow up your fort and your railroad and burn down your home."

"A laugh?" Bart said. He felt his anger and hatred settle. A snicker was coming on. "A laugh? Randy, you son of a bitch." His shoulders bounced on a couple of chuckles, racking the left one with pain. "Just a joke!"

"Yes, I swear, it was just a joke," Randy cried, sniggering uncertainly.

It was ludicrous! Bart laughed straight up at the skies of his barony. "*Just* a joke, your hide! It was the joke of all jokes, Randy! By golly, you got me with this one!"

They enjoyed a strange moment of camaraderie, shaking their heads, blinking tears of joy from their eyes. Then the smile wilted on Randy's face as he looked down at Dan Tolliver's corpse.

"You did it, didn't you, Bart? You really did forge those papers."

Bart heard the order given to advance, and he looked up the canyon. A wounded man on a tired horse would get nowhere. He had nothing left. "You told me once, Randy, that one of these practical jokes was going to get me in trouble." Resting the butt of the Marlin on his hip, he nudged his stallion back up the canyon. "I guess you were right. Adios."

He left Randy at Shakehand Springs with the dead mountain man. He would find the cavalry waiting for him around the bluff. When he glanced back, Randy was shaking his head, and scratching it.

"Hold it, Young!" a voice ordered, just before the baron prepared to charge the soldiers.

Looking up to the west, he saw Lin Yarborough against the glow of the evening sky. The sun was setting on his barony. He raked his spurs along the stallion's ribs, whirled the rifle from his hip, and blasted the sky over the head of the lawmen.

Yarborough was hell on fugitives. Bart felt two hammer blows hit him between the shoulders and the hips as he flailed the rifle on its lever again, working a fresh shell into the chamber. The line of horse soldiers appeared before him as a marshal's bullet sang against a rock. He loosed a round over the troops and one-handed the Marlin's action as he charged.

Every sense he had groped for life. He smelled the sharp fragrance of evergreens, saw tree-broken rays of sun streaking dust above the cavalry, felt the powerful surge of the good horse under him. He tasted his own blood. He heard Colonel Semple's saber ring from its scabbard, found its glint against the mountain.

He fired another round, but couldn't find the strength to sling the rifle's action open again. His left arm was flopping loosely at his side. He smiled up at the Lost Barony of the Sacramentos. The colonel's saber fell, and the whole line of rifles saluted him in unison.

In the instant it took for the bullets to reach him, Don Bartolome sensed a presence, and turned slowly to see Antonio loping beside him, grinning wide. The fourth baron joined the fifth. Then came the third baron from the trees, and the second from the sky. Then Nepomeceno himself appeared, with a silver-studded saddle and a white sombrero. They rode five abreast through the fusillade, and up the mountainside. They drew rein on the summit, looked over their barony, and swapped riddles until the thunder drove them home.